THE BATMAN STRIKES! CRIME TIME

™

Written by:

Bill Matheny

Illustrated by:

Terry Beatty

Christopher Jones

Colored by:

Heroic Age

Lettered by:

Phil Balsman

Pat Brosseau

Jared K. Fletcher

Nick J. Napolitano

Batman created by **Bob Kane**

Dan DiDio
VP-Executive Editor

Joan Hilty
Nachie Castro
Editors-original series

Harvey Richards
Assistant Editor-original series

Scott Nybakken
Editor-collected edition

Robbin Brosterman
Senior Art Director

Paul Levitz
President & Publisher

Georg Brewer
VP-Design & Retail Product
Development

Richard Bruning
Senior VP-Creative Director

Patrick Caldon
Senior VP-Finance & Operations

Chris Caramalis
VP-Finance

Terri Cunningham
VP-Managing Editor

Stephanie Fierman
Senior VP-Sales & Marketing

Alison Gill
VP-Manufacturing

Rich Johnson
VP-Book Trade Sales

Hank Kanalz
VP-General Manager, WildStorm

Lillian Laserson
Senior VP & General Counsel

Jim Lee
Editorial Director-WildStorm

Paula Lowitt
Senior VP-Business & Legal Affairs

David McKillips
VP-Advertising & Custom Publishing

John Nee
VP-Business Development

Gregory Noveck
Senior VP-Creative Affairs

Cheryl Rubin
Senior VP-Brand Management

Bob Wayne
VP-Sales

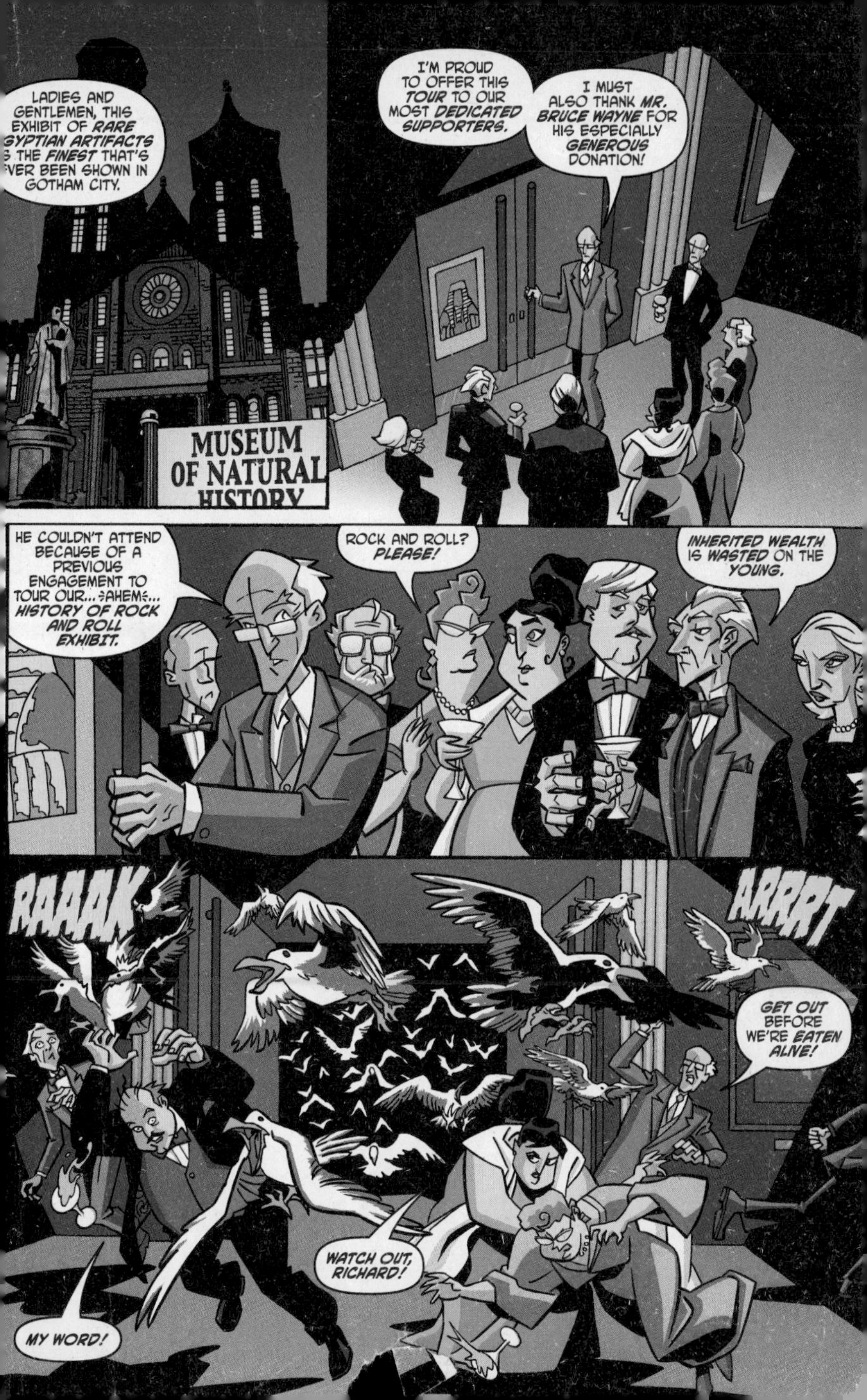
LADIES AND GENTLEMEN, THIS EXHIBIT OF RARE GYPTIAN ARTIFACTS S THE FINEST THAT'S VER BEEN SHOWN IN GOTHAM CITY.
MUSEUM OF NATURAL HISTORY
I'M PROUD TO OFFER THIS TOUR TO OUR MOST DEDICATED SUPPORTERS.
I MUST ALSO THANK MR. BRUCE WAYNE FOR HIS ESPECIALLY GENEROUS DONATION!
HE COULDN'T ATTEND BECAUSE OF A PREVIOUS ENGAGEMENT TO TOUR OUR... *AHEM*... HISTORY OF ROCK AND ROLL EXHIBIT.
ROCK AND ROLL? PLEASE!
INHERITED WEALTH IS WASTED ON THE YOUNG.
RAAAK
ARRRT
GET OUT BEFORE WE'RE EATEN ALIVE!
WATCH OUT, RICHARD!
MY WORD!

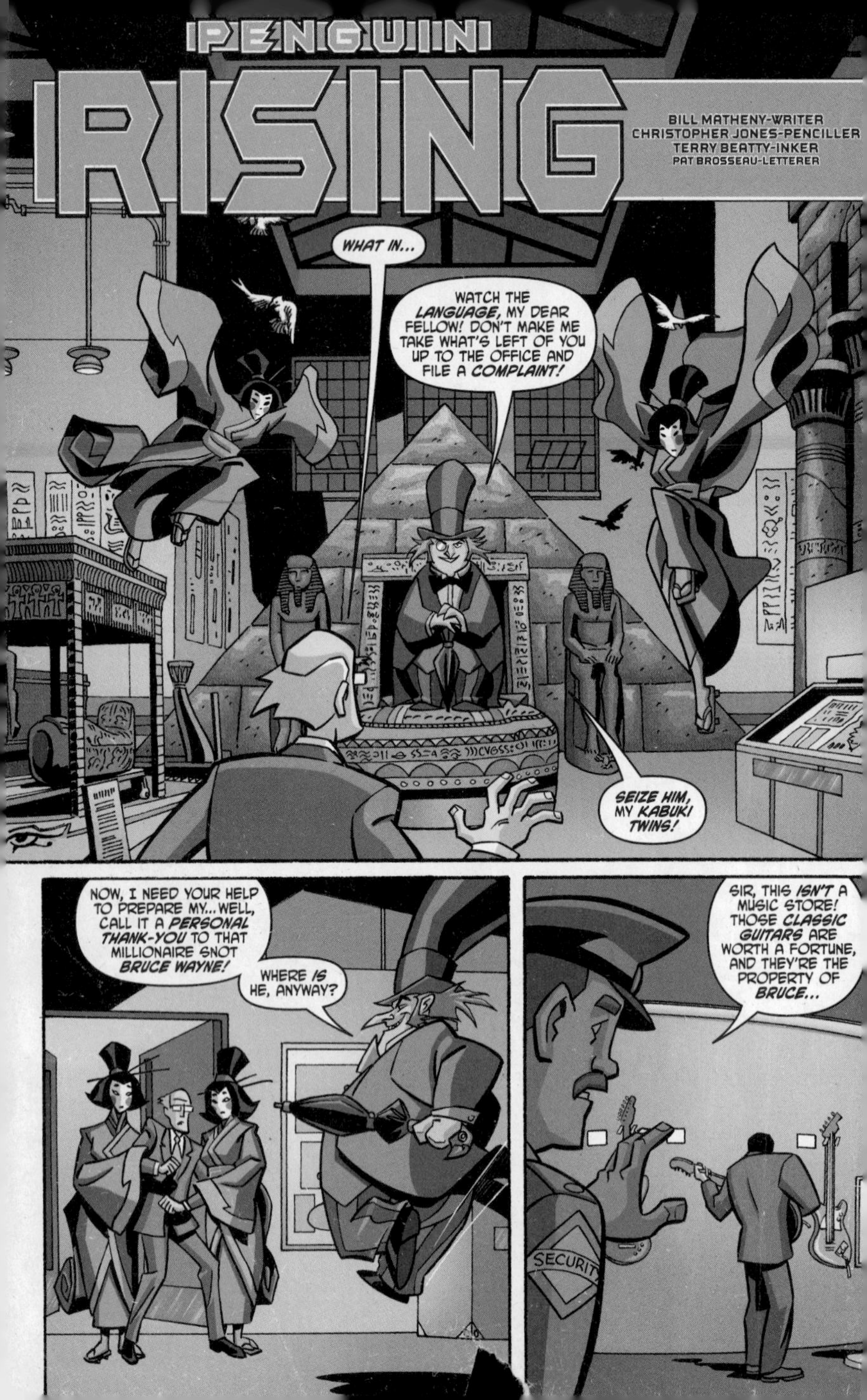
PENGUIN
RISING
BILL MATHENY-WRITER
CHRISTOPHER JONES-PENCILLER
TERRY BEATTY-INKER
PAT BROSSEAU-LETTERER
WHAT IN...
WATCH THE LANGUAGE, MY DEAR FELLOW! DON'T MAKE ME TAKE WHAT'S LEFT OF YOU UP TO THE OFFICE AND FILE A COMPLAINT!
SEIZE HIM, MY KABUKI TWINS!
NOW, I NEED YOUR HELP TO PREPARE MY... WELL, CALL IT A PERSONAL THANK-YOU TO THAT MILLIONAIRE SNOT BRUCE WAYNE!
WHERE IS HE, ANYWAY?
SIR, THIS ISN'T A MUSIC STORE! THOSE CLASSIC GUITARS ARE WORTH A FORTUNE, AND THEY'RE THE PROPERTY OF BRUCE...
SECURIT

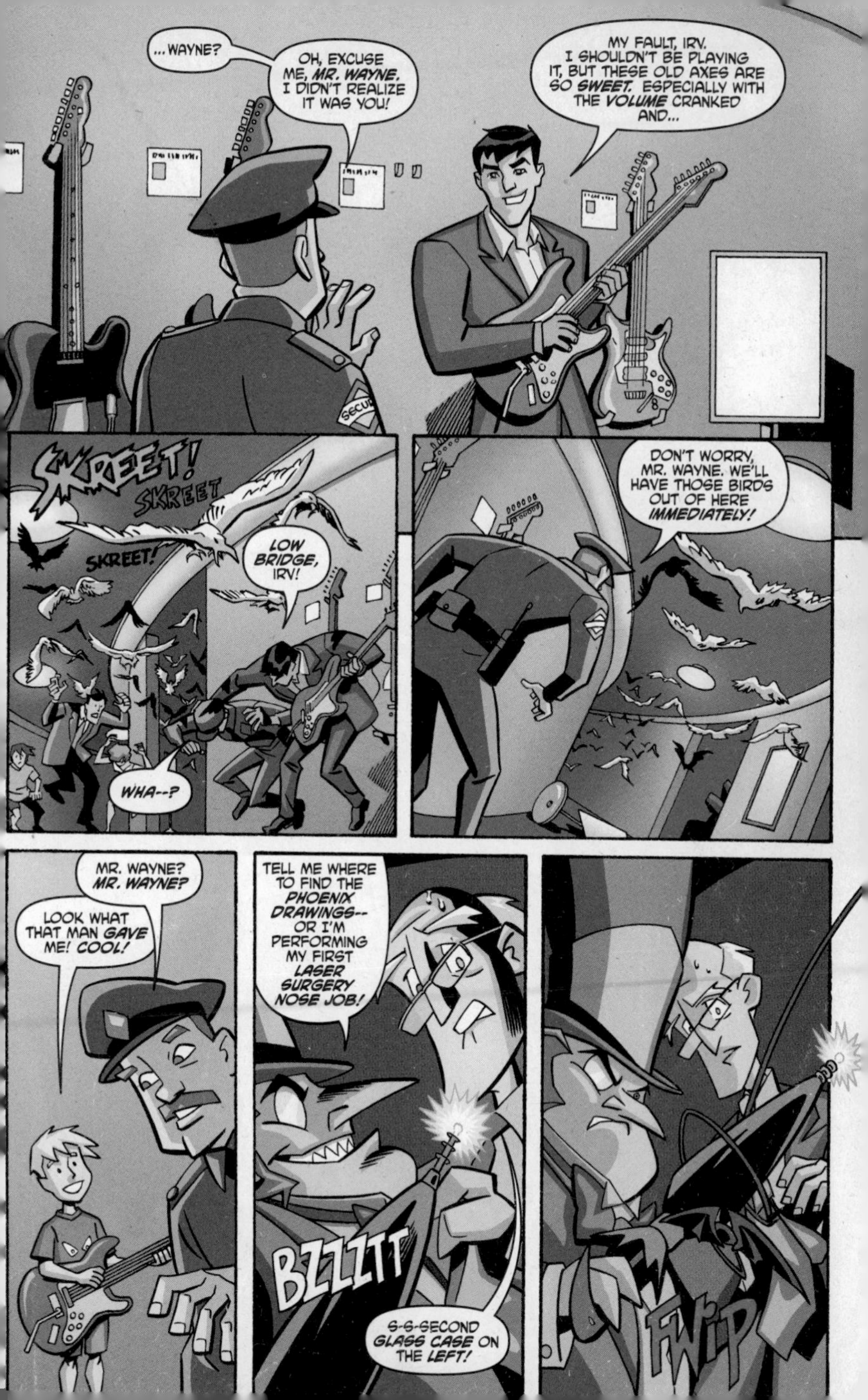

...WAYNE?
OH, EXCUSE ME, MR. WAYNE. I DIDN'T REALIZE IT WAS YOU!
MY FAULT, IRV. I SHOULDN'T BE PLAYING IT, BUT THESE OLD AXES ARE SO SWEET. ESPECIALLY WITH THE VOLUME CRANKED AND...
SKREET!
SKREET
SKREET!
LOW BRIDGE, IRV!
WHA--?
DON'T WORRY, MR. WAYNE. WE'LL HAVE THOSE BIRDS OUT OF HERE IMMEDIATELY!
MR. WAYNE? MR. WAYNE?
LOOK WHAT THAT MAN GAVE ME! COOL!
TELL ME WHERE TO FIND THE PHOENIX DRAWINGS-- OR I'M PERFORMING MY FIRST LASER SURGERY NOSE JOB!
BZZZTT
S-S-SECOND GLASS CASE ON THE LEFT!
FWIP

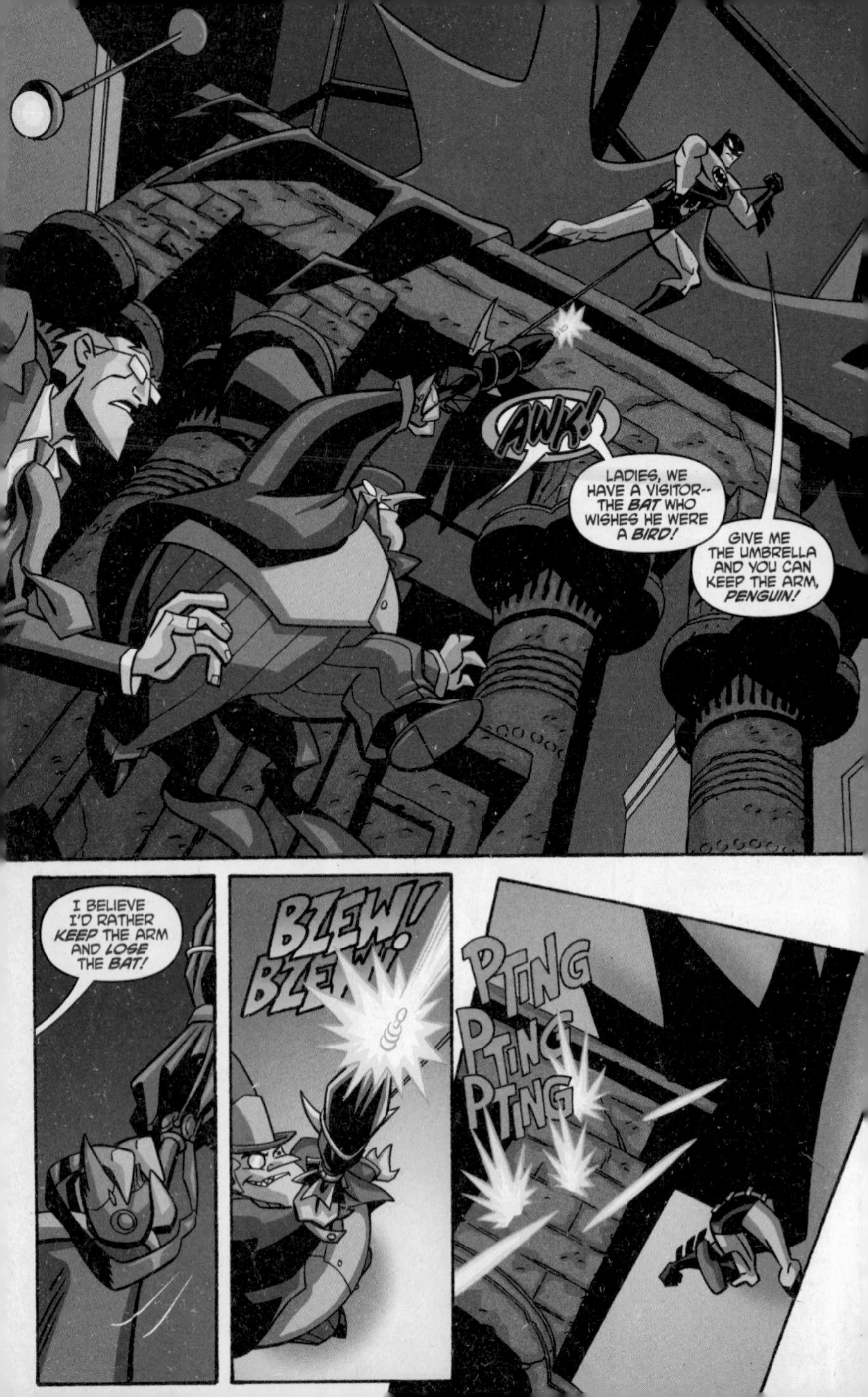
AWK!
LADIES, WE HAVE A VISITOR-- THE BAT WHO WISHES HE WERE A BIRD!
GIVE ME THE UMBRELLA AND YOU CAN KEEP THE ARM, PENGUIN!
I BELIEVE I'D RATHER KEEP THE ARM AND LOSE THE BAT!
BZEW! BZEW!
PTING PTING PTING

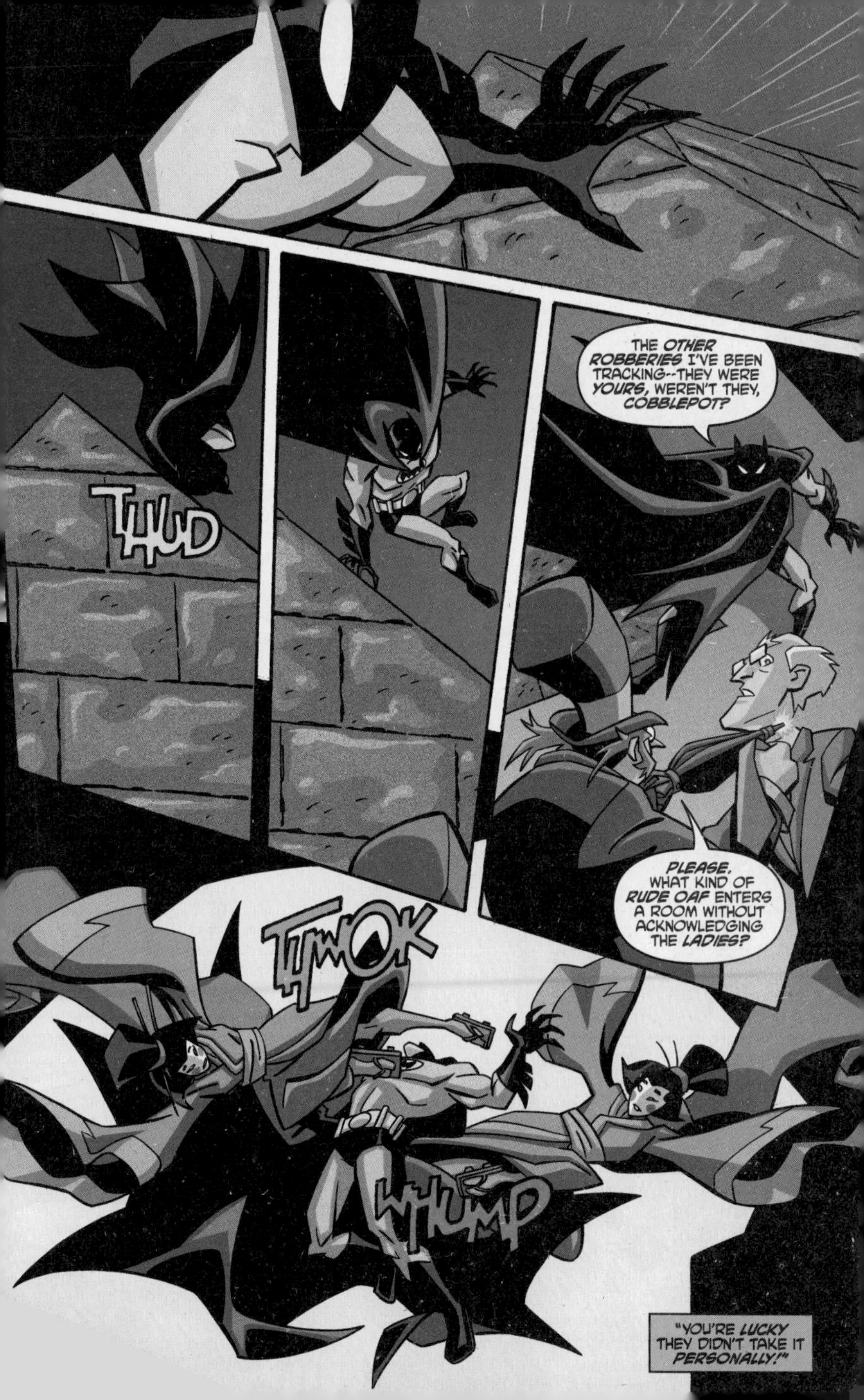
THUD
THE OTHER ROBBERIES I'VE BEEN TRACKING--THEY WERE YOURS, WEREN'T THEY, COBBLEPOT?
PLEASE. WHAT KIND OF RUDE OAF ENTERS A ROOM WITHOUT ACKNOWLEDGING THE LADIES?
THWOK
WHUMP
"YOU'RE LUCKY THEY DIDN'T TAKE IT PERSONALLY!"

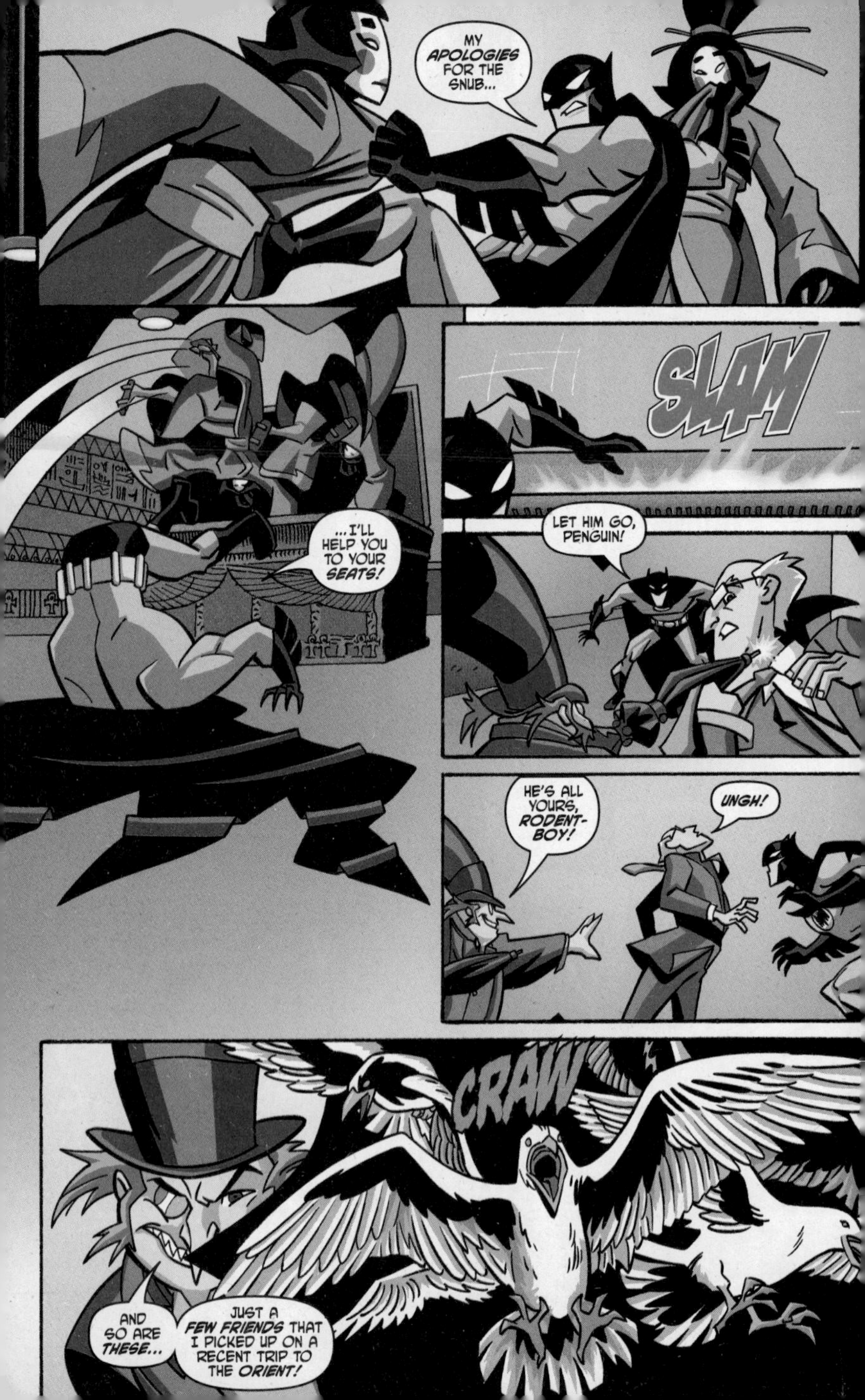
MY APOLOGIES FOR THE SNUB...
...I'LL HELP YOU TO YOUR SEATS!
SLAM
LET HIM GO, PENGUIN!
HE'S ALL YOURS, RODENT-BOY!
UNGH!
CRAW
AND SO ARE THESE...
JUST A FEW FRIENDS THAT I PICKED UP ON A RECENT TRIP TO THE ORIENT!

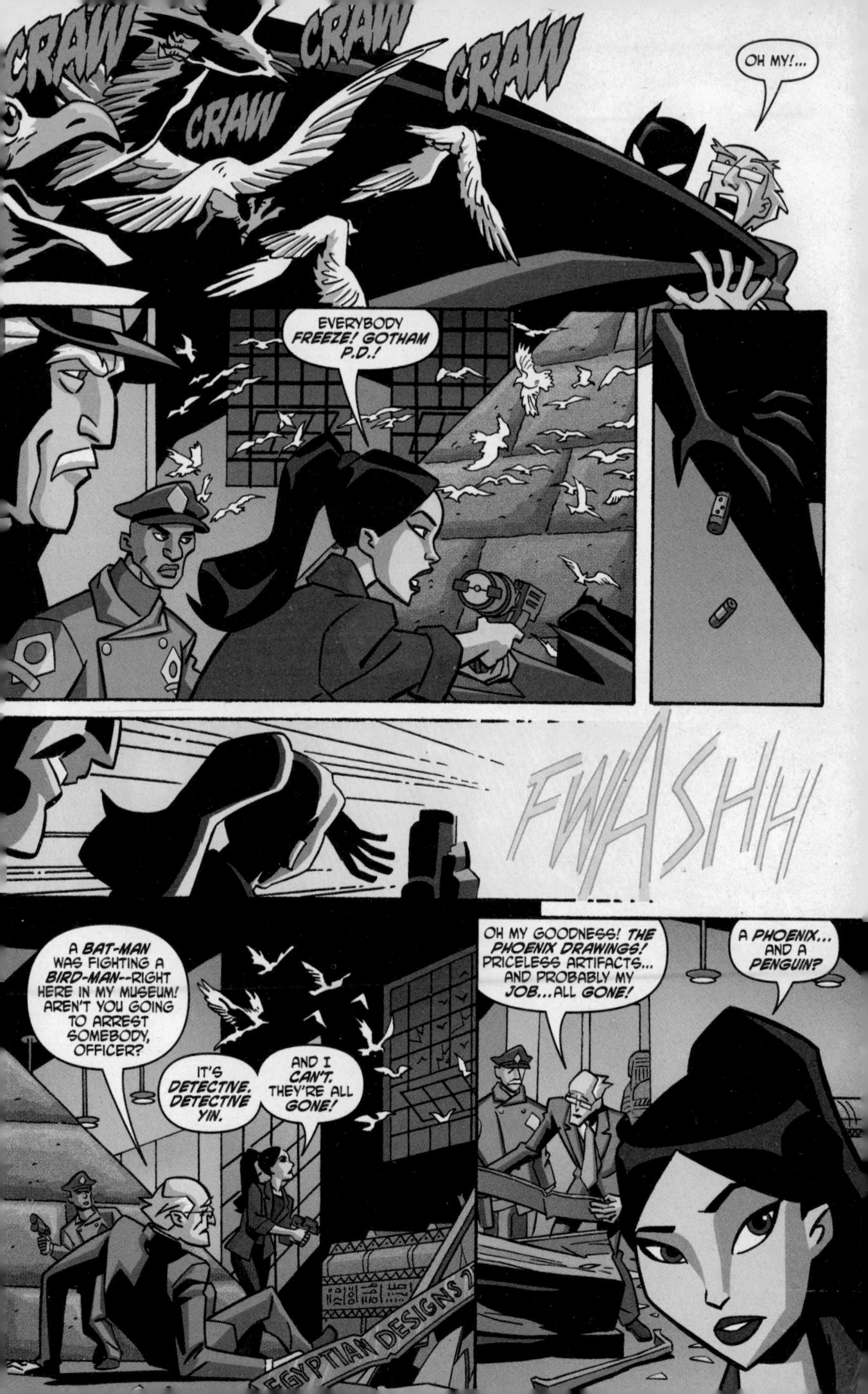
CRAW
CRAW
CRAW
CRAW
OH MY!...
EVERYBODY FREEZE! GOTHAM P.D.!
FWASHH
A BAT-MAN WAS FIGHTING A BIRD-MAN--RIGHT HERE IN MY MUSEUM! AREN'T YOU GOING TO ARREST SOMEBODY, OFFICER?
IT'S DETECTIVE. DETECTIVE YIN.
AND I CAN'T. THEY'RE ALL GONE!
EGYPTIAN DESIGNS
OH MY GOODNESS! THE PHOENIX DRAWINGS! PRICELESS ARTIFACTS... AND PROBABLY MY JOB...ALL GONE!
A PHOENIX... AND A PENGUIN?

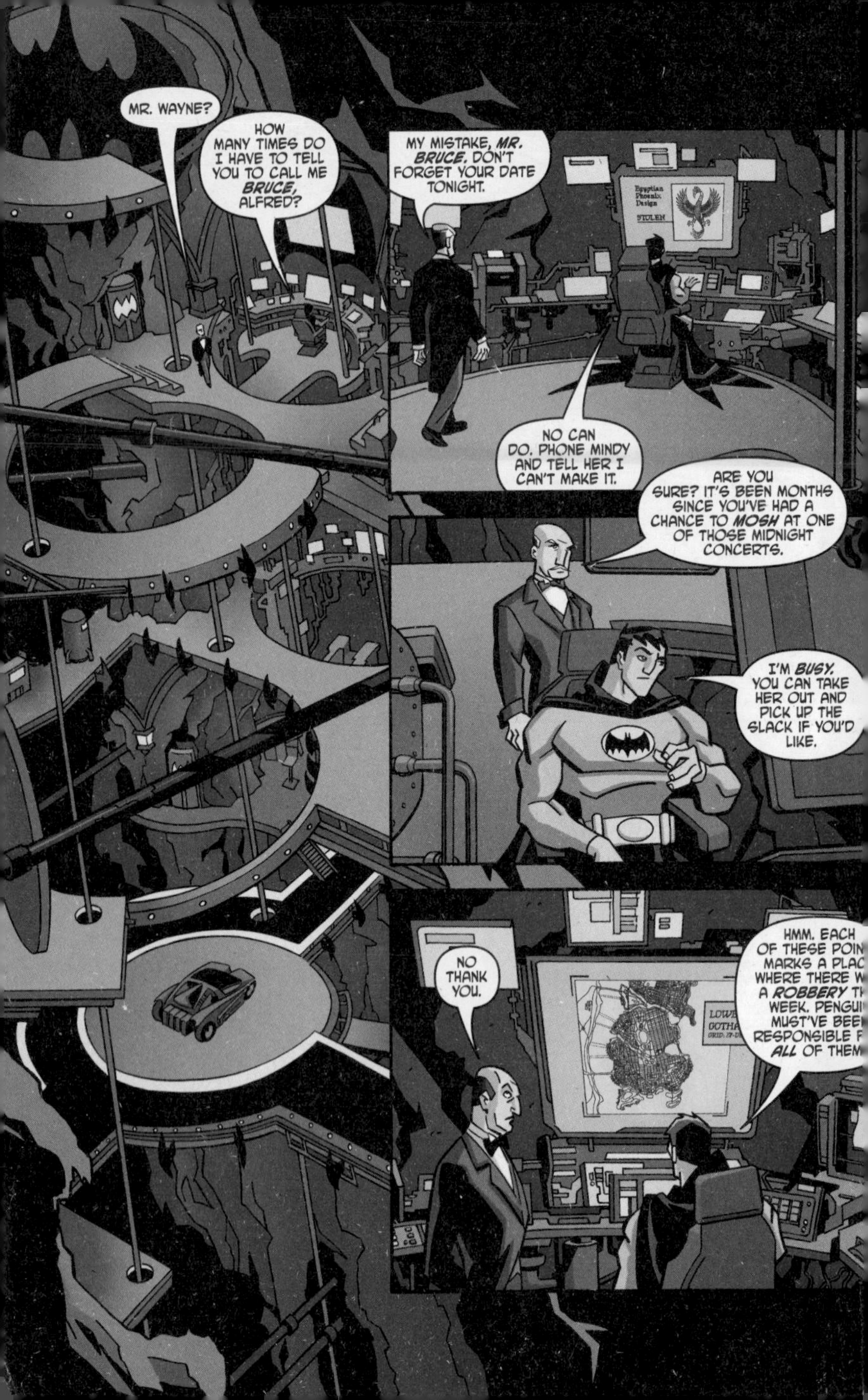

MR. WAYNE?
HOW MANY TIMES DO I HAVE TO TELL YOU TO CALL ME *BRUCE*, ALFRED?
MY MISTAKE, *MR. BRUCE*. DON'T FORGET YOUR DATE TONIGHT.
Egyptian Phoenix Design
STOLEN
NO CAN DO. PHONE MINDY AND TELL HER I CAN'T MAKE IT.
ARE YOU SURE? IT'S BEEN MONTHS SINCE YOU'VE HAD A CHANCE TO *MOSH* AT ONE OF THOSE MIDNIGHT CONCERTS.
I'M *BUSY*. YOU CAN TAKE HER OUT AND PICK UP THE SLACK IF YOU'D LIKE.
NO THANK YOU.
HMM. EACH OF THESE POIN MARKS A PLAC WHERE THERE W A *ROBBERY* T WEEK. PENGU MUST'VE BEE RESPONSIBLE F *ALL* OF THEM

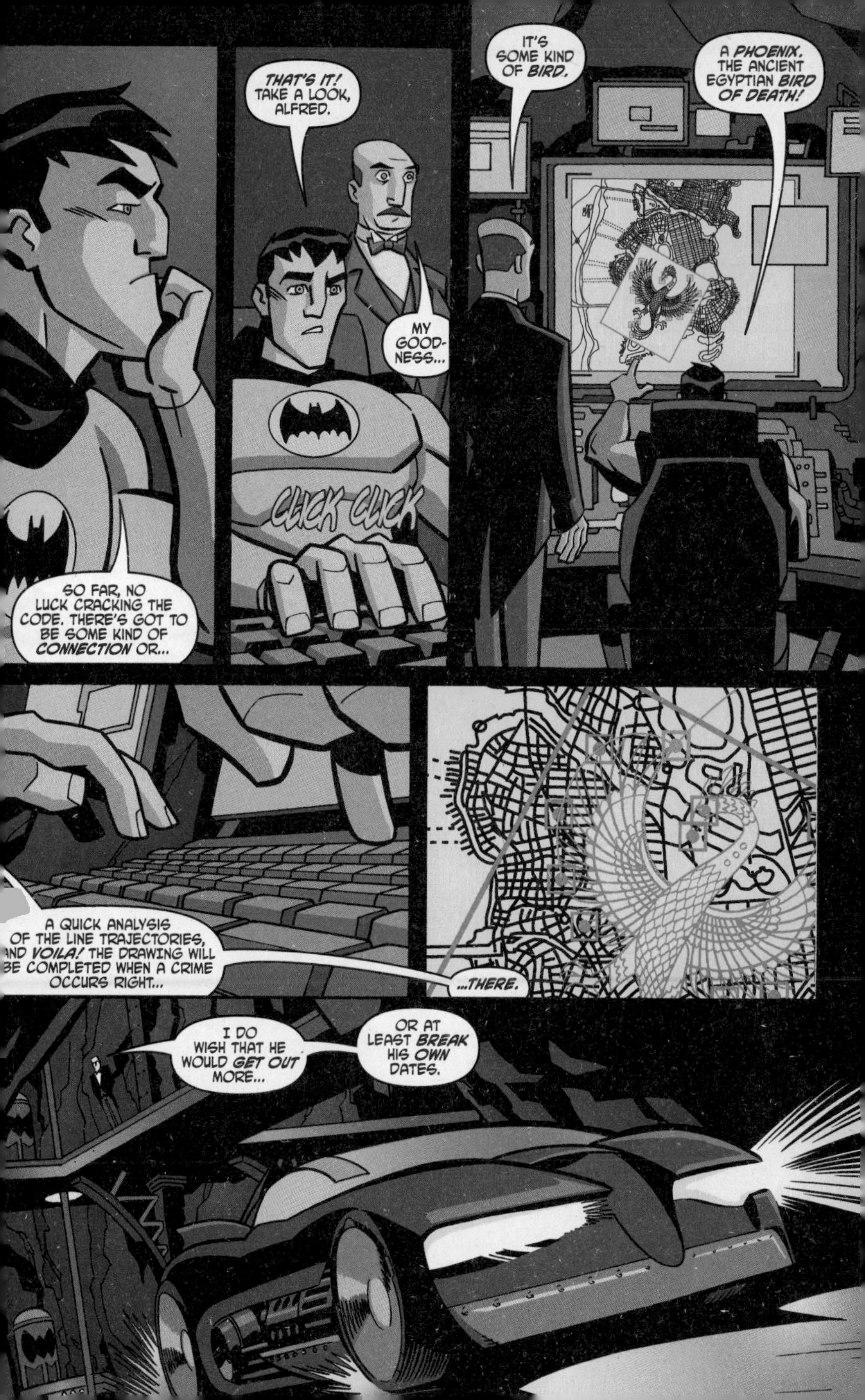
SO FAR, NO LUCK CRACKING THE CODE. THERE'S GOT TO BE SOME KIND OF *CONNECTION* OR...
THAT'S IT! TAKE A LOOK, ALFRED.
CLICK CLICK
MY GOOD-NESS...
IT'S SOME KIND OF *BIRD.*
A *PHOENIX.* THE ANCIENT EGYPTIAN *BIRD OF DEATH!*
A QUICK ANALYSIS OF THE LINE TRAJECTORIES, AND *VOILA!* THE DRAWING WILL BE COMPLETED WHEN A CRIME OCCURS RIGHT...
...*THERE.*
I DO WISH THAT HE WOULD *GET OUT* MORE...
OR AT LEAST *BREAK* HIS *OWN* DATES.

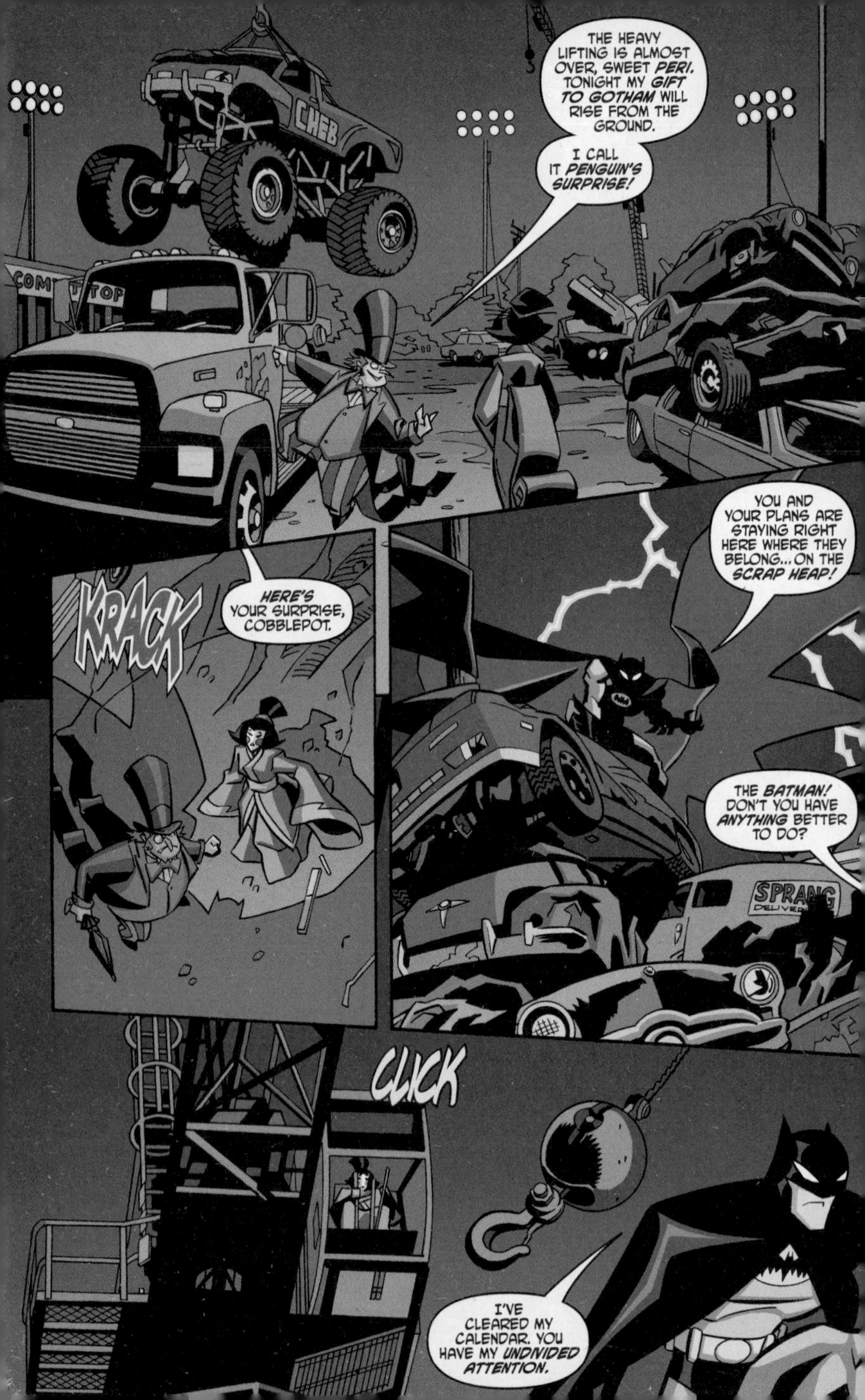

CHEB
COM TOP
THE HEAVY LIFTING IS ALMOST OVER, SWEET *PERI.* TONIGHT MY *GIFT TO GOTHAM* WILL RISE FROM THE GROUND.
I CALL IT *PENGUIN'S SURPRISE!*
KRACK
HERE'S YOUR SURPRISE, COBBLEPOT.
YOU AND YOUR PLANS ARE STAYING RIGHT HERE WHERE THEY BELONG... ON THE *SCRAP HEAP!*
THE *BATMAN!* DON'T YOU HAVE *ANYTHING* BETTER TO DO?
SPRANG
CLICK
I'VE CLEARED MY CALENDAR. YOU HAVE MY *UNDIVIDED ATTENTION.*

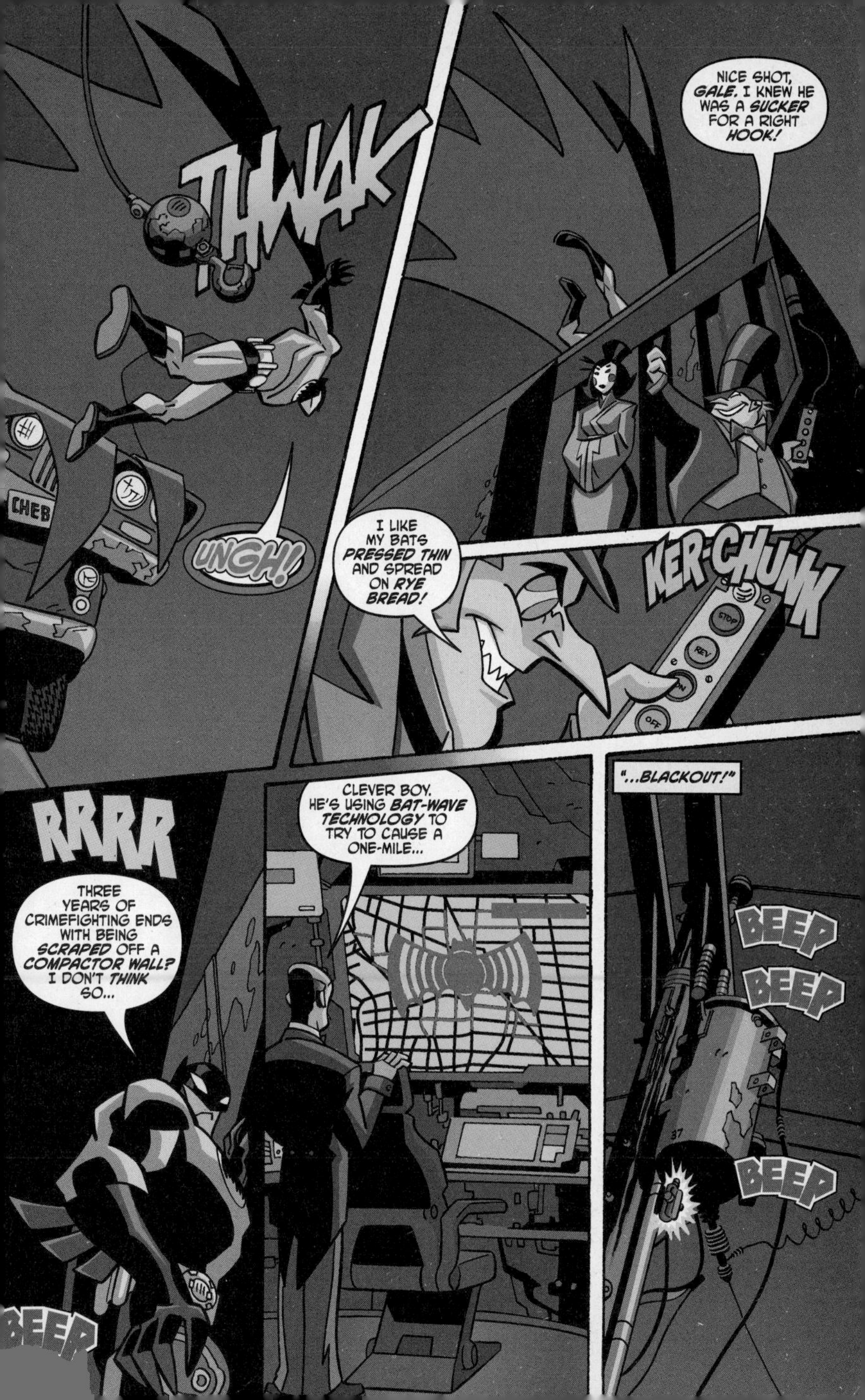
THWAK
NICE SHOT, GALE. I KNEW HE WAS A SUCKER FOR A RIGHT HOOK!
CHEB
UNGH!
I LIKE MY BATS PRESSED THIN AND SPREAD ON RYE BREAD!
KER-CHUNK
STOP
REV
ON
OFF
RRRR
THREE YEARS OF CRIMEFIGHTING ENDS WITH BEING SCRAPED OFF A COMPACTOR WALL? I DON'T THINK SO...
BEEP
CLEVER BOY. HE'S USING BAT-WAVE TECHNOLOGY TO TRY TO CAUSE A ONE-MILE...
"...BLACKOUT!"
BEEP
BEEP
BEEP

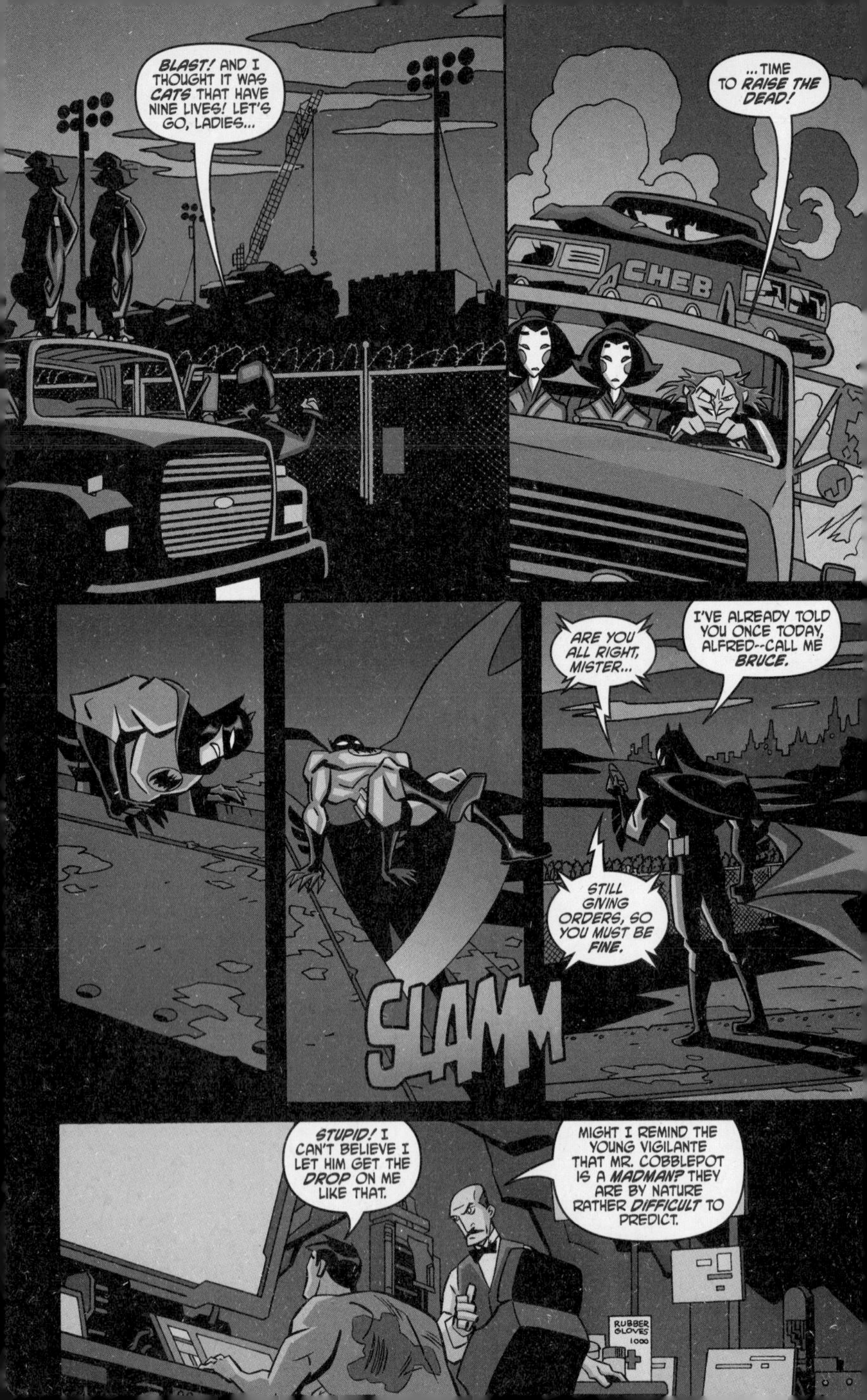

BLAST! AND I THOUGHT IT WAS CATS THAT HAVE NINE LIVES! LET'S GO, LADIES...
...TIME TO RAISE THE DEAD!
CHEB
ARE YOU ALL RIGHT, MISTER...
I'VE ALREADY TOLD YOU ONCE TODAY, ALFRED--CALL ME BRUCE.
STILL GIVING ORDERS, SO YOU MUST BE FINE.
SLAMM
STUPID! I CAN'T BELIEVE I LET HIM GET THE DROP ON ME LIKE THAT.
MIGHT I REMIND THE YOUNG VIGILANTE THAT MR. COBBLEPOT IS A MADMAN? THEY ARE BY NATURE RATHER DIFFICULT TO PREDICT.
RUBBER GLOVES 1000

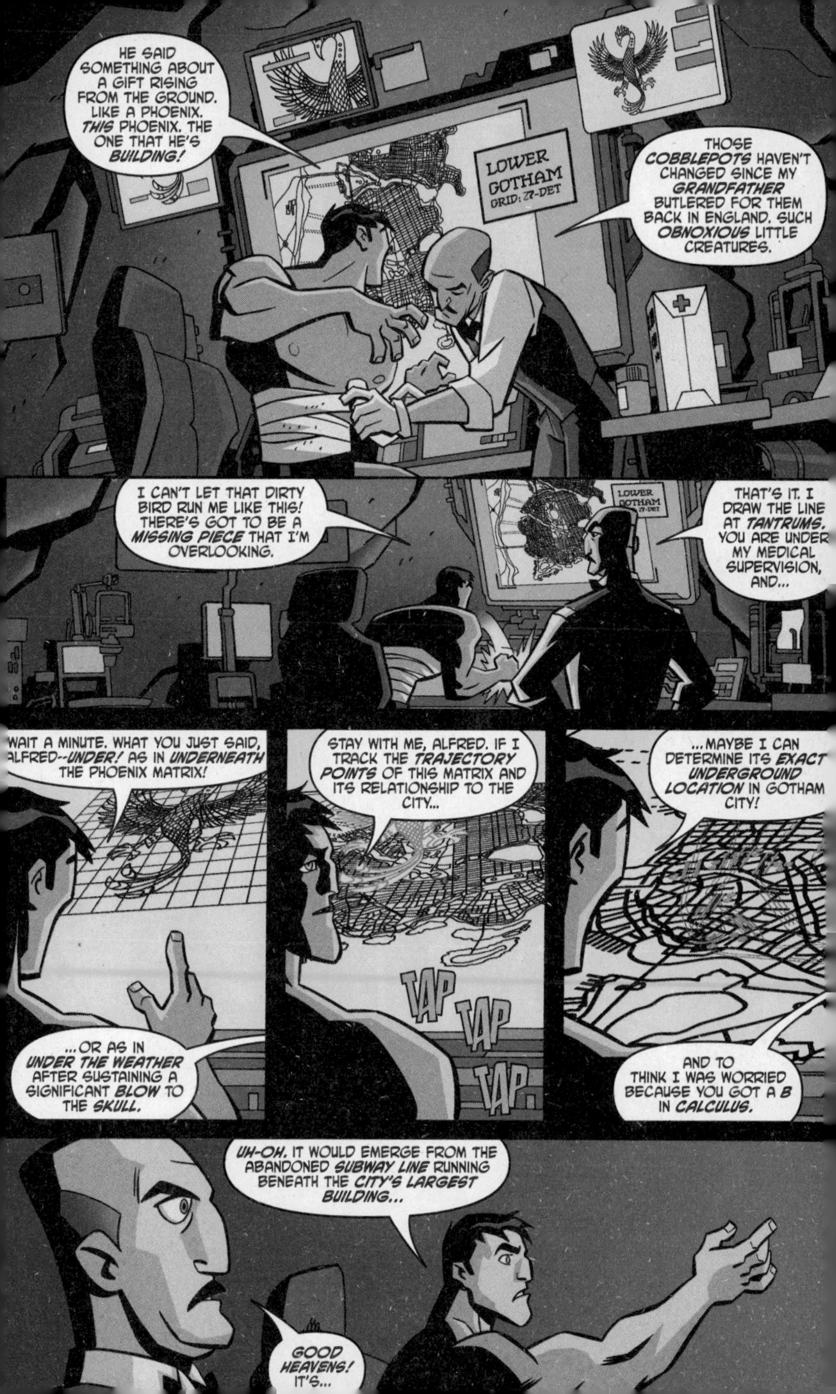
HE SAID SOMETHING ABOUT A GIFT RISING FROM THE GROUND. LIKE A PHOENIX. THIS PHOENIX. THE ONE THAT HE'S BUILDING!
LOWER GOTHAM GRID: 27-DET
THOSE COBBLEPOTS HAVEN'T CHANGED SINCE MY GRANDFATHER BUTLERED FOR THEM BACK IN ENGLAND. SUCH OBNOXIOUS LITTLE CREATURES.
I CAN'T LET THAT DIRTY BIRD RUN ME LIKE THIS! THERE'S GOT TO BE A MISSING PIECE THAT I'M OVERLOOKING.
THAT'S IT. I DRAW THE LINE AT TANTRUMS. YOU ARE UNDER MY MEDICAL SUPERVISION, AND...
WAIT A MINUTE. WHAT YOU JUST SAID, ALFRED--UNDER! AS IN UNDERNEATH THE PHOENIX MATRIX!
...OR AS IN UNDER THE WEATHER AFTER SUSTAINING A SIGNIFICANT BLOW TO THE SKULL.
STAY WITH ME, ALFRED. IF I TRACK THE TRAJECTORY POINTS OF THIS MATRIX AND ITS RELATIONSHIP TO THE CITY...
TAP TAP TAP
...MAYBE I CAN DETERMINE ITS EXACT UNDERGROUND LOCATION IN GOTHAM CITY!
AND TO THINK I WAS WORRIED BECAUSE YOU GOT A B IN CALCULUS.
UH-OH. IT WOULD EMERGE FROM THE ABANDONED SUBWAY LINE RUNNING BENEATH THE CITY'S LARGEST BUILDING...
GOOD HEAVENS! IT'S...

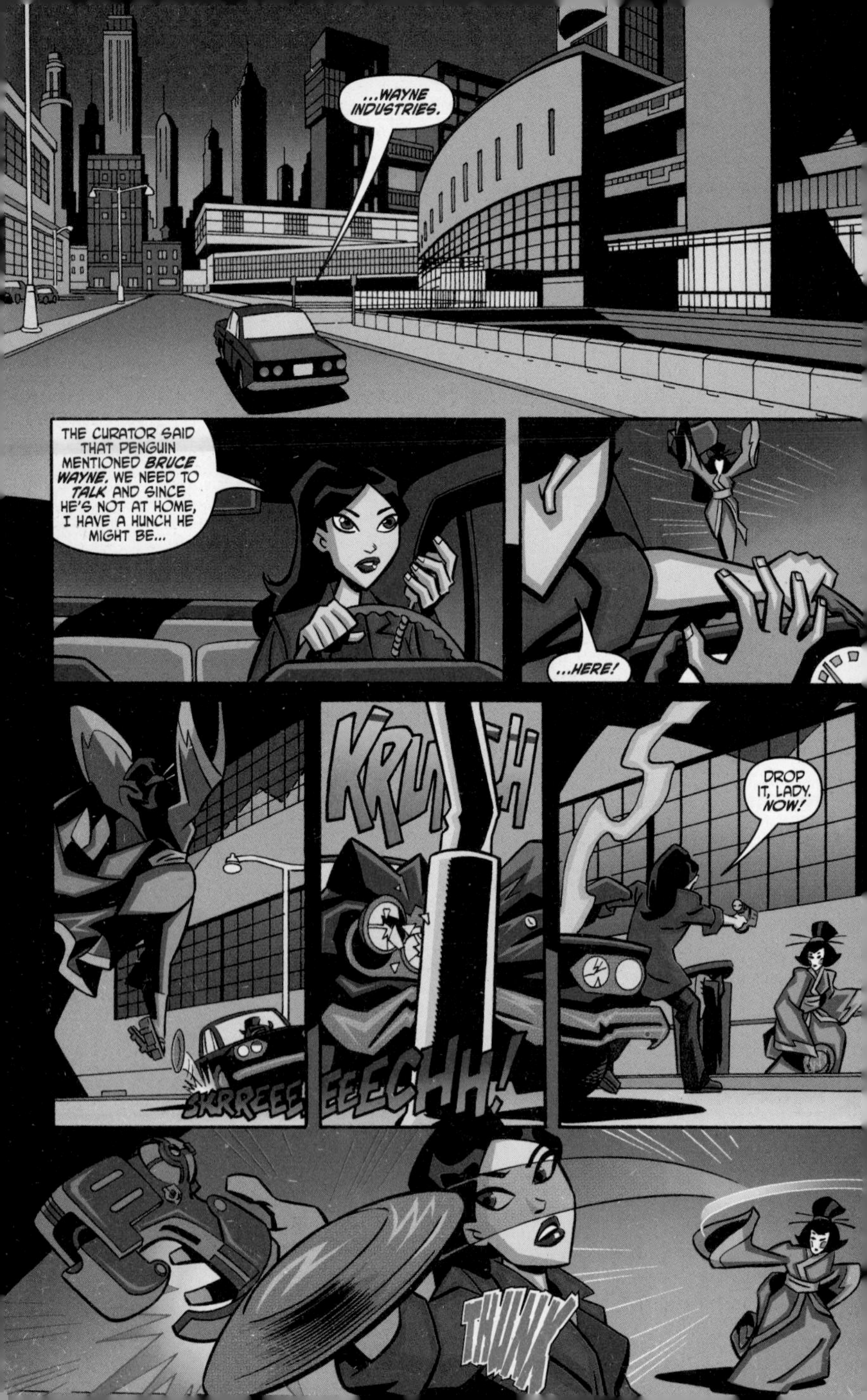
...WAYNE INDUSTRIES.
THE CURATOR SAID THAT PENGUIN MENTIONED BRUCE WAYNE. WE NEED TO TALK AND SINCE HE'S NOT AT HOME, I HAVE A HUNCH HE MIGHT BE...
...HERE!
KRUNCH
SKRREEEEEECHH!
DROP IT, LADY. NOW!
THUNK

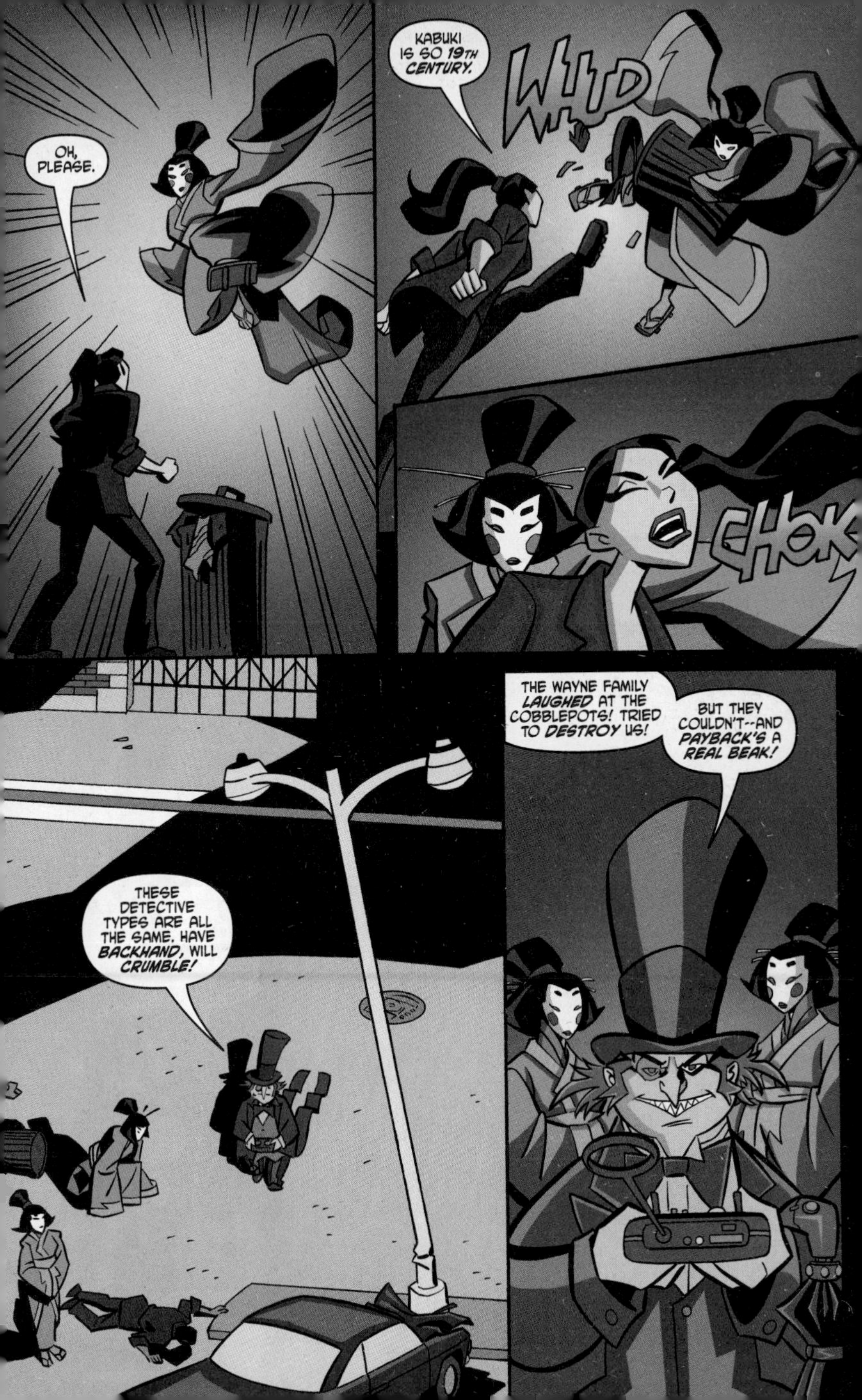
OH, PLEASE.
KABUKI IS SO 19TH CENTURY.
WHUD
CHOK
THESE DETECTIVE TYPES ARE ALL THE SAME. HAVE BACKHAND, WILL CRUMBLE!
THE WAYNE FAMILY LAUGHED AT THE COBBLEPOTS! TRIED TO DESTROY US!
BUT THEY COULDN'T--AND PAYBACK'S A REAL BEAK!

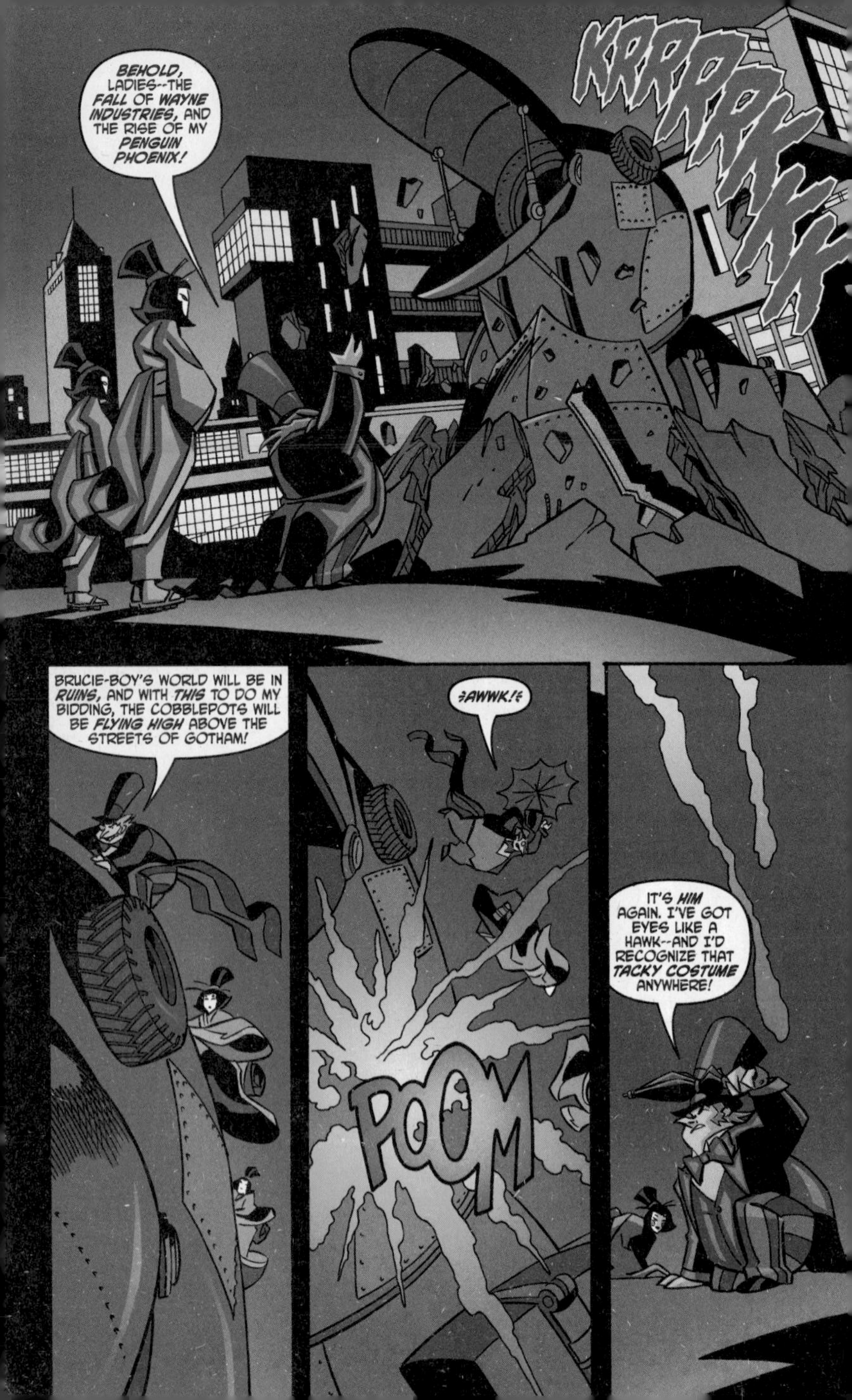
KRRRRKKKK
BEHOLD, LADIES--THE FALL OF WAYNE INDUSTRIES, AND THE RISE OF MY PENGUIN PHOENIX!
BRUCIE-BOY'S WORLD WILL BE IN RUINS, AND WITH THIS TO DO MY BIDDING, THE COBBLEPOTS WILL BE FLYING HIGH ABOVE THE STREETS OF GOTHAM!
AWWK!
POOM
IT'S HIM AGAIN. I'VE GOT EYES LIKE A HAWK--AND I'D RECOGNIZE THAT TACKY COSTUME ANYWHERE!

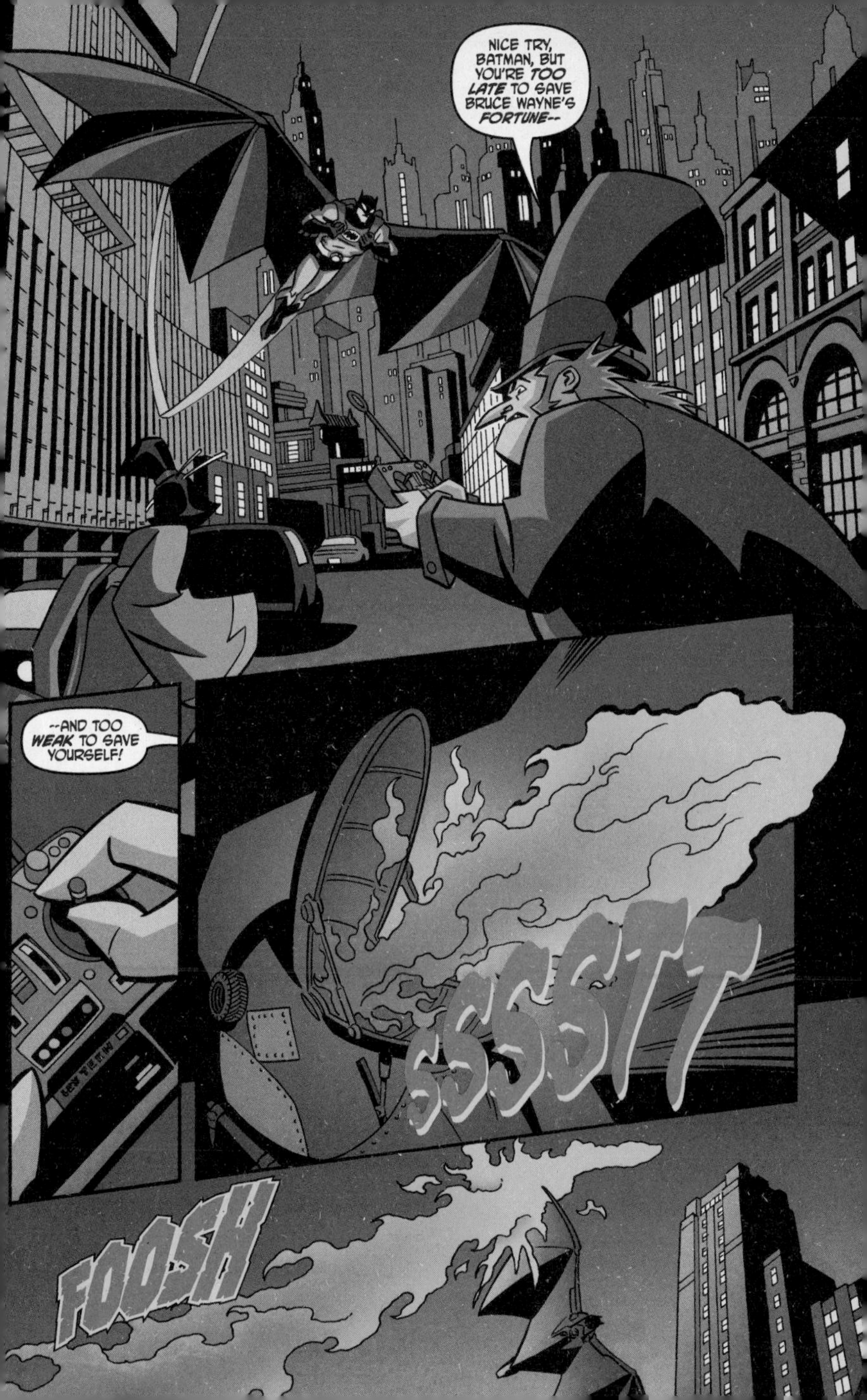
NICE TRY, BATMAN, BUT YOU'RE *TOO LATE* TO SAVE BRUCE WAYNE'S *FORTUNE*--
--AND TOO *WEAK* TO SAVE YOURSELF!
SSSSTT
FOOSH

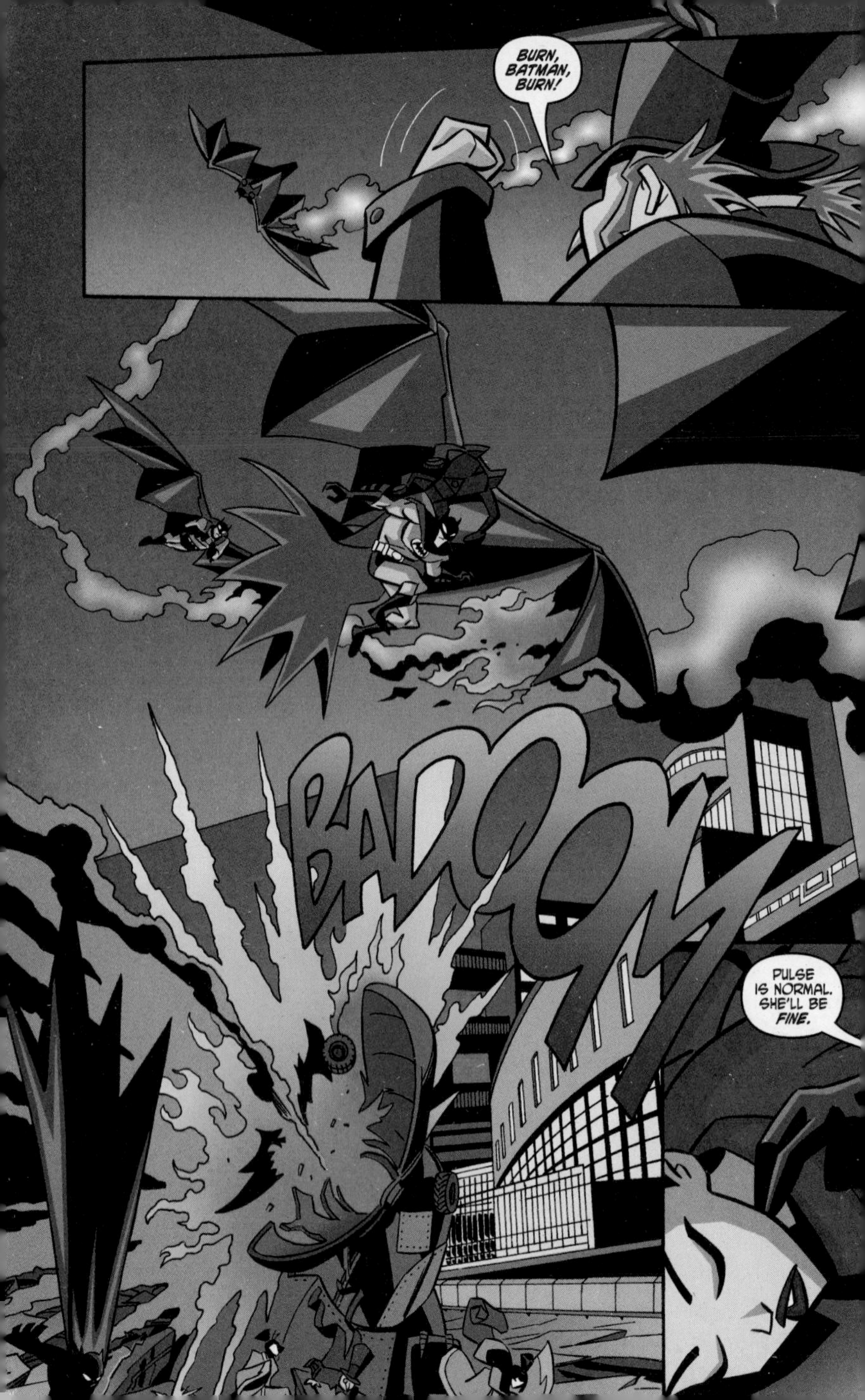
BURN, BATMAN, BURN!
BADOOM
PULSE IS NORMAL. SHE'LL BE FINE.

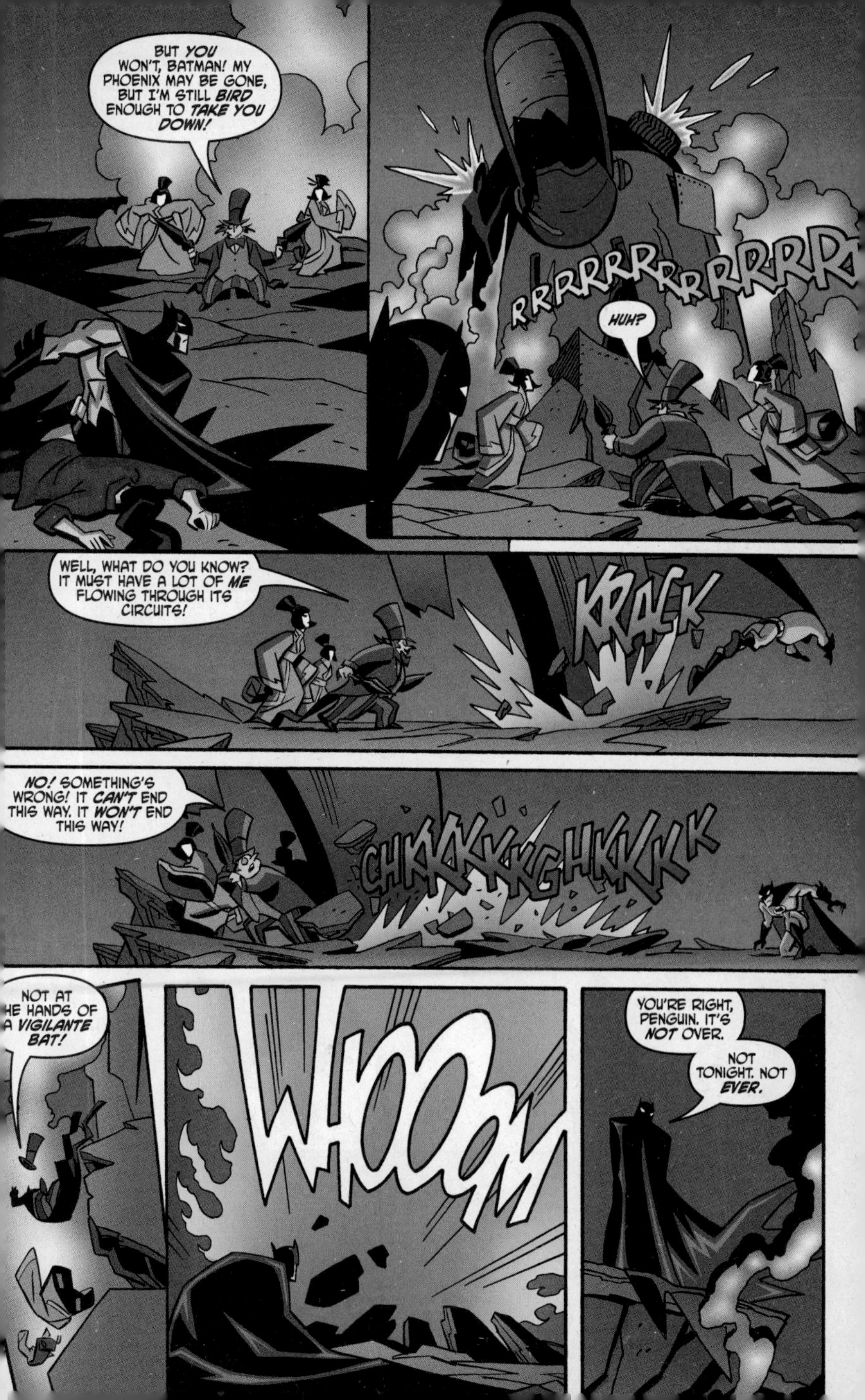
BUT YOU WON'T, BATMAN! MY PHOENIX MAY BE GONE, BUT I'M STILL BIRD ENOUGH TO TAKE YOU DOWN!
RRRRRRRRRRRRR
HUH?
WELL, WHAT DO YOU KNOW? IT MUST HAVE A LOT OF ME FLOWING THROUGH ITS CIRCUITS!
KRACK
NO! SOMETHING'S WRONG! IT CAN'T END THIS WAY. IT WON'T END THIS WAY!
CHKKKKGHKKKK
NOT AT HE HANDS OF A VIGILANTE BAT!
WHOOM
YOU'RE RIGHT, PENGUIN. IT'S NOT OVER.
NOT TONIGHT. NOT EVER.

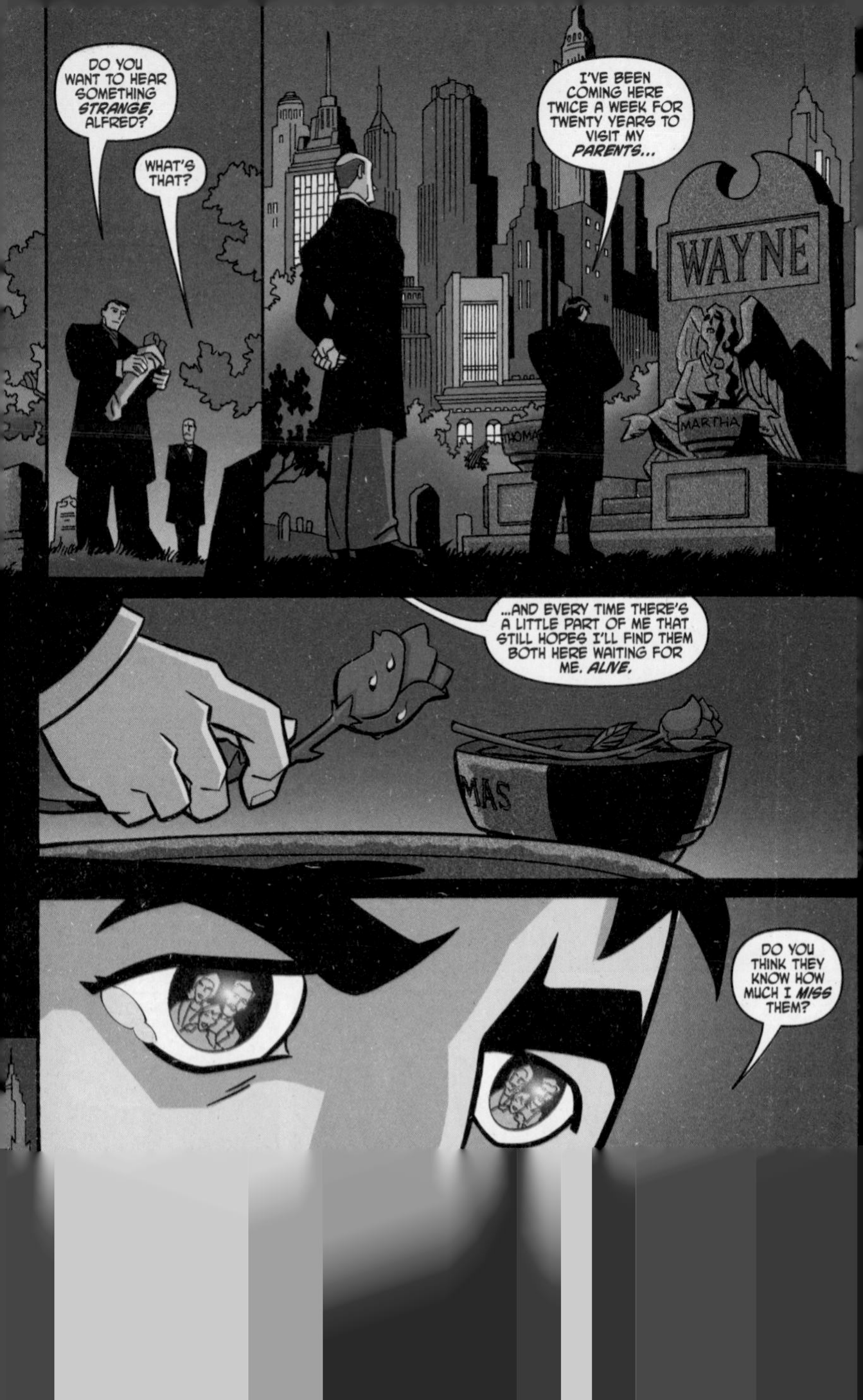
DO YOU WANT TO HEAR SOMETHING *STRANGE*, ALFRED?
WHAT'S THAT?
I'VE BEEN COMING HERE TWICE A WEEK FOR TWENTY YEARS TO VISIT MY *PARENTS...*
WAYNE
THOMAS
MARTHA
...AND EVERY TIME THERE'S A LITTLE PART OF ME THAT STILL HOPES I'LL FIND THEM BOTH HERE WAITING FOR ME. *ALIVE.*
MAS
DO YOU THINK THEY KNOW HOW MUCH I *MISS* THEM?

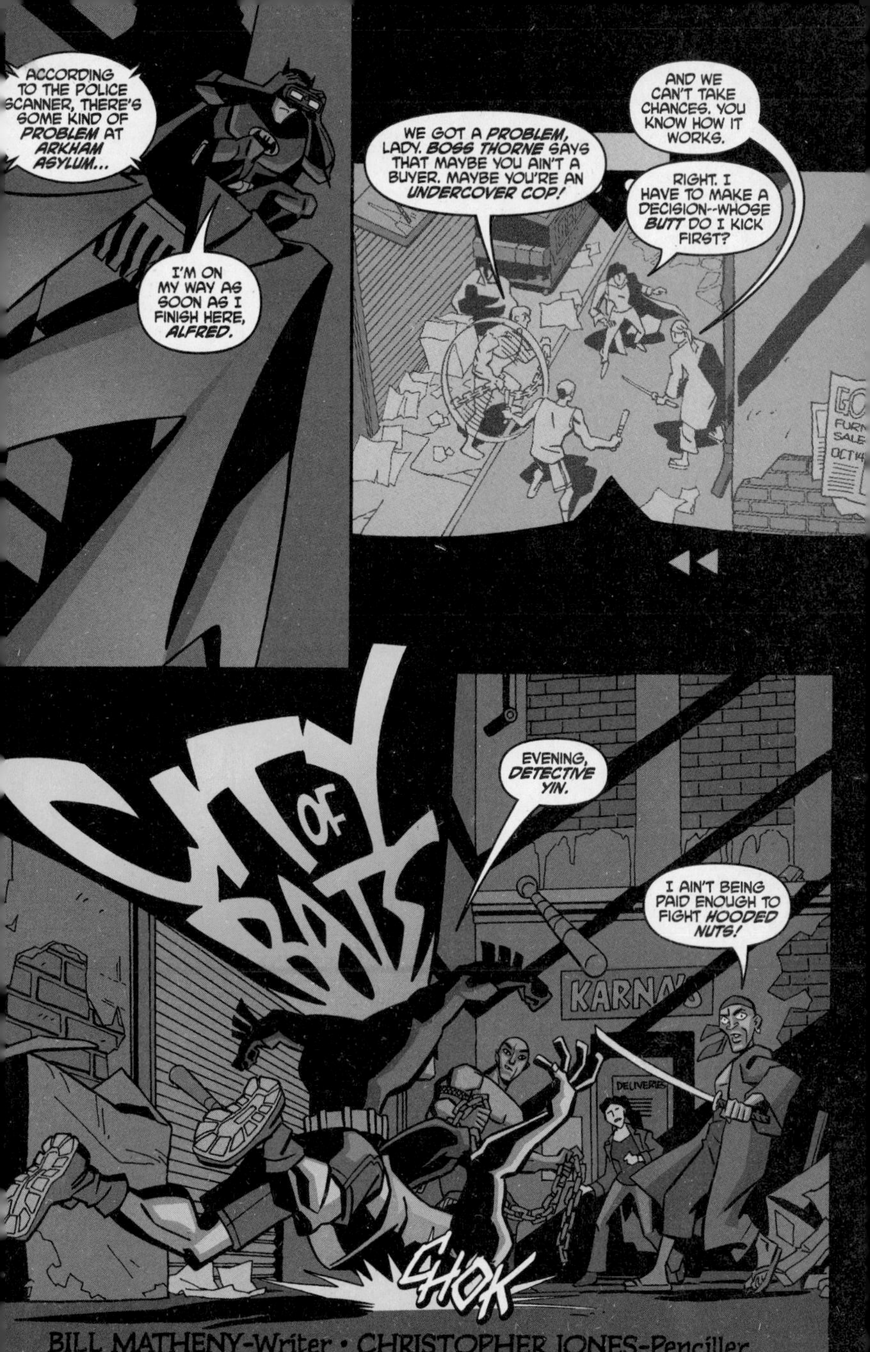
ACCORDING TO THE POLICE SCANNER, THERE'S SOME KIND OF *PROBLEM* AT *ARKHAM ASYLUM...*
I'M ON MY WAY AS SOON AS I FINISH HERE, *ALFRED.*
WE GOT A *PROBLEM,* LADY. *BOSS THORNE* SAYS THAT MAYBE YOU AIN'T A BUYER. MAYBE YOU'RE AN *UNDERCOVER COP!*
AND WE CAN'T TAKE CHANCES. YOU KNOW HOW IT WORKS.
RIGHT. I HAVE TO MAKE A DECISION--WHOSE *BUTT* DO I KICK FIRST?
CITY OF BATS
EVENING, *DETECTIVE YIN.*
I AIN'T BEING PAID ENOUGH TO FIGHT *HOODED NUTS!*
CHOK

BILL MATHENY-Writer • CHRISTOPHER JONES-Penciller
TERRY BEATTY-Inker • NICK J. NAPOLITANO-Letterer

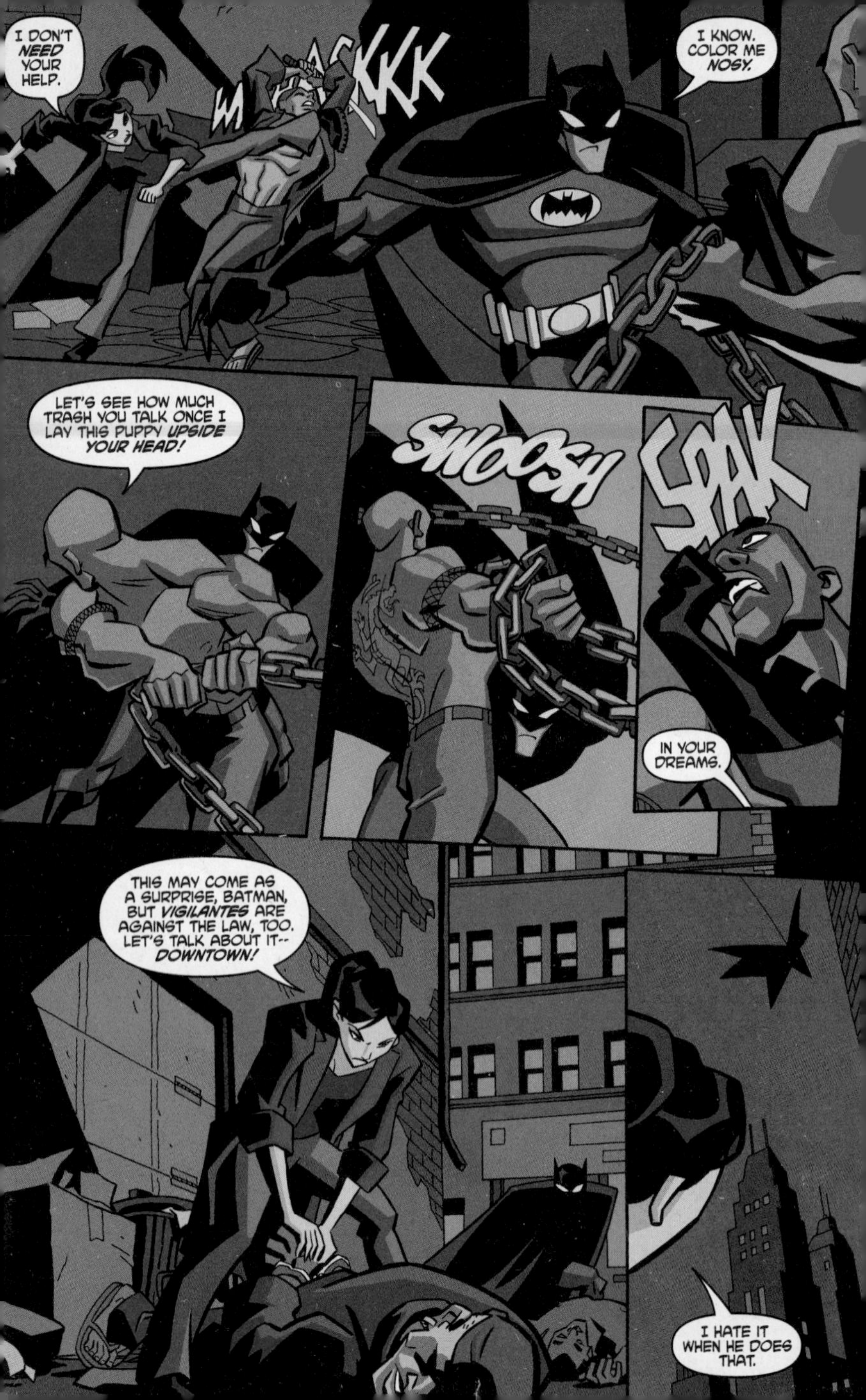
I DON'T NEED YOUR HELP.
I KNOW. COLOR ME NOSY.
LET'S SEE HOW MUCH TRASH YOU TALK ONCE I LAY THIS PUPPY UPSIDE YOUR HEAD!
SWOOSH
SPAK
IN YOUR DREAMS.
THIS MAY COME AS A SURPRISE, BATMAN, BUT VIGILANTES ARE AGAINST THE LAW, TOO. LET'S TALK ABOUT IT-- DOWNTOWN!
I HATE IT WHEN HE DOES THAT.

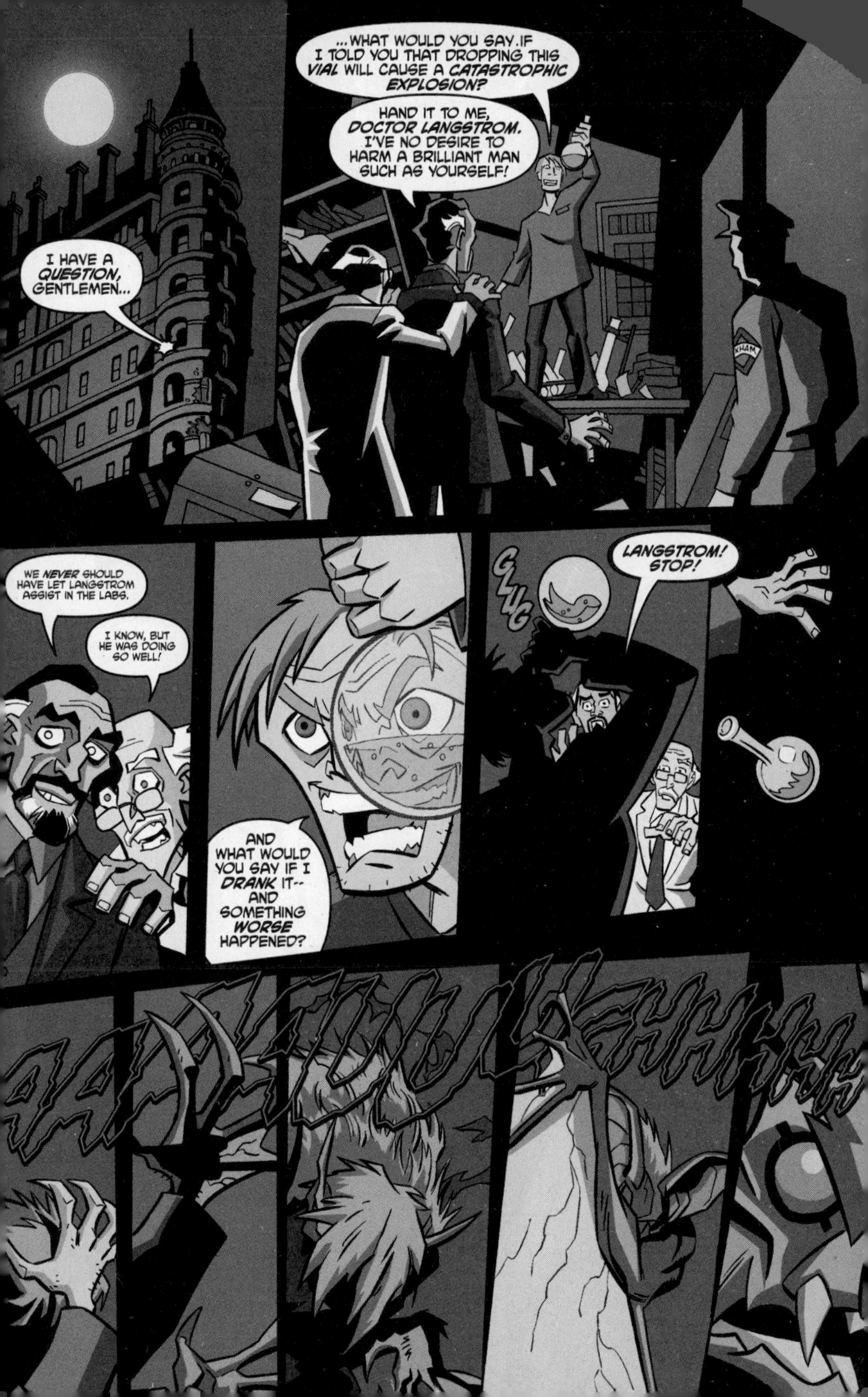
I HAVE A QUESTION, GENTLEMEN...
...WHAT WOULD YOU SAY IF I TOLD YOU THAT DROPPING THIS VIAL WILL CAUSE A CATASTROPHIC EXPLOSION?
HAND IT TO ME, DOCTOR LANGSTROM. I'VE NO DESIRE TO HARM A BRILLIANT MAN SUCH AS YOURSELF!
KHAM
WE NEVER SHOULD HAVE LET LANGSTROM ASSIST IN THE LABS.
I KNOW, BUT HE WAS DOING SO WELL!
AND WHAT WOULD YOU SAY IF I DRANK IT-- AND SOMETHING WORSE HAPPENED?
GLUG
LANGSTROM! STOP!

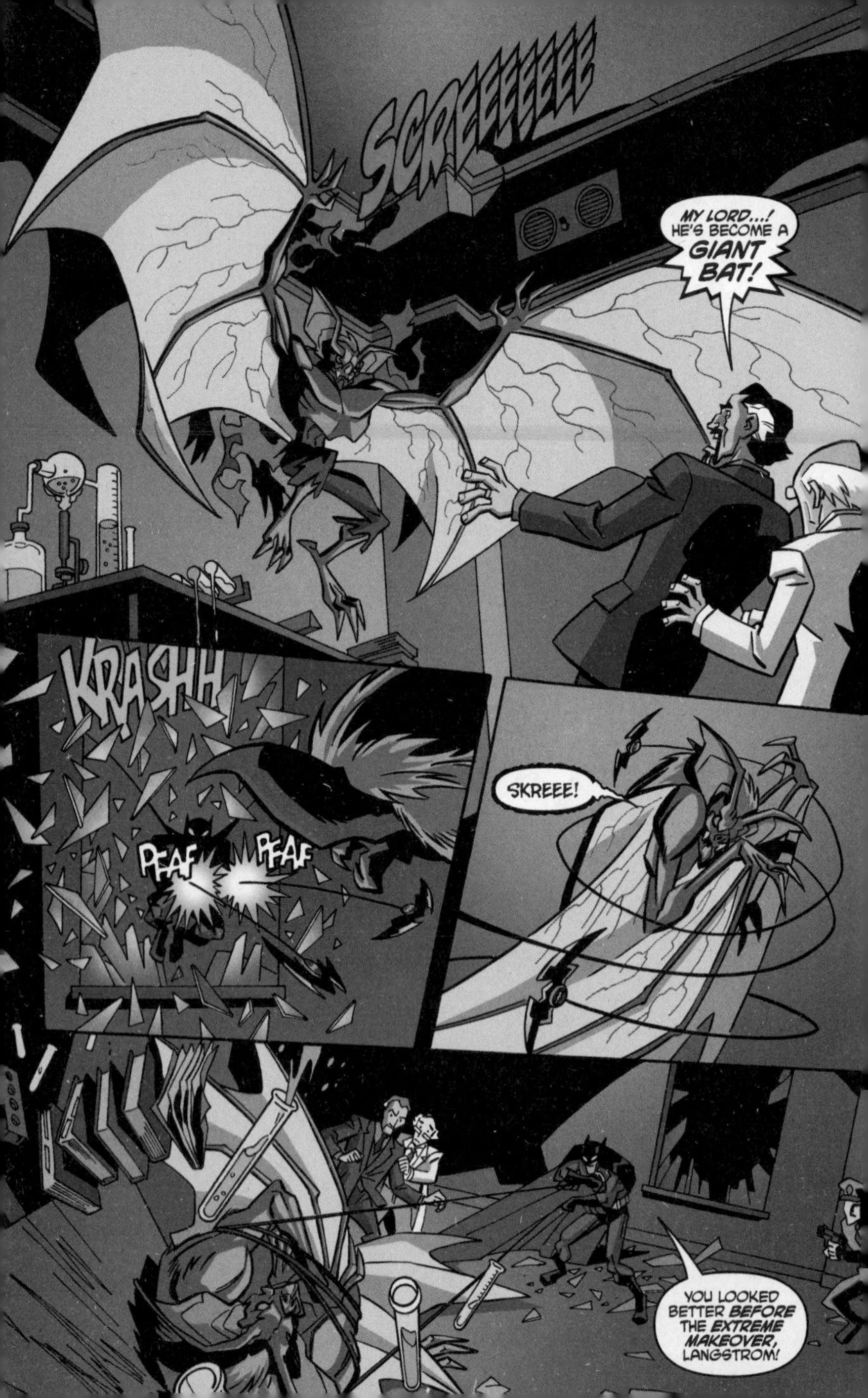
SCREEEEEEE
MY LORD...! HE'S BECOME A GIANT BAT!
KRASHH
PFAF
PFAF
SKREEE!
YOU LOOKED BETTER BEFORE THE EXTREME MAKEOVER, LANGSTROM!

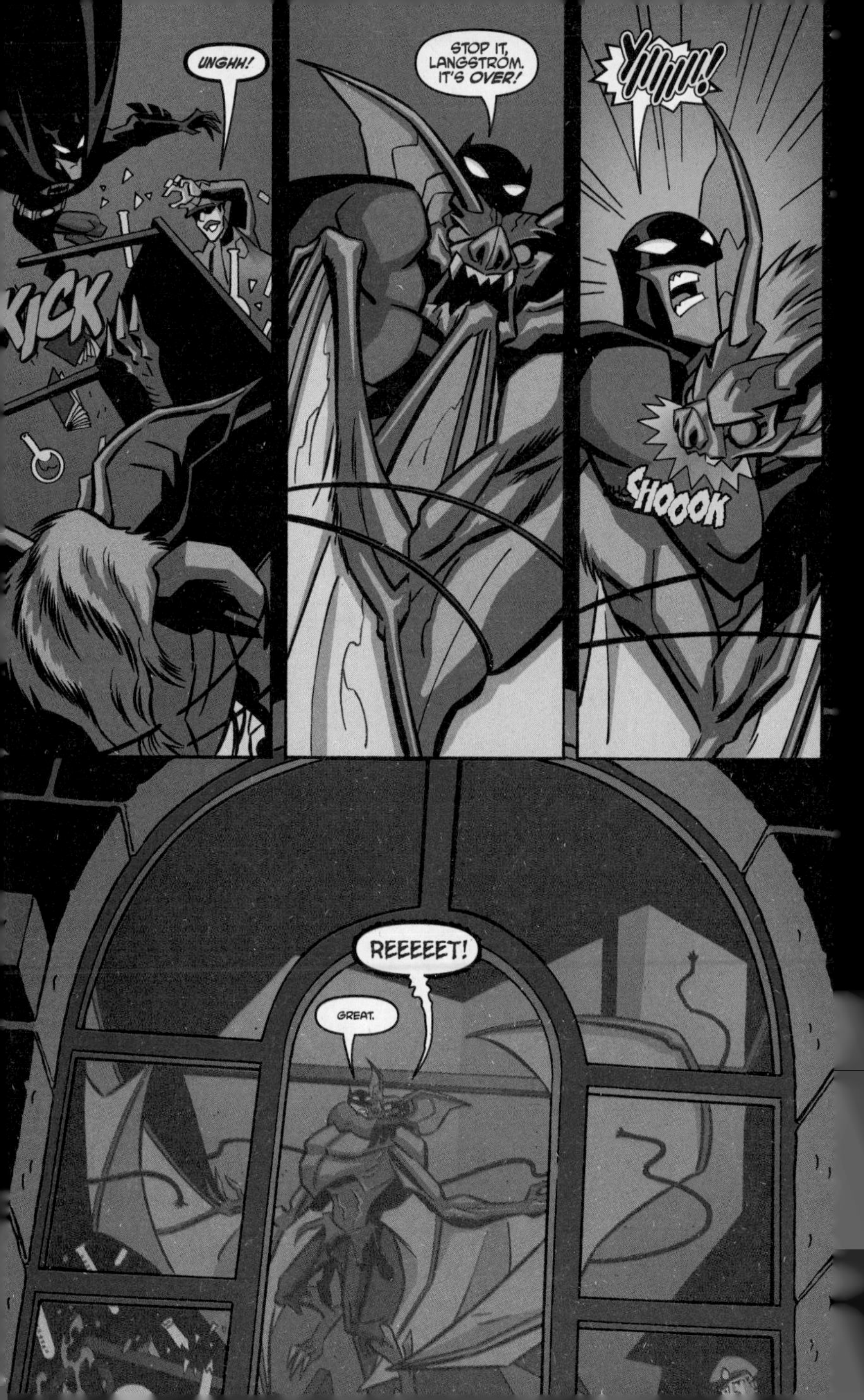
UNGHH!
KICK
STOP IT, LANGSTROM. IT'S OVER!
YIIIIII!
CHOOOK
REEEEEET!
GREAT.

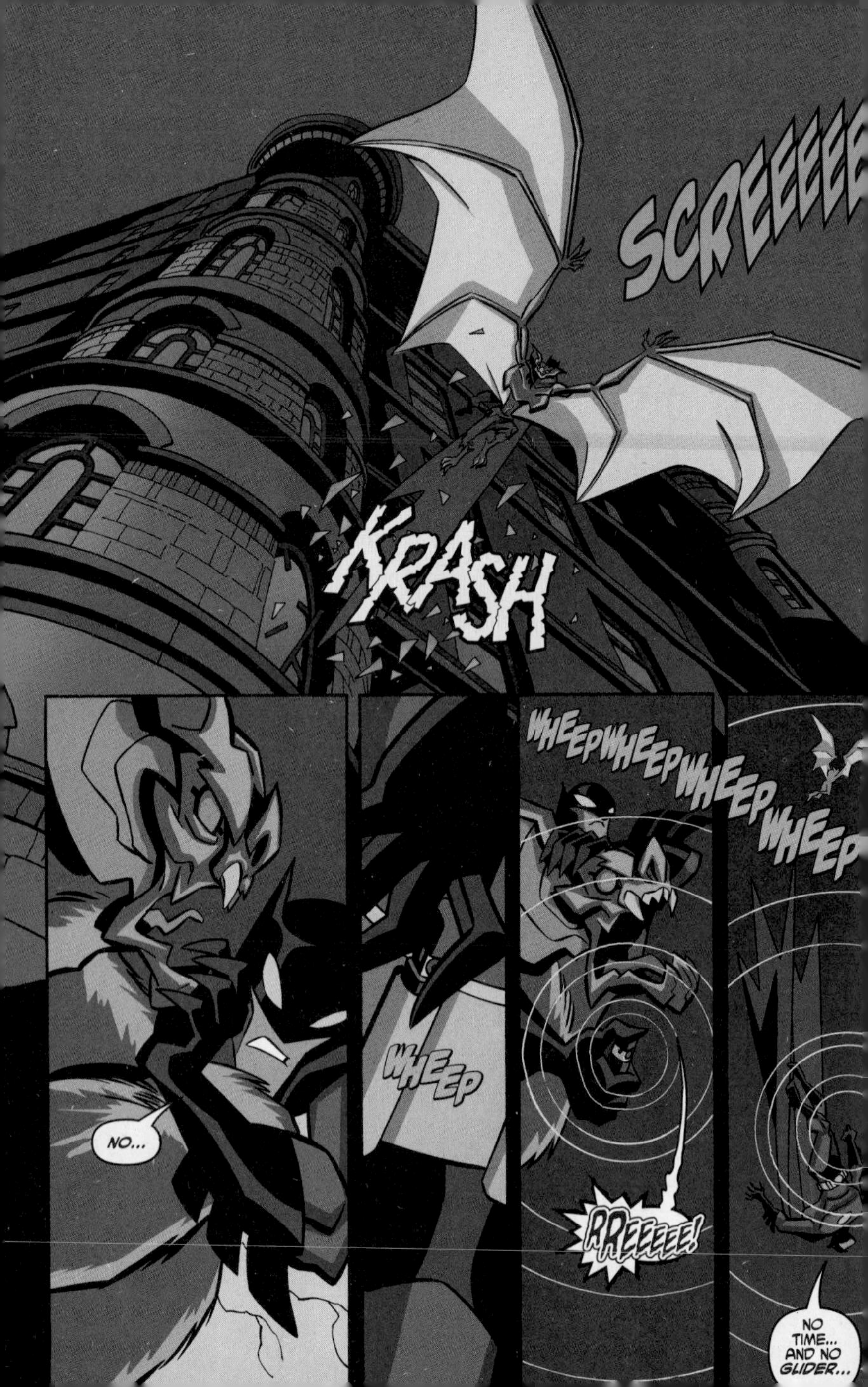
SCREEEEE
KRASH
NO...
WHEEP
WHEEPWHEEPWHEEPWHEEP
RREEEEEE!
NO TIME... AND NO GLIDER...

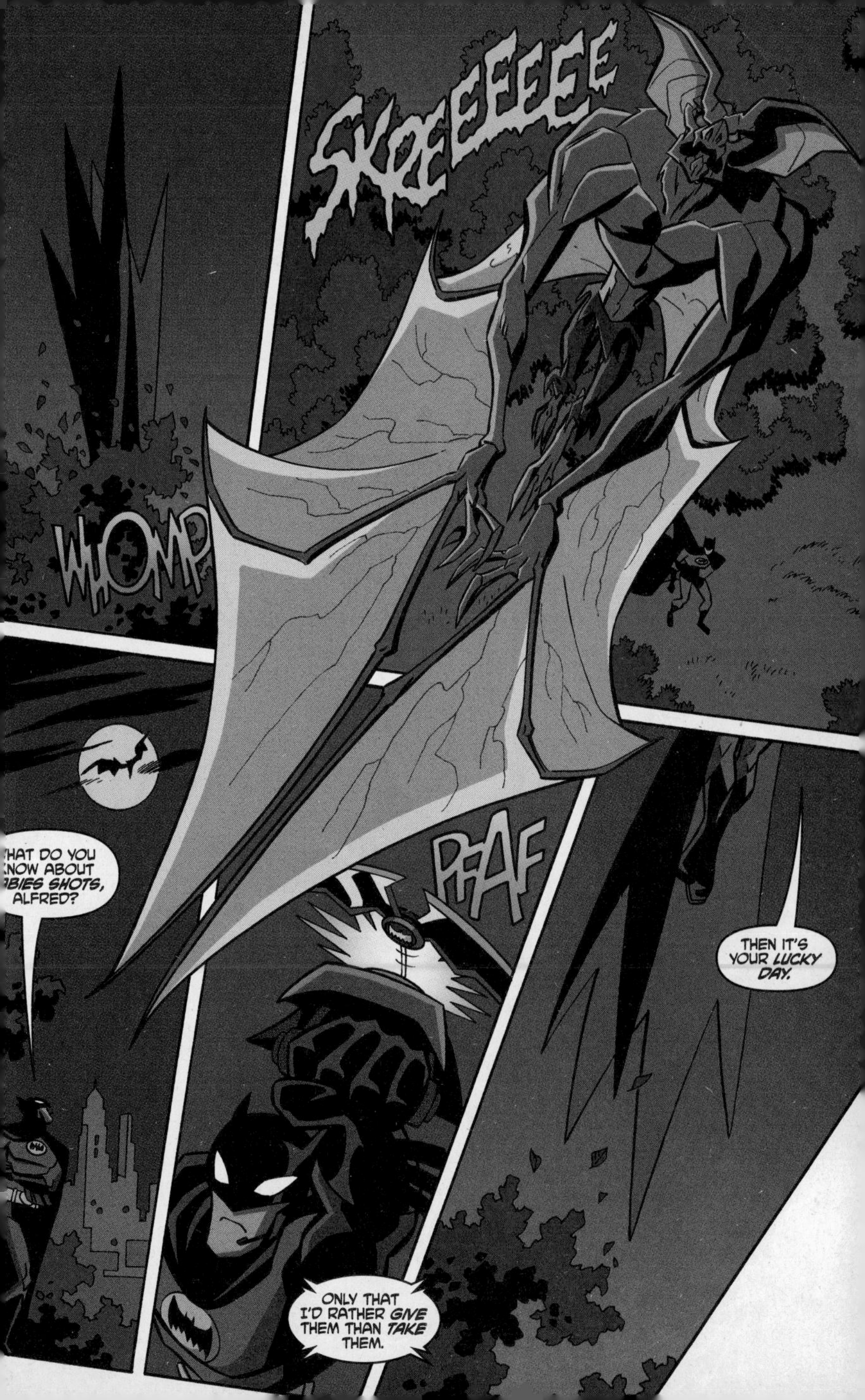
SKREEEEEEE
WHOMP
PFAF
HAT DO YOU
NOW ABOUT
BIES SHOTS,
ALFRED?
ONLY THAT I'D RATHER GIVE THEM THAN TAKE THEM.
THEN IT'S YOUR LUCKY DAY.

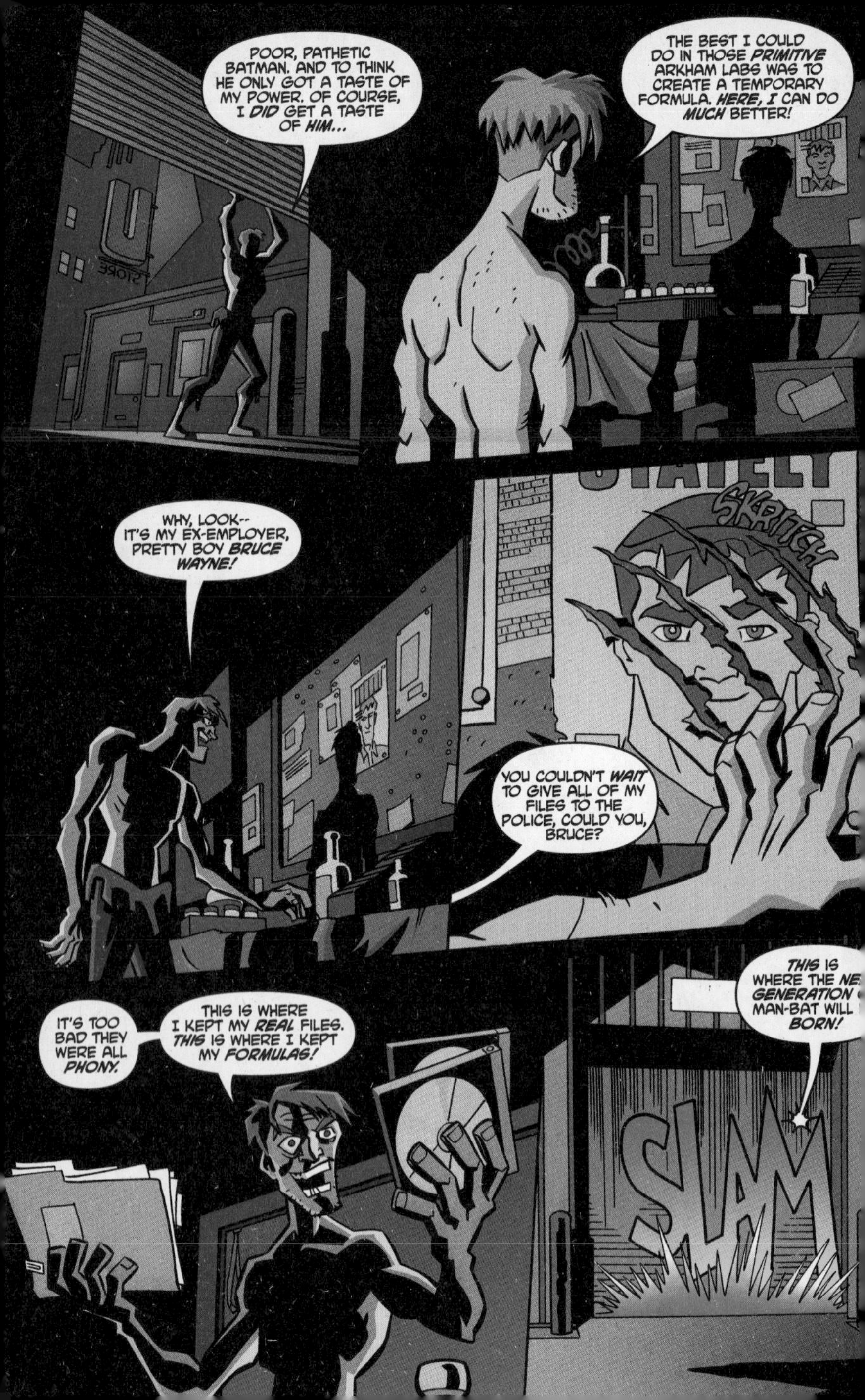
POOR, PATHETIC BATMAN. AND TO THINK HE ONLY GOT A TASTE OF MY POWER. OF COURSE, I *DID* GET A TASTE OF *HIM...*
THE BEST I COULD DO IN THOSE *PRIMITIVE* ARKHAM LABS WAS TO CREATE A TEMPORARY FORMULA. *HERE, I* CAN DO *MUCH* BETTER!
WHY, LOOK-- IT'S MY EX-EMPLOYER, PRETTY BOY *BRUCE WAYNE!*
SKRITCH
YOU COULDN'T *WAIT* TO GIVE ALL OF MY FILES TO THE POLICE, COULD YOU, BRUCE?
IT'S TOO BAD THEY WERE ALL *PHONY.*
THIS IS WHERE I KEPT MY *REAL* FILES. *THIS* IS WHERE I KEPT MY *FORMULAS!*
THIS IS WHERE THE NE *GENERATION* MAN-BAT WILL *BORN!*
SLAM

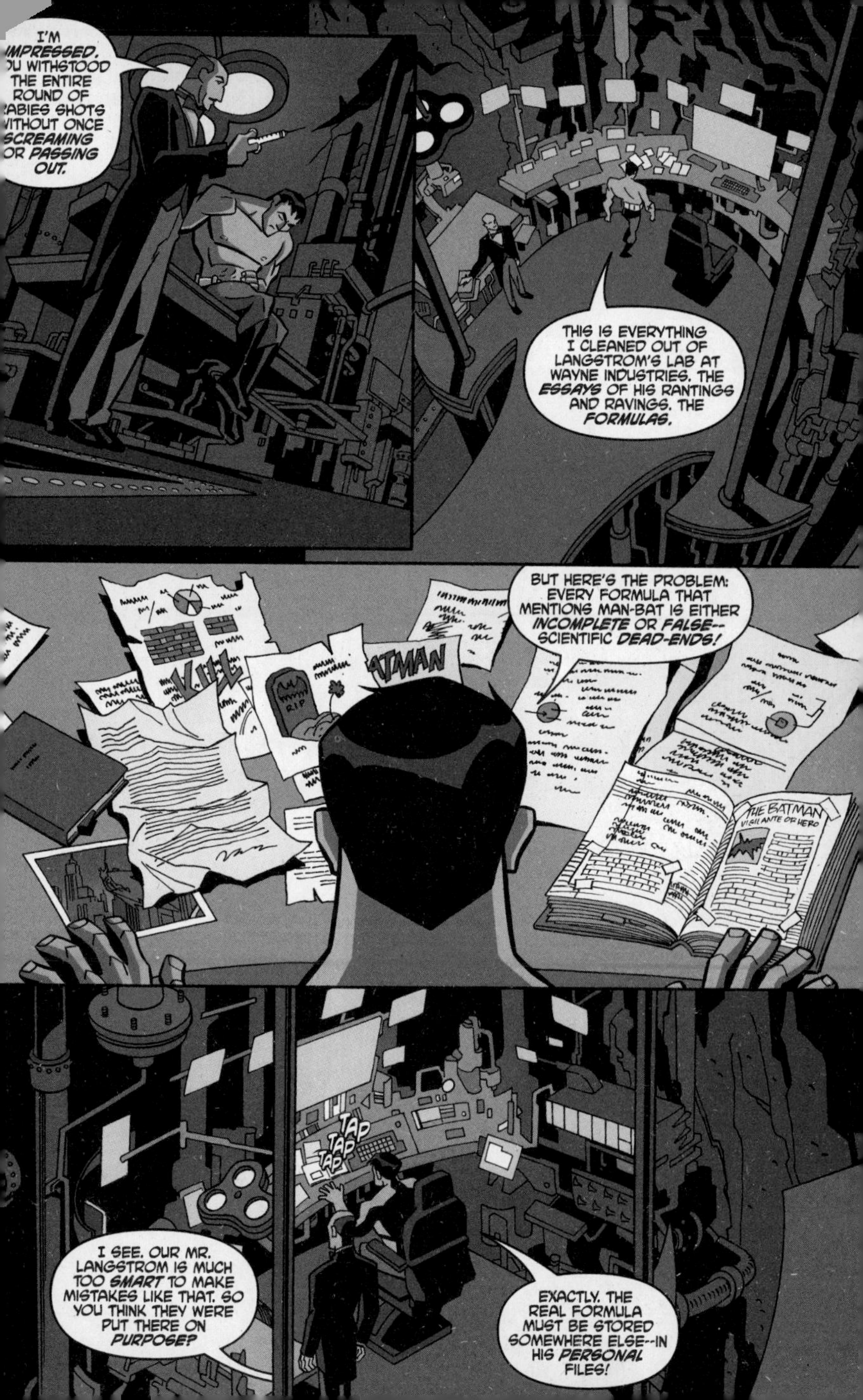
I'M IMPRESSED. OU WITHSTOOD THE ENTIRE ROUND OF ABIES SHOTS ITHOUT ONCE SCREAMING OR PASSING OUT.
THIS IS EVERYTHING I CLEANED OUT OF LANGSTROM'S LAB AT WAYNE INDUSTRIES. THE ESSAYS OF HIS RANTINGS AND RAVINGS. THE FORMULAS.
ATMAN
RIP
THE BATMAN
VIGILANTE OR HERO
BUT HERE'S THE PROBLEM: EVERY FORMULA THAT MENTIONS MAN-BAT IS EITHER INCOMPLETE OR FALSE-- SCIENTIFIC DEAD-ENDS!
TAP TAP TAP
I SEE. OUR MR. LANGSTROM IS MUCH TOO SMART TO MAKE MISTAKES LIKE THAT. SO YOU THINK THEY WERE PUT THERE ON PURPOSE?
EXACTLY. THE REAL FORMULA MUST BE STORED SOMEWHERE ELSE--IN HIS PERSONAL FILES!

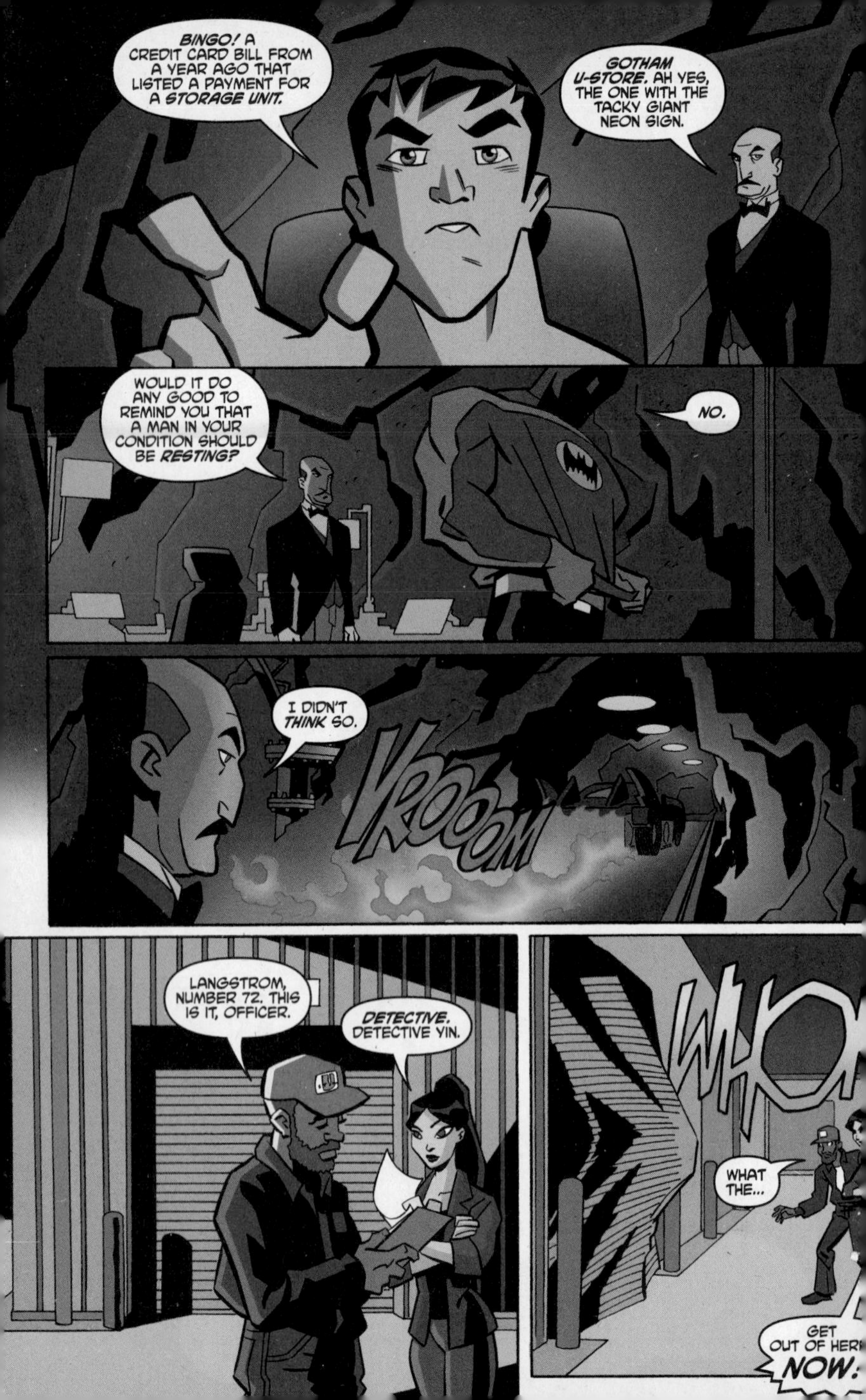
BINGO! A CREDIT CARD BILL FROM A YEAR AGO THAT LISTED A PAYMENT FOR A STORAGE UNIT.
GOTHAM U-STORE. AH YES, THE ONE WITH THE TACKY GIANT NEON SIGN.
WOULD IT DO ANY GOOD TO REMIND YOU THAT A MAN IN YOUR CONDITION SHOULD BE RESTING?
NO.
I DIDN'T THINK SO.
VROOOM
LANGSTROM, NUMBER 72. THIS IS IT, OFFICER.
DETECTIVE. DETECTIVE YIN.
WHAT THE...
GET OUT OF HER
NOW:

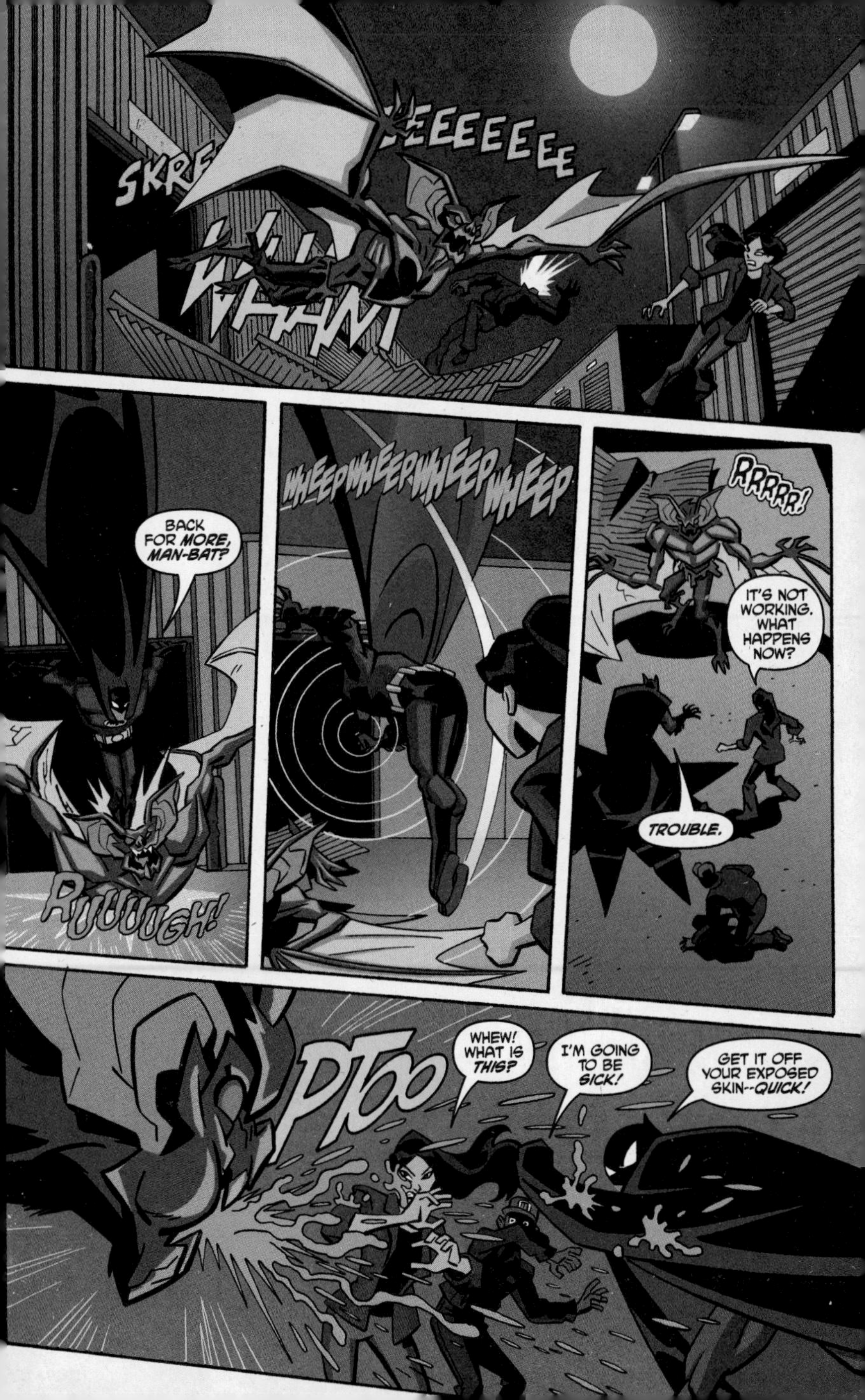

SKREEEEEEEEEE
WHAM
BACK FOR MORE, MAN-BAT?
RUUUUGH!
WHEEPWHEEPWHEEPWHEEP
RRRRR!
IT'S NOT WORKING. WHAT HAPPENS NOW?
TROUBLE.
PTOO
WHEW! WHAT IS THIS?
I'M GOING TO BE SICK!
GET IT OFF YOUR EXPOSED SKIN--QUICK!

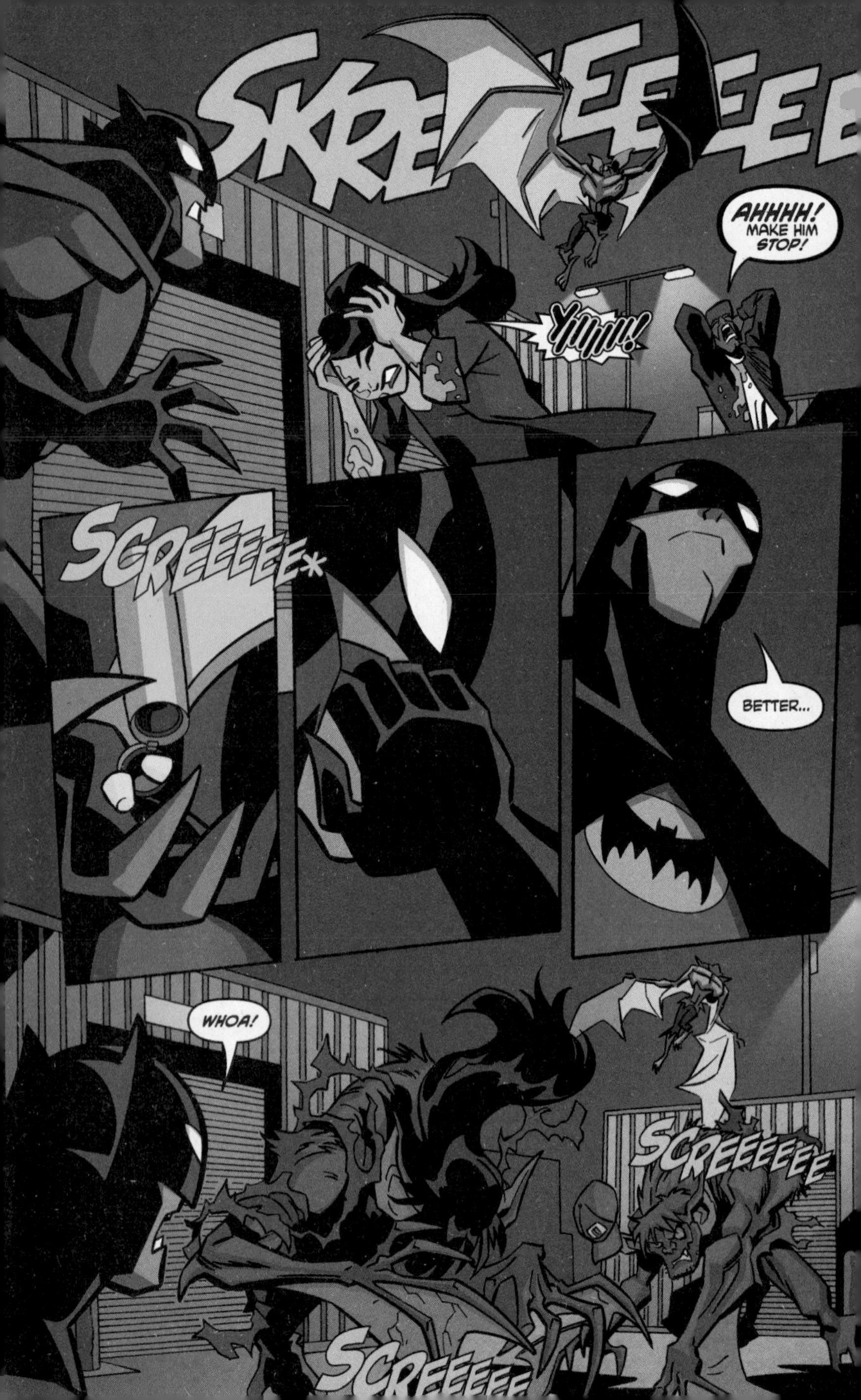
SKREEEEEEEE
AHHHH! MAKE HIM STOP!
YIIIIII!
SCREEEEEE*
BETTER...
WHOA!
SCREEEEEE
SCREEEEEE

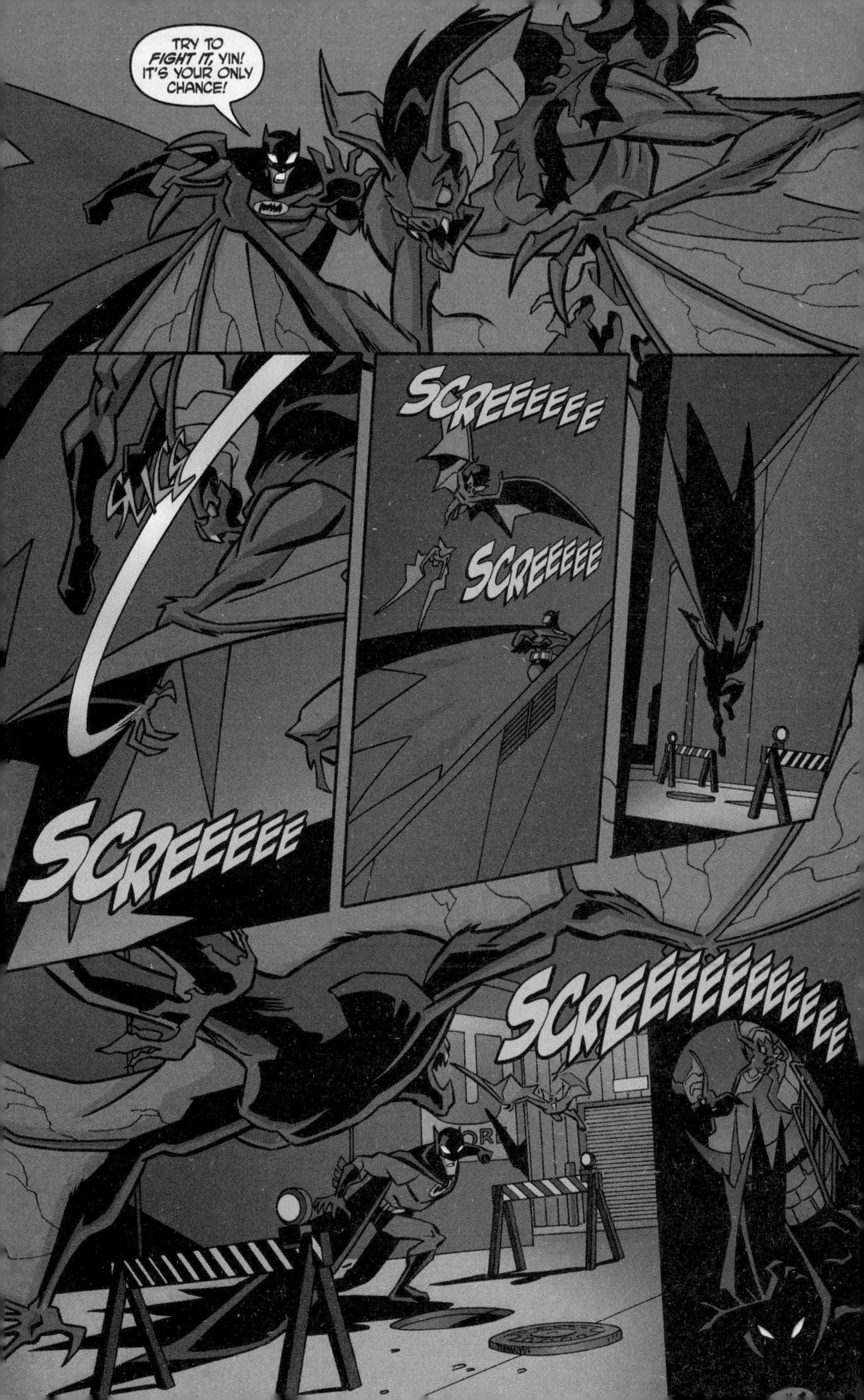
TRY TO *FIGHT IT,* YIN! IT'S YOUR ONLY CHANCE!
SLICE
SCREEEEEE
SCREEEEEEE
SCREEEEE
SCREEEEEEEEEEE

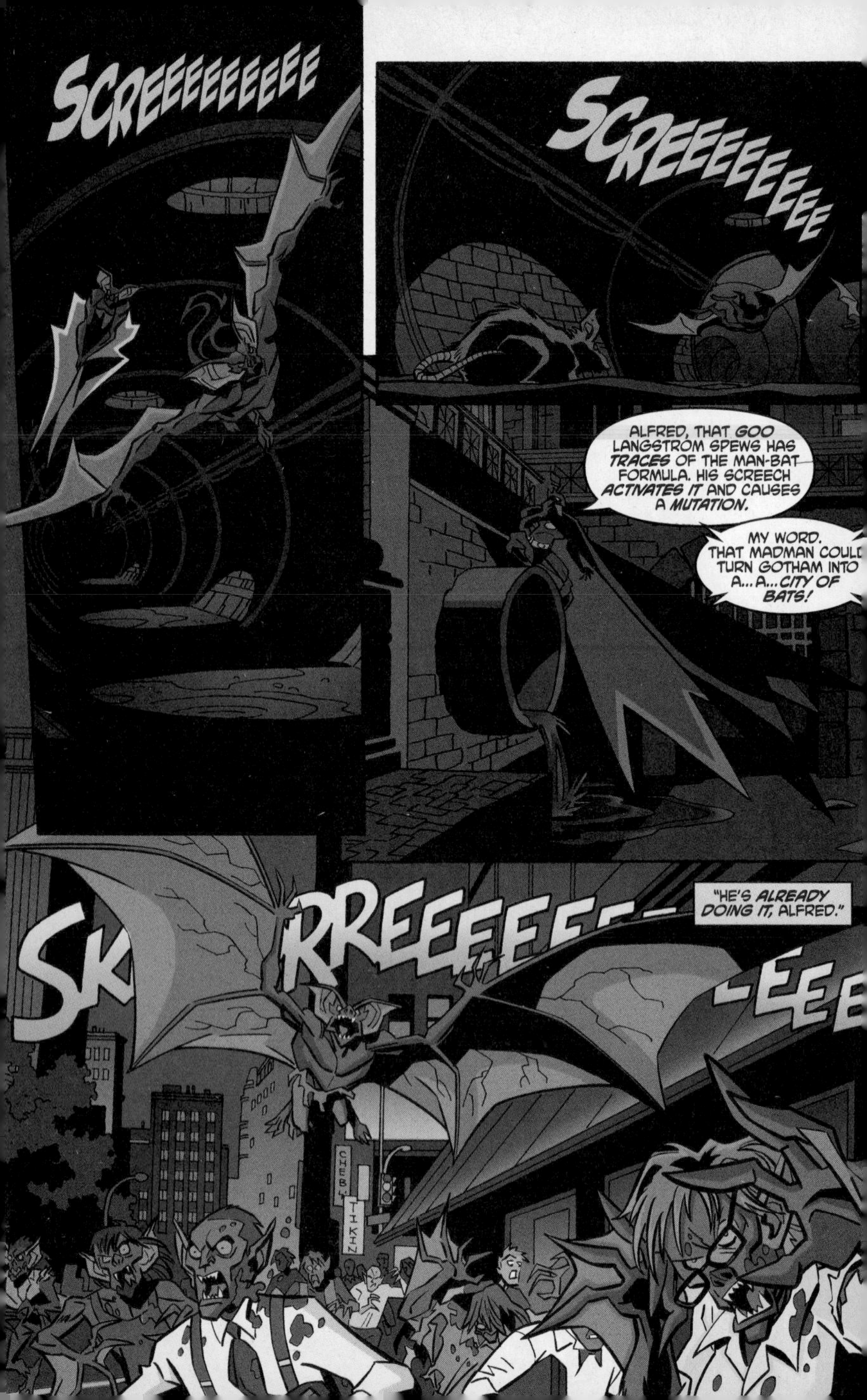
SCREEEEEEEEE
SCREEEEEEEEE
ALFRED, THAT GOO LANGSTROM SPEWS HAS TRACES OF THE MAN-BAT FORMULA. HIS SCREECH ACTIVATES IT AND CAUSES A MUTATION.
MY WORD. THAT MADMAN COULD TURN GOTHAM INTO A...A...CITY OF BATS!
"HE'S ALREADY DOING IT, ALFRED."
SKRREEEEE--
-EEEE

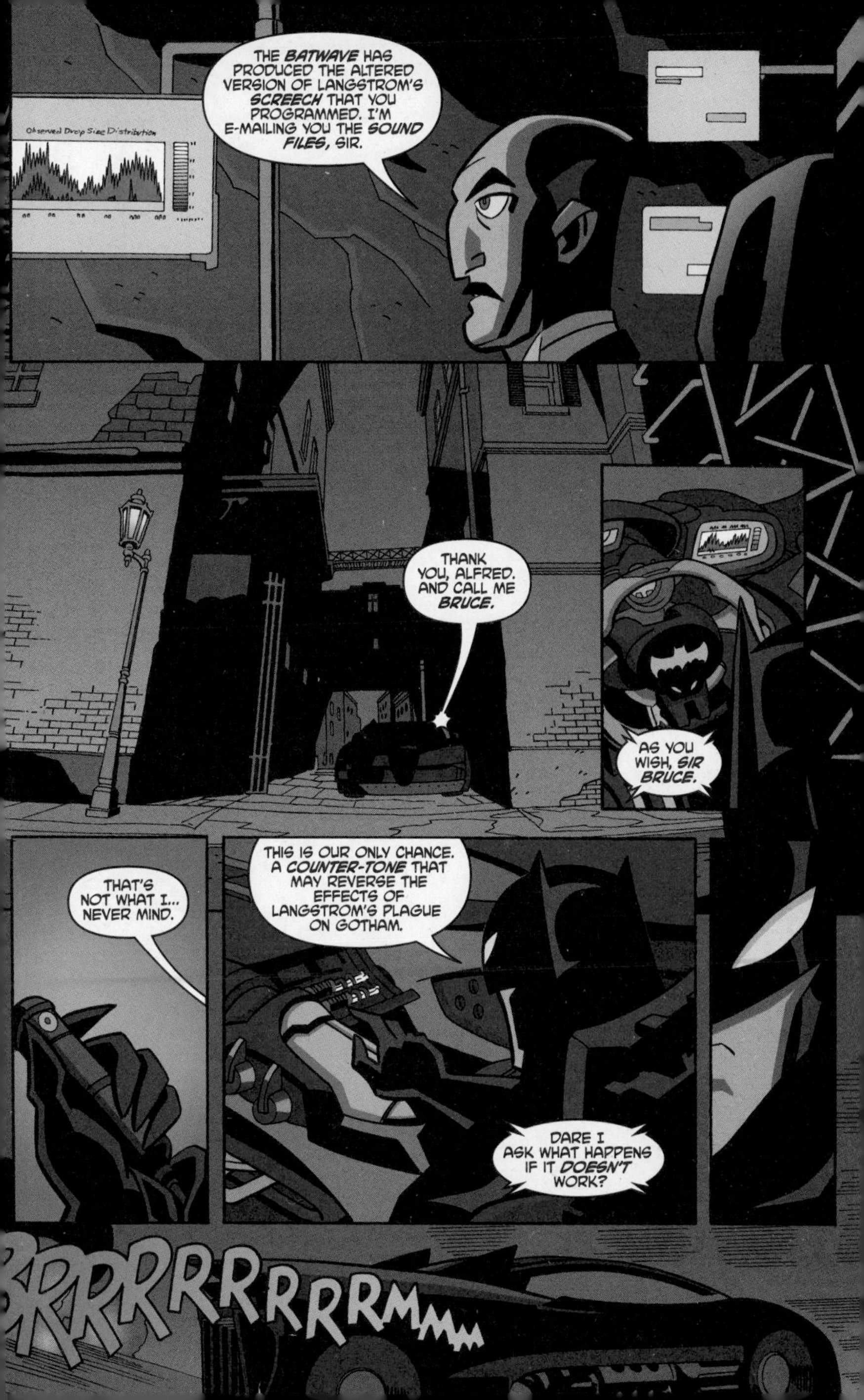
THE BATWAVE HAS PRODUCED THE ALTERED VERSION OF LANGSTROM'S SCREECH THAT YOU PROGRAMMED. I'M E-MAILING YOU THE SOUND FILES, SIR.
Observed Drop Size Distribution
THANK YOU, ALFRED. AND CALL ME BRUCE.
AS YOU WISH, SIR BRUCE.
THAT'S NOT WHAT I... NEVER MIND.
THIS IS OUR ONLY CHANCE. A COUNTER-TONE THAT MAY REVERSE THE EFFECTS OF LANGSTROM'S PLAGUE ON GOTHAM.
DARE I ASK WHAT HAPPENS IF IT DOESN'T WORK?
RRRRRRRRRRMMMM

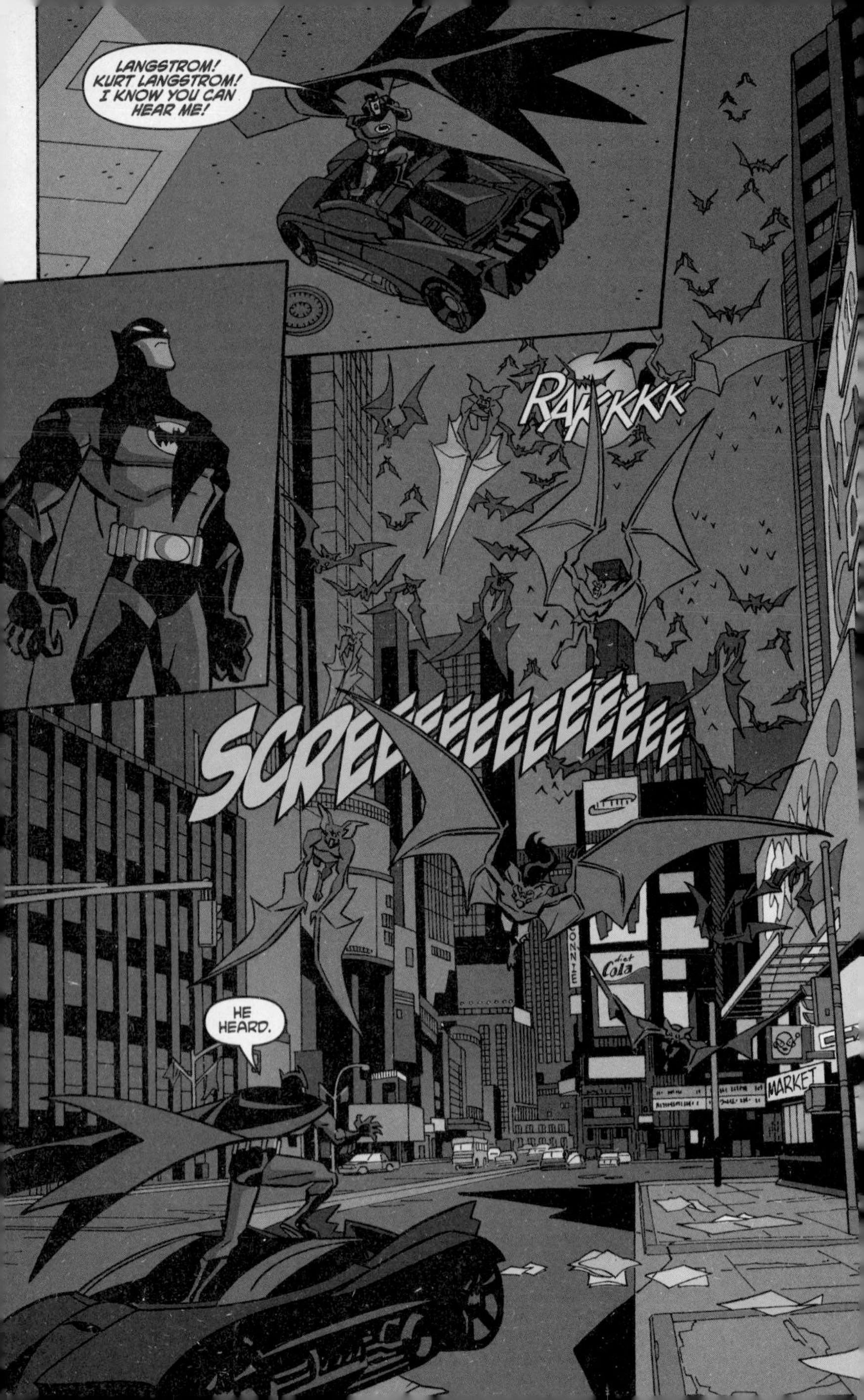
LANGSTROM! KURT LANGSTROM! I KNOW YOU CAN HEAR ME!
RAKKKK
SCREEEEEEEEEEEE
HE HEARD.
diet Cola
MARKET

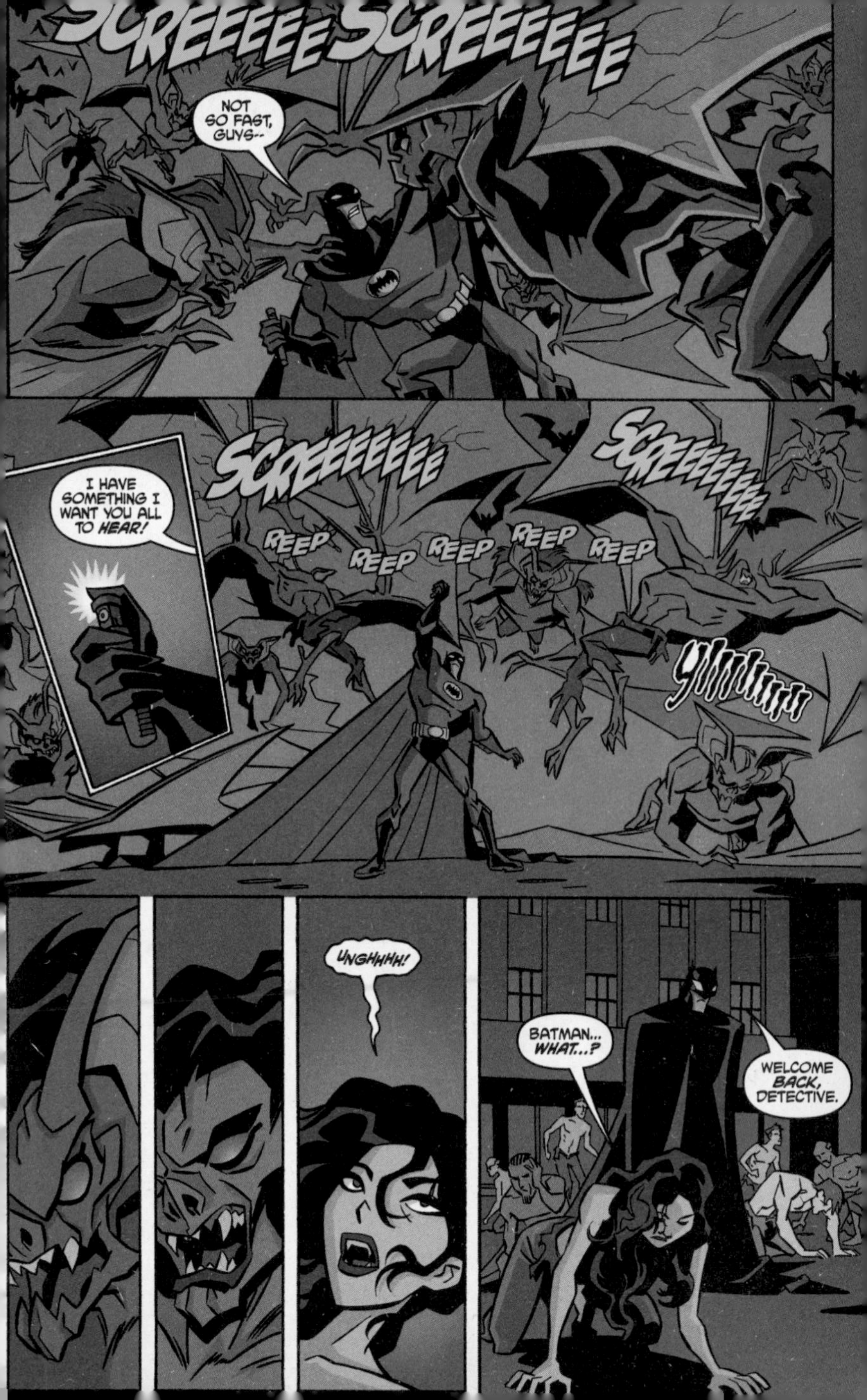
SCREEEEEE SCREEEEEEE
NOT SO FAST, GUYS--
SCREEEEEEEE
SCREEEEEEEEE
I HAVE SOMETHING I WANT YOU ALL TO *HEAR!*
REEP
REEP
REEP
REEP
REEP
UNGHHHH!
BATMAN... *WHAT...?*
WELCOME *BACK,* DETECTIVE.

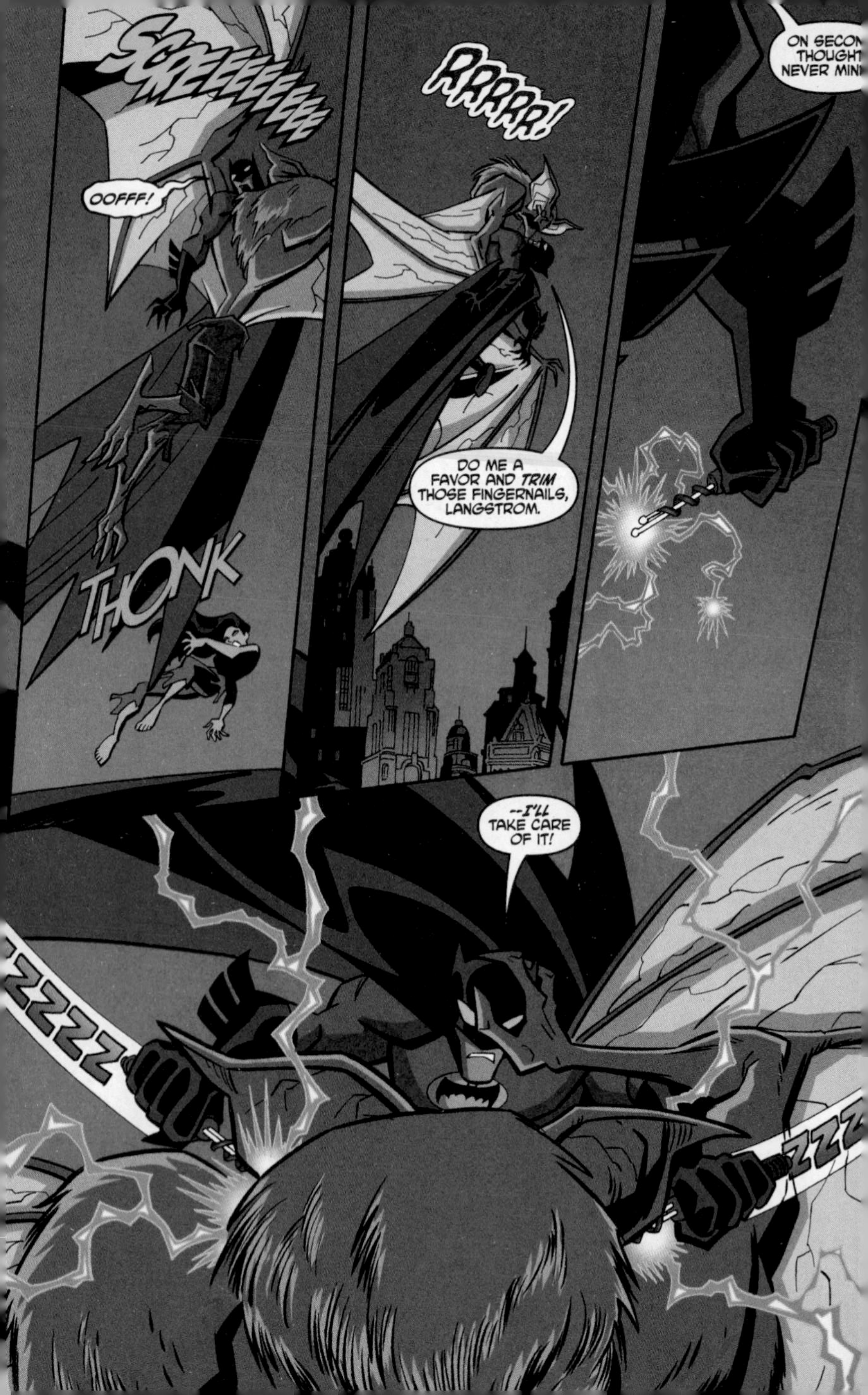
SCREEEEEEEEE
OOFFF!
THONK
RRRRR!
DO ME A FAVOR AND TRIM THOSE FINGERNAILS, LANGSTROM.
ON SECON THOUGHT NEVER MIN
--I'LL TAKE CARE OF IT!
ZZZZZ
ZZZ

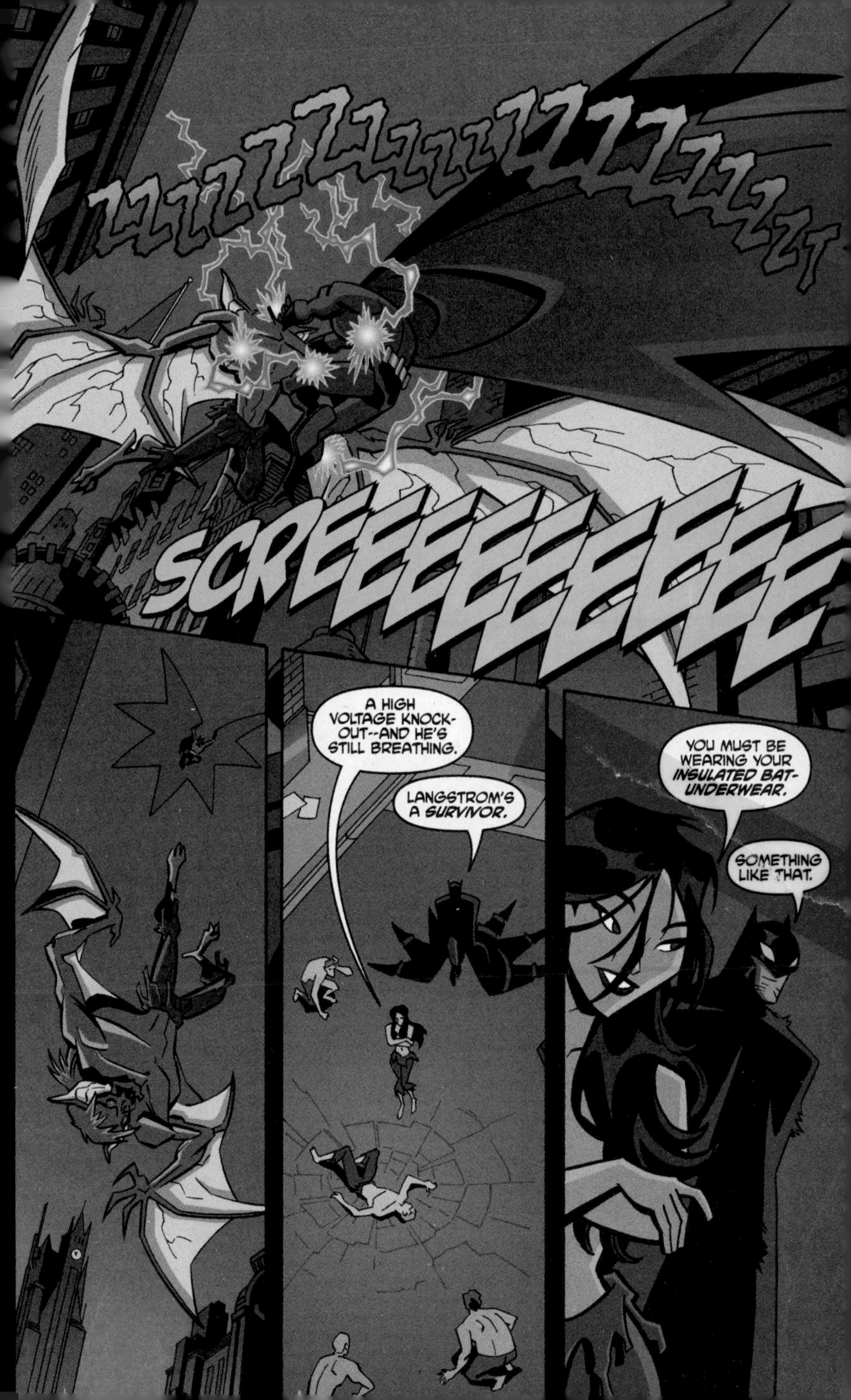
ZZZZZZZZZZZZZZZZZZZZZZZT
SCREEEEEEEEEEE
A HIGH VOLTAGE KNOCK-OUT--AND HE'S STILL BREATHING.
LANGSTROM'S A *SURVIVOR.*
YOU MUST BE WEARING YOUR *INSULATED BAT-UNDERWEAR.*
SOMETHING LIKE THAT.

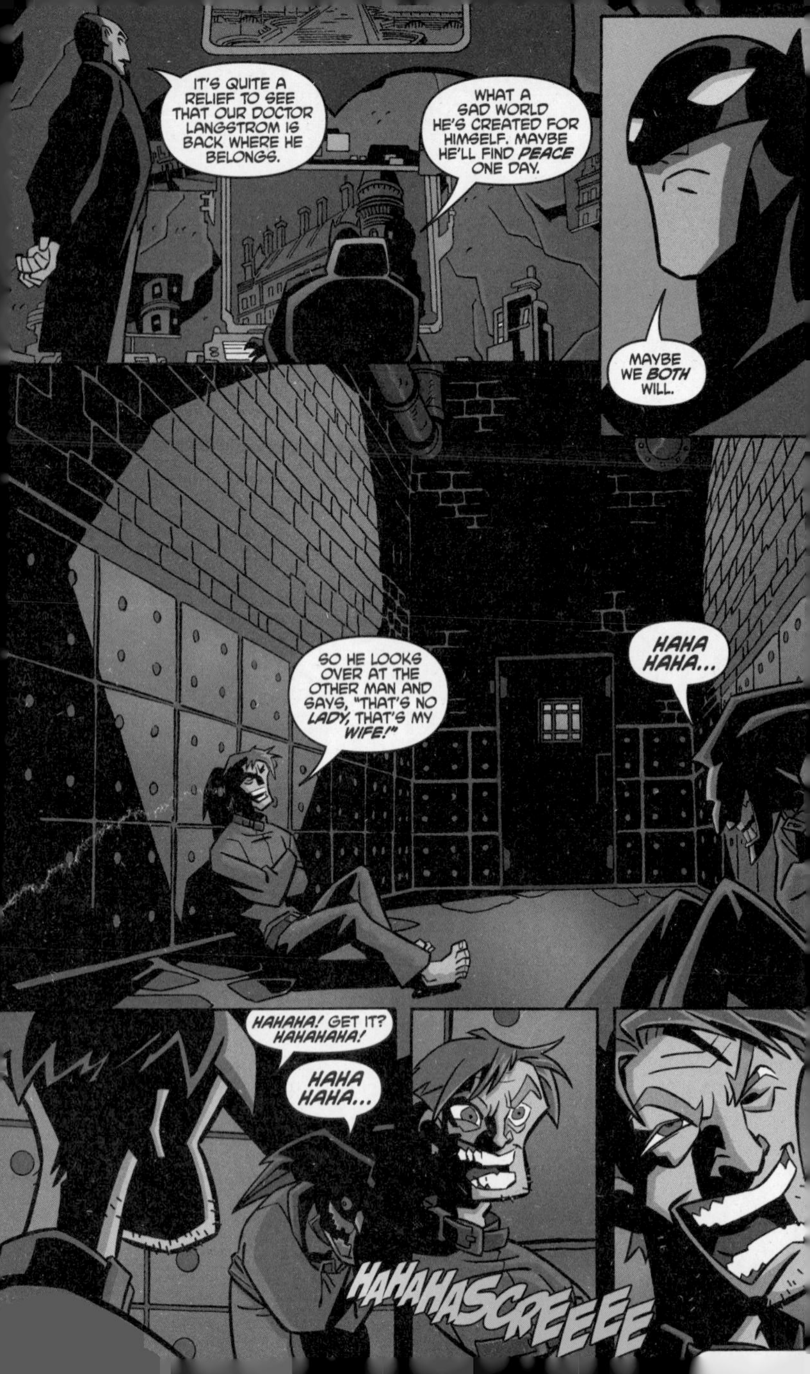
IT'S QUITE A RELIEF TO SEE THAT OUR DOCTOR LANGSTROM IS BACK WHERE HE BELONGS.
WHAT A SAD WORLD HE'S CREATED FOR HIMSELF. MAYBE HE'LL FIND *PEACE* ONE DAY.
MAYBE WE *BOTH* WILL.
SO HE LOOKS OVER AT THE OTHER MAN AND SAYS, "THAT'S NO *LADY,* THAT'S MY *WIFE!"*
HAHA HAHA...
HAHAHA! GET IT? *HAHAHAHA!*
HAHA HAHA...
HAHAHASCREEEEE

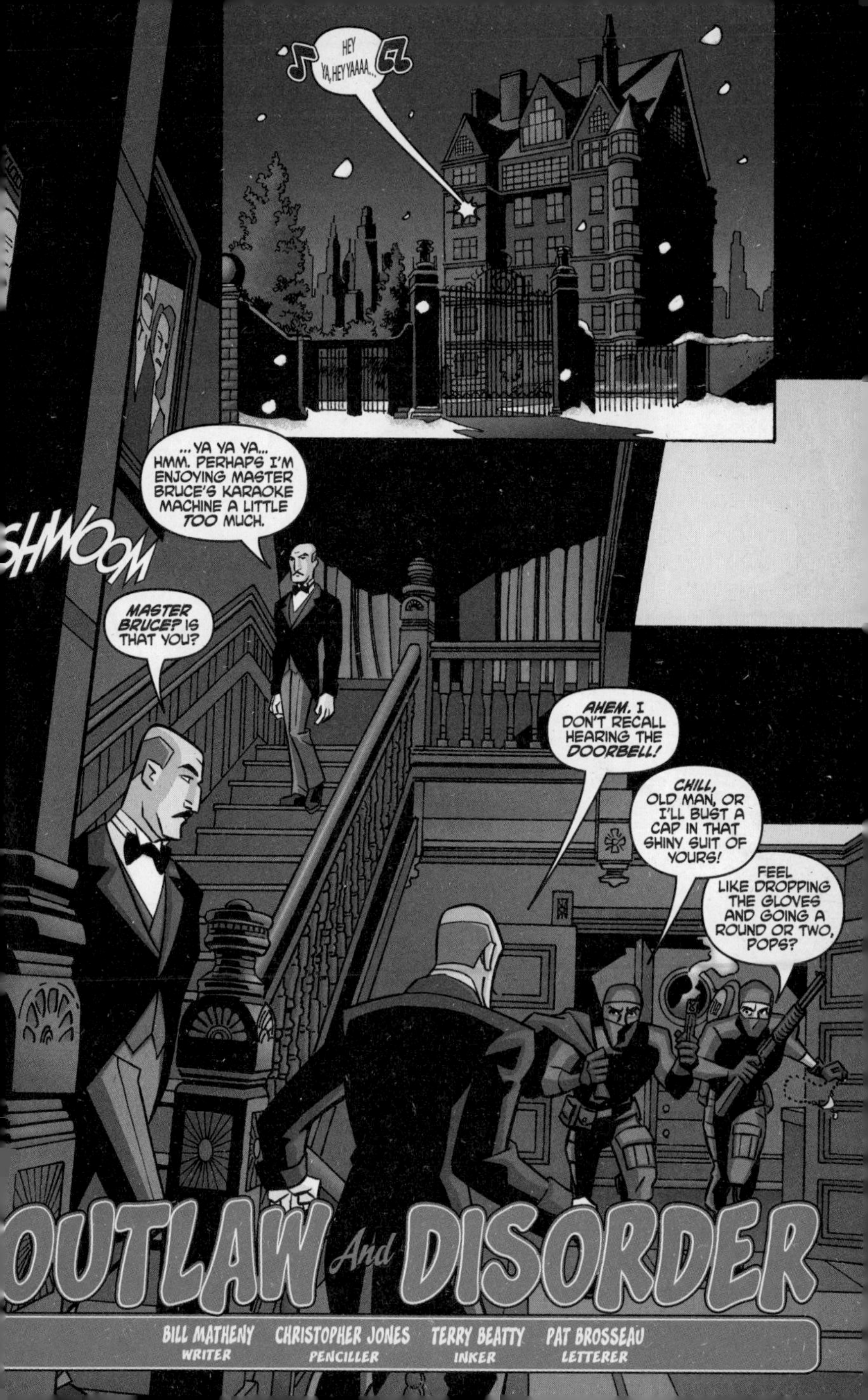
HEY YA, HEY YAAAA...
...YA YA YA... HMM. PERHAPS I'M ENJOYING MASTER BRUCE'S KARAOKE MACHINE A LITTLE TOO MUCH.
SHWOOM
MASTER BRUCE? IS THAT YOU?
AHEM. I DON'T RECALL HEARING THE DOORBELL!
CHILL, OLD MAN, OR I'LL BUST A CAP IN THAT SHINY SUIT OF YOURS!
FEEL LIKE DROPPING THE GLOVES AND GOING A ROUND OR TWO, POPS?
OUTLAW And DISORDER
BILL MATHENY WRITER
CHRISTOPHER JONES PENCILLER
TERRY BEATTY INKER
PAT BROSSEAU LETTERER

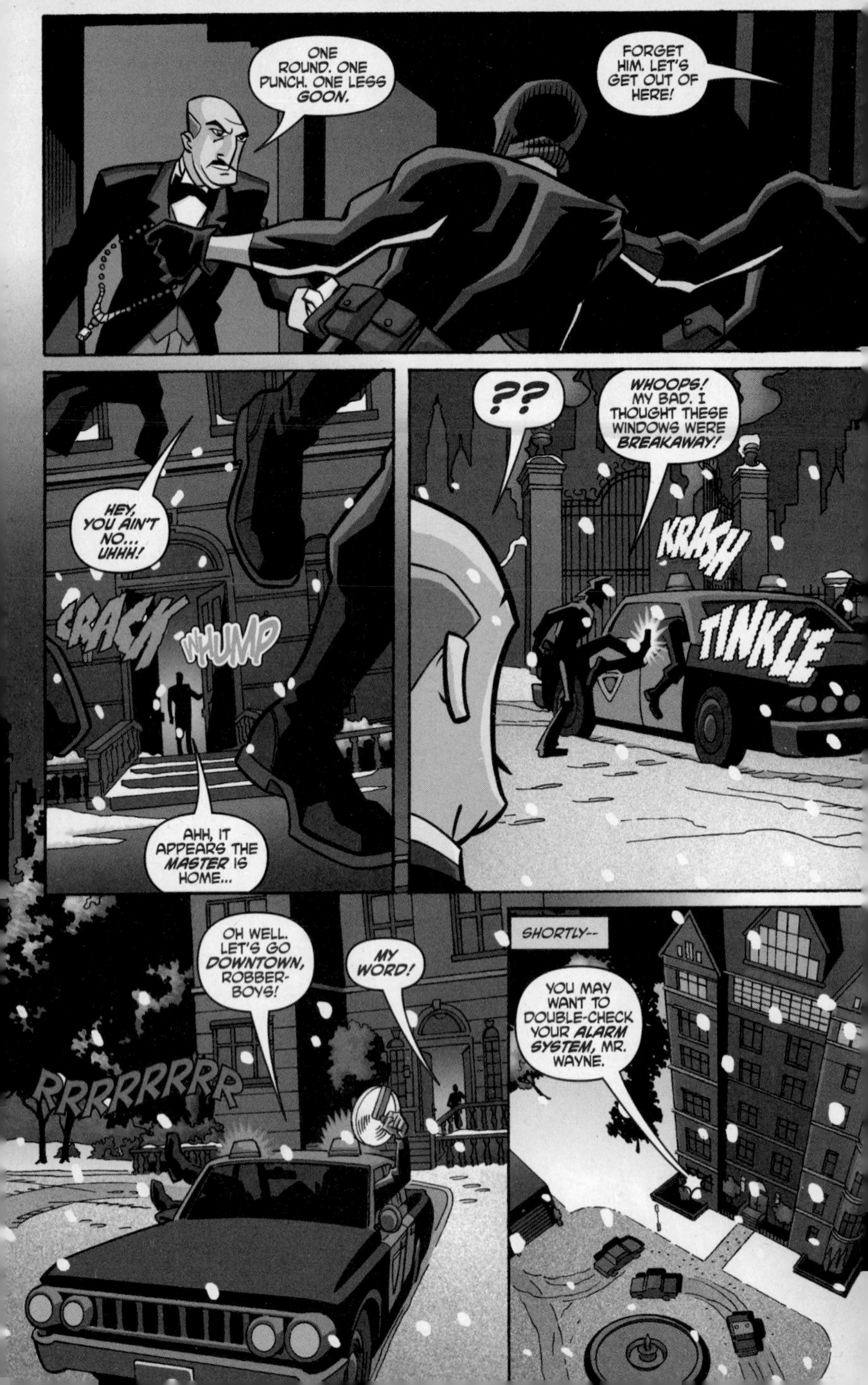
ONE ROUND. ONE PUNCH. ONE LESS GOON.
FORGET HIM. LET'S GET OUT OF HERE!
HEY, YOU AIN'T NO... UHHH!
CRACK
WHUMP
AHH, IT APPEARS THE MASTER IS HOME...
??
WHOOPS! MY BAD. I THOUGHT THESE WINDOWS WERE BREAKAWAY!
KRASH
TINKLE
OH WELL. LET'S GO DOWNTOWN, ROBBER-BOYS!
MY WORD!
RRRRRRRR
SHORTLY--
YOU MAY WANT TO DOUBLE-CHECK YOUR ALARM SYSTEM, MR. WAYNE.

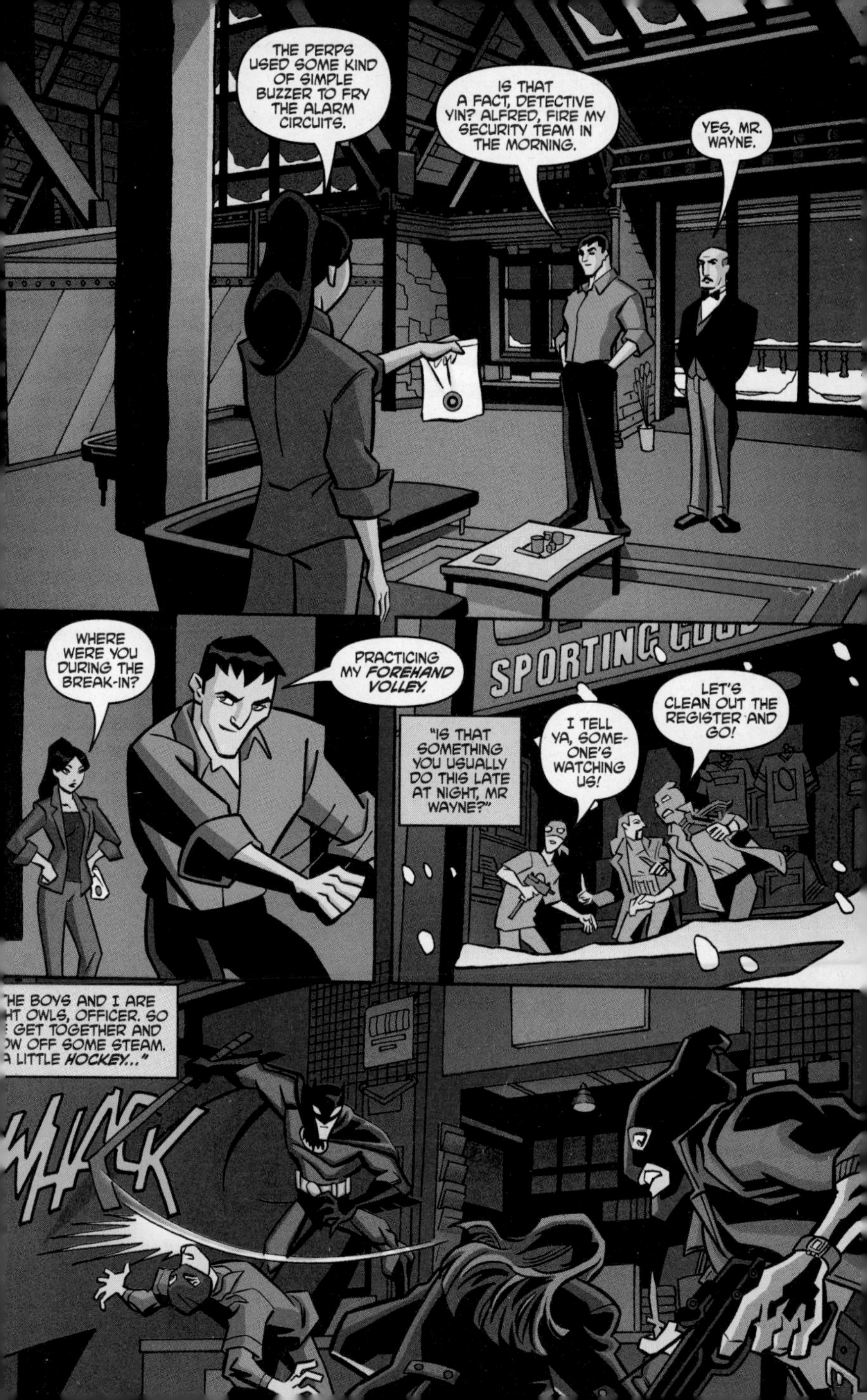
THE PERPS USED SOME KIND OF SIMPLE BUZZER TO FRY THE ALARM CIRCUITS.
IS THAT A FACT, DETECTIVE YIN? ALFRED, FIRE MY SECURITY TEAM IN THE MORNING.
YES, MR. WAYNE.
WHERE WERE YOU DURING THE BREAK-IN?
PRACTICING MY *FOREHAND VOLLEY.*
SPORTING
"IS THAT SOMETHING YOU USUALLY DO THIS LATE AT NIGHT, MR WAYNE?"
I TELL YA, SOME-ONE'S WATCHING US!
LET'S CLEAN OUT THE REGISTER AND GO!
HE BOYS AND I ARE HT OWLS, OFFICER. SO GET TOGETHER AND W OFF SOME STEAM. A LITTLE *HOCKEY...*"
WHACK

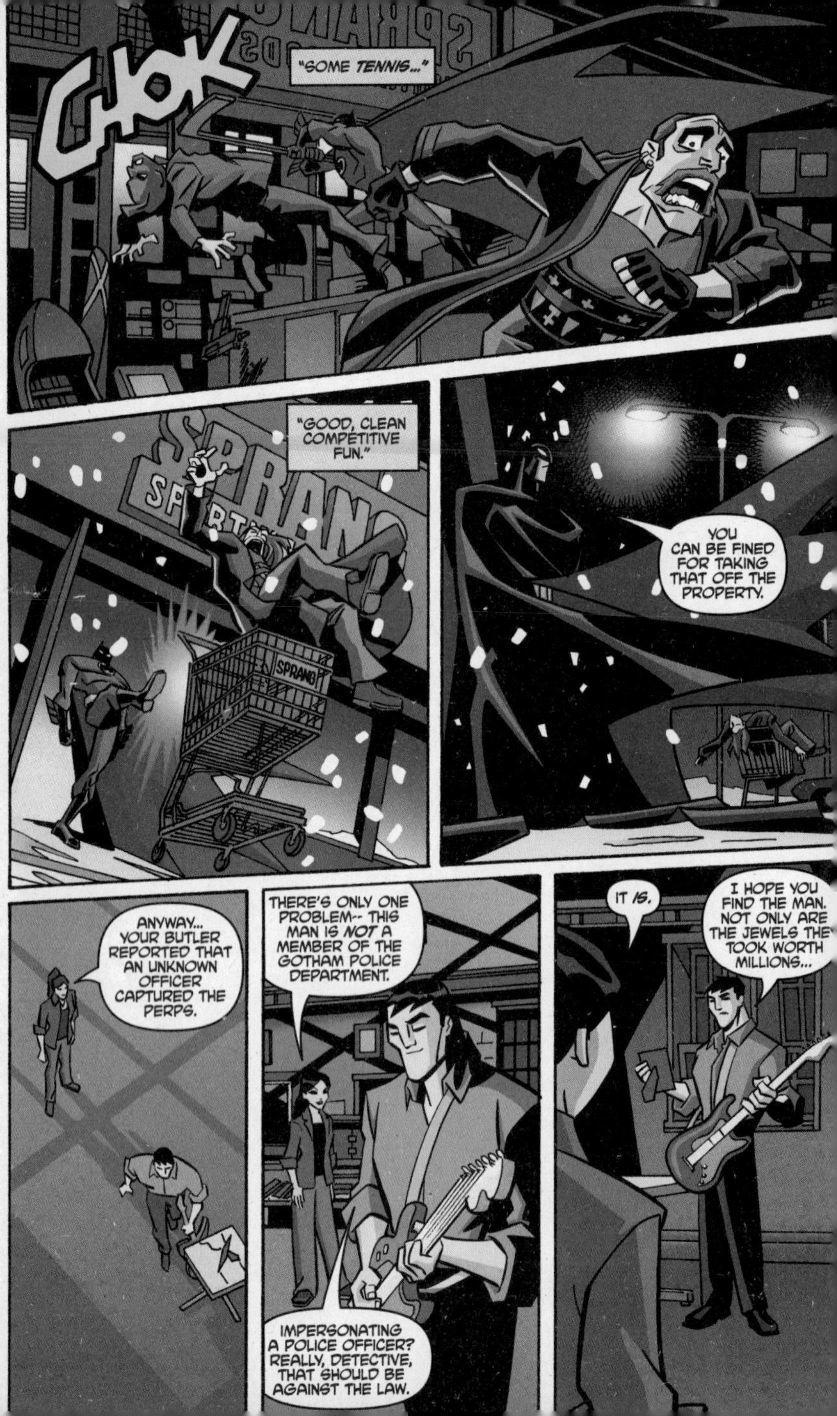
CHOK
"SOME TENNIS..."
"GOOD, CLEAN COMPETITIVE FUN."
SPRANG
YOU CAN BE FINED FOR TAKING THAT OFF THE PROPERTY.
ANYWAY... YOUR BUTLER REPORTED THAT AN UNKNOWN OFFICER CAPTURED THE PERPS.
THERE'S ONLY ONE PROBLEM-- THIS MAN IS *NOT* A MEMBER OF THE GOTHAM POLICE DEPARTMENT.
IMPERSONATING A POLICE OFFICER? REALLY, DETECTIVE, THAT SHOULD BE AGAINST THE LAW.
IT *IS*.
I HOPE YOU FIND THE MAN. NOT ONLY ARE THE JEWELS THE TOOK WORTH MILLIONS...

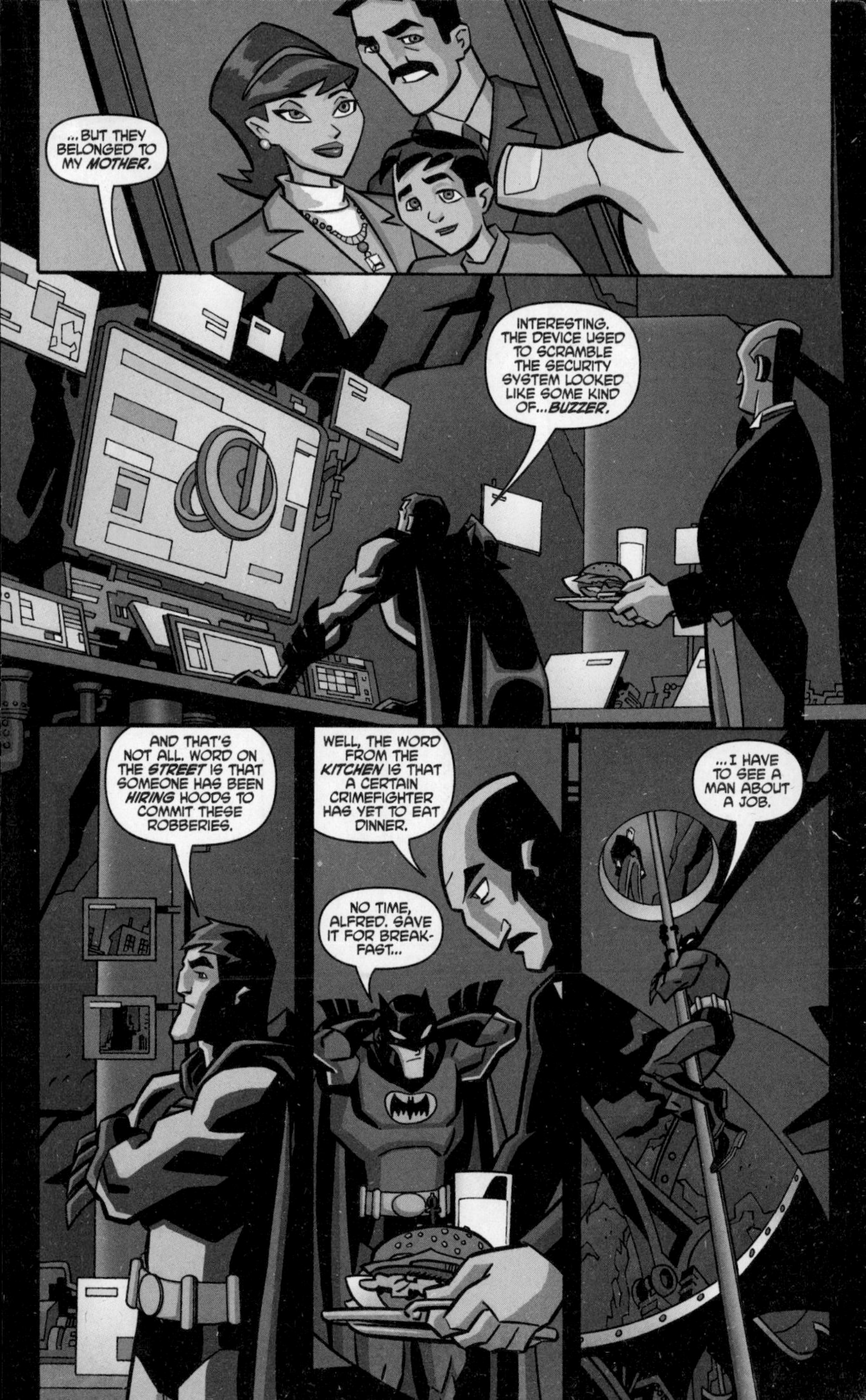
...BUT THEY BELONGED TO MY MOTHER.
INTERESTING. THE DEVICE USED TO SCRAMBLE THE SECURITY SYSTEM LOOKED LIKE SOME KIND OF...BUZZER.
AND THAT'S NOT ALL. WORD ON THE STREET IS THAT SOMEONE HAS BEEN HIRING HOODS TO COMMIT THESE ROBBERIES.
WELL, THE WORD FROM THE KITCHEN IS THAT A CERTAIN CRIMEFIGHTER HAS YET TO EAT DINNER.
NO TIME, ALFRED. SAVE IT FOR BREAK-FAST...
...I HAVE TO SEE A MAN ABOUT A JOB.

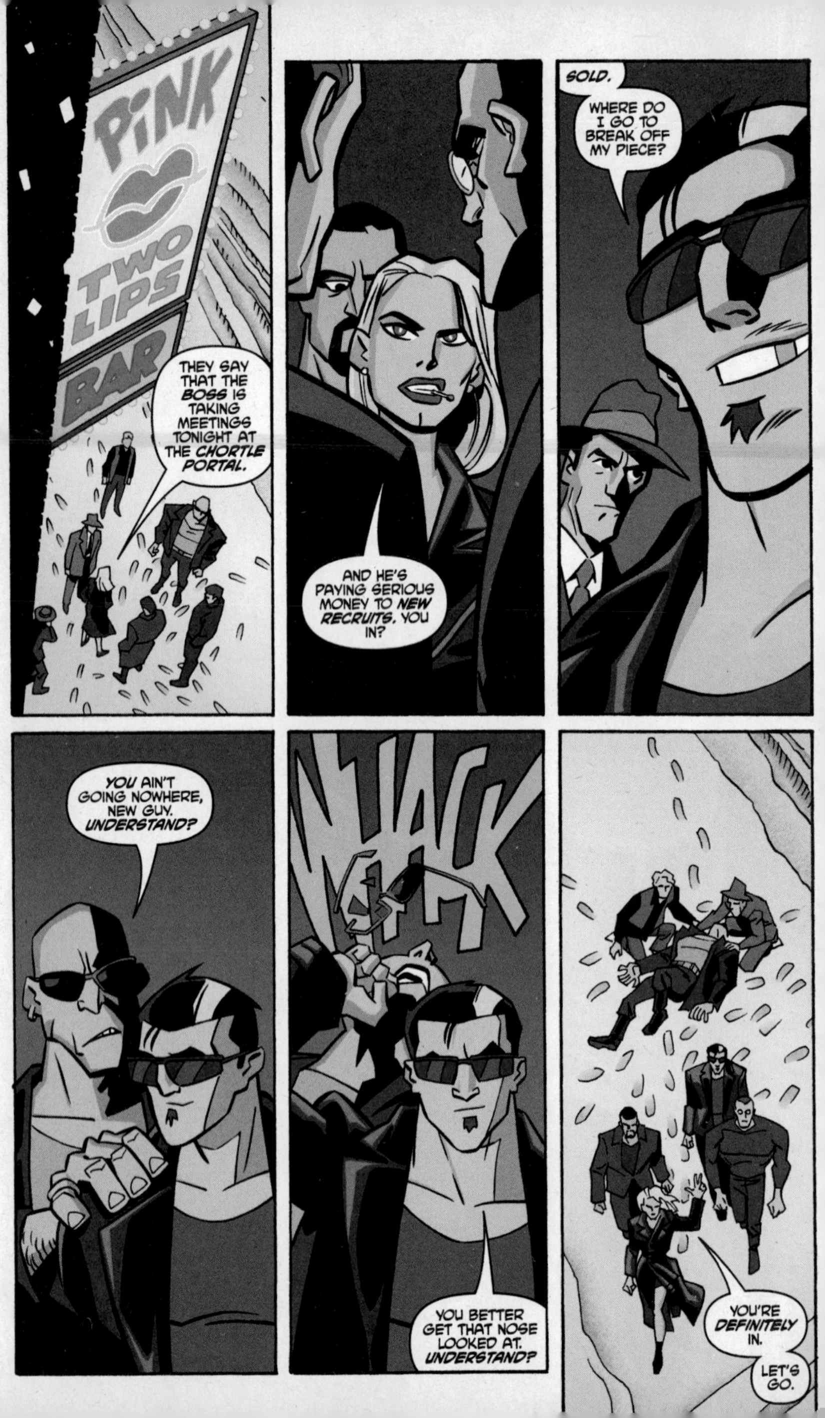
PINK
TWO LIPS
BAR
THEY SAY THAT THE BOSS IS TAKING MEETINGS TONIGHT AT THE CHORTLE PORTAL.
AND HE'S PAYING SERIOUS MONEY TO NEW RECRUITS. YOU IN?
SOLD.
WHERE DO I GO TO BREAK OFF MY PIECE?
YOU AIN'T GOING NOWHERE, NEW GUY. UNDERSTAND?
WHACK
YOU BETTER GET THAT NOSE LOOKED AT. UNDERSTAND?
YOU'RE DEFINITELY IN.
LET'S GO.

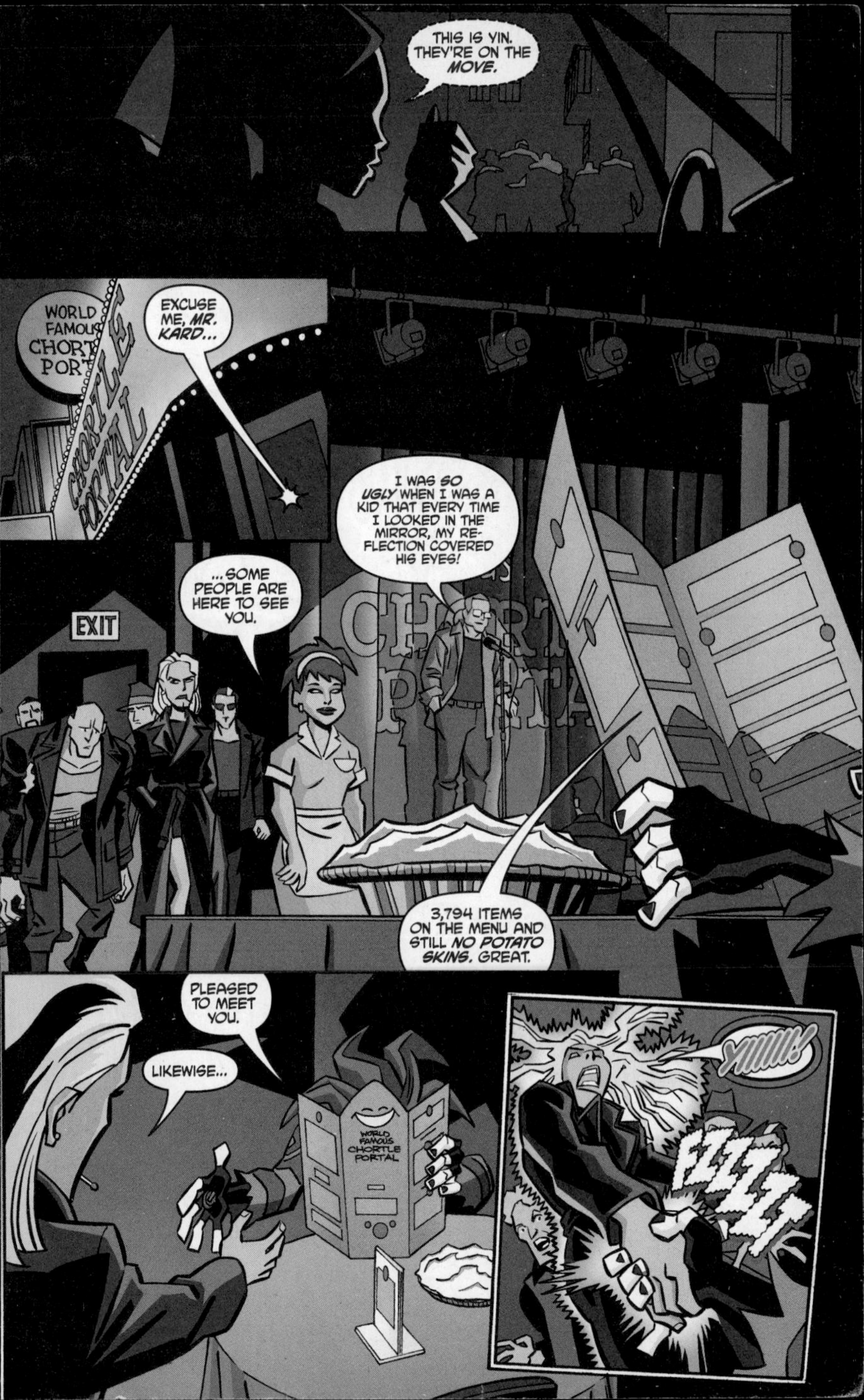
THIS IS YIN. THEY'RE ON THE *MOVE.*
WORLD FAMOUS CHORTLE PORTAL
EXCUSE ME, *MR. KARD*...
I WAS *SO UGLY* WHEN I WAS A KID THAT EVERY TIME I LOOKED IN THE MIRROR, MY RE-FLECTION COVERED HIS EYES!
...SOME PEOPLE ARE HERE TO SEE YOU.
EXIT
3,794 ITEMS ON THE MENU AND STILL *NO POTATO SKINS.* GREAT.
PLEASED TO MEET YOU.
LIKEWISE...
WORLD FAMOUS CHORTLE PORTAL
YIIIIII!
FZZZT

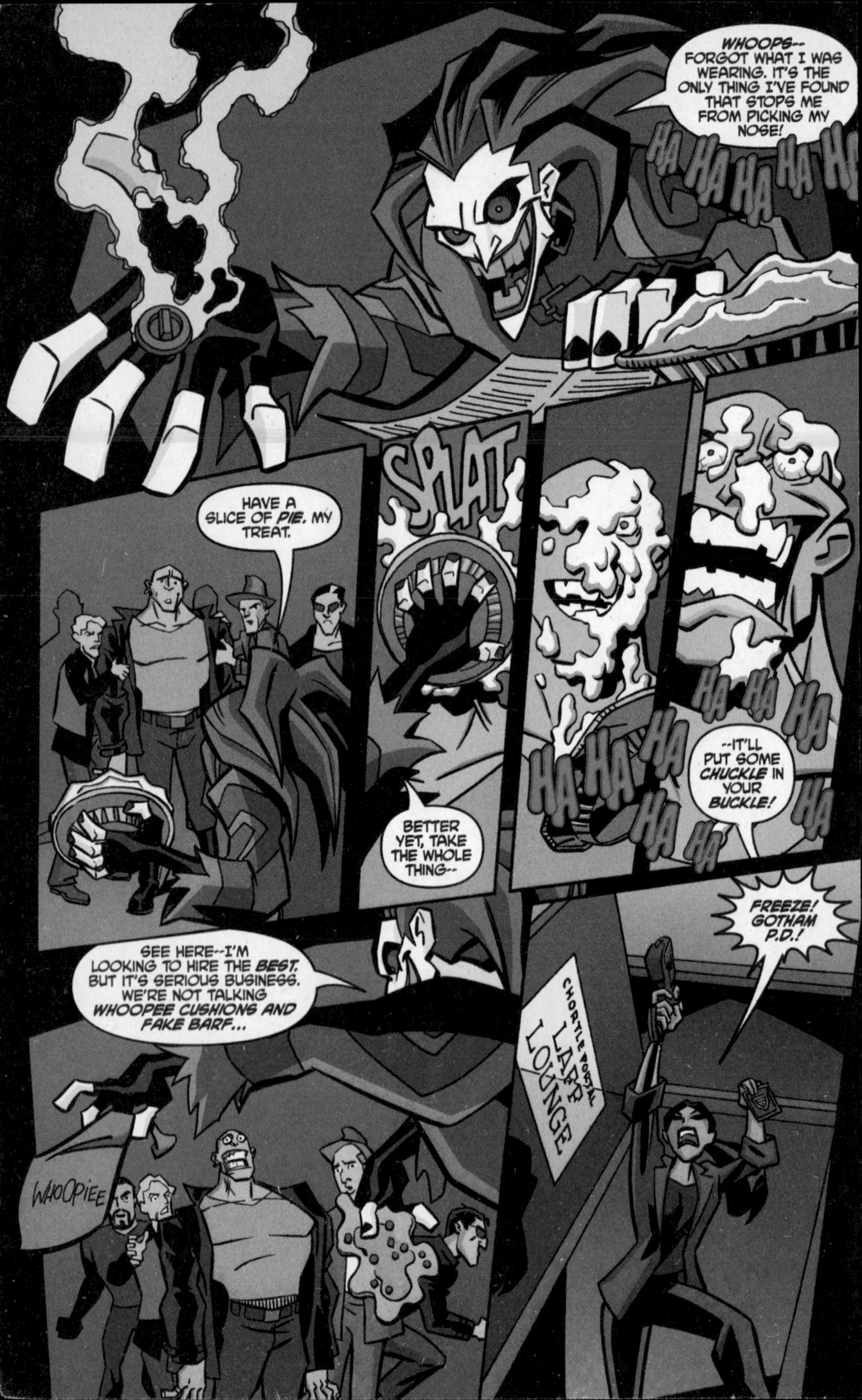
WHOOPS-- FORGOT WHAT I WAS WEARING. IT'S THE ONLY THING I'VE FOUND THAT STOPS ME FROM PICKING MY NOSE!
HA HA HA HA HA
HAVE A SLICE OF PIE, MY TREAT.
SPLAT
BETTER YET, TAKE THE WHOLE THING--
HA HA HA HA HA HA HA HA HA HA
--IT'LL PUT SOME CHUCKLE IN YOUR BUCKLE!
SEE HERE--I'M LOOKING TO HIRE THE BEST. BUT IT'S SERIOUS BUSINESS. WE'RE NOT TALKING WHOOPEE CUSHIONS AND FAKE BARF...
WHOOPIEE
CHORTLE PORTAL LAFF LOUNGE
FREEZE! GOTHAM P.D.!

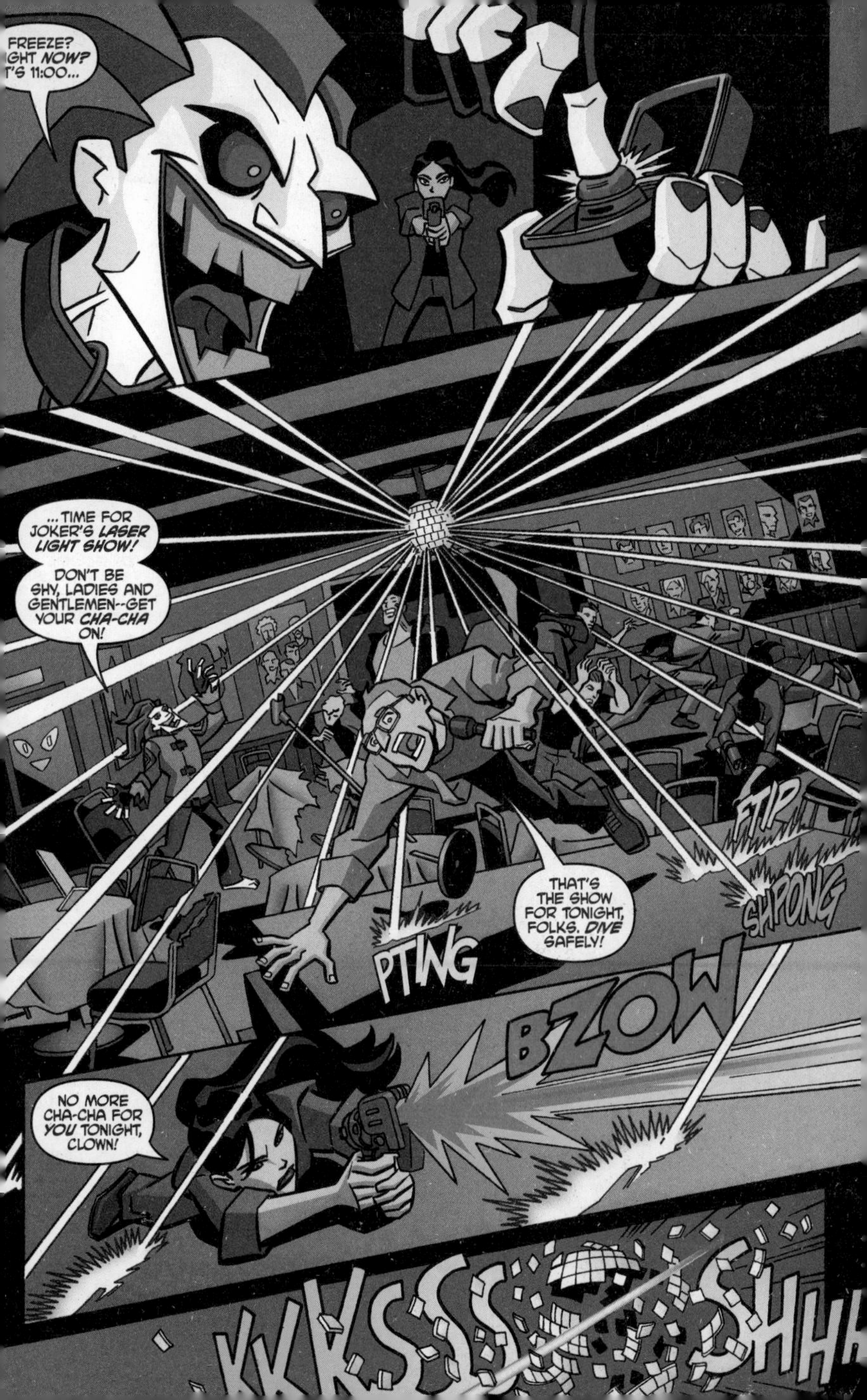
FREEZE?
IGHT NOW?
T'S 11:00...
...TIME FOR JOKER'S LASER LIGHT SHOW!
DON'T BE SHY, LADIES AND GENTLEMEN--GET YOUR CHA-CHA ON!
THAT'S THE SHOW FOR TONIGHT, FOLKS. DIVE SAFELY!
FTIP
SHPONG
PTING
BZOW
NO MORE CHA-CHA FOR YOU TONIGHT, CLOWN!
KKKSSSSSHHH

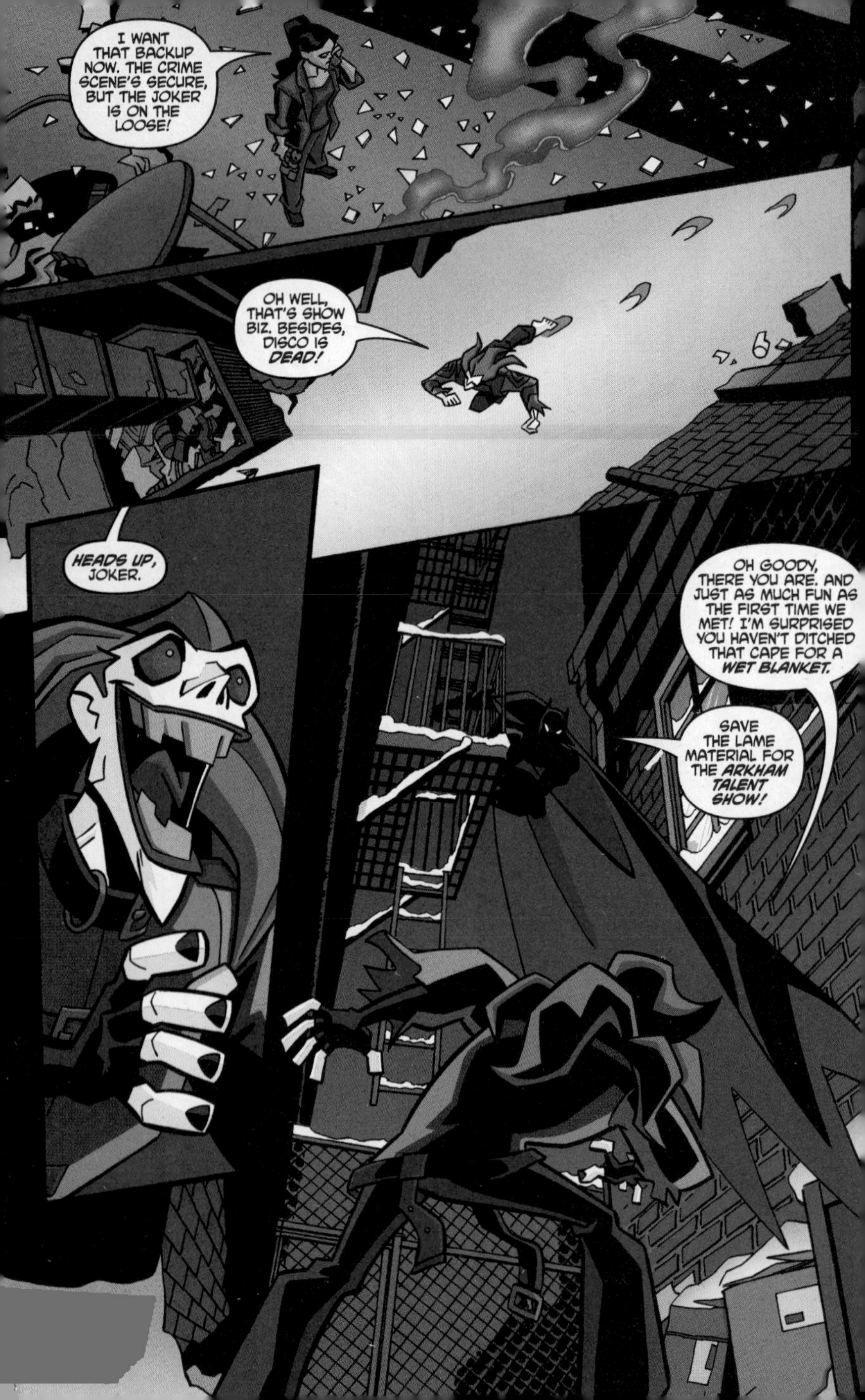
I WANT THAT BACKUP NOW. THE CRIME SCENE'S SECURE, BUT THE JOKER IS ON THE LOOSE!
OH WELL, THAT'S SHOW BIZ. BESIDES, DISCO IS *DEAD!*
HEADS UP, JOKER.
OH GOODY, THERE YOU ARE. AND JUST AS MUCH FUN AS THE FIRST TIME WE MET! I'M SURPRISED YOU HAVEN'T DITCHED THAT CAPE FOR A *WET BLANKET.*
SAVE THE LAME MATERIAL FOR THE *ARKHAM TALENT SHOW!*

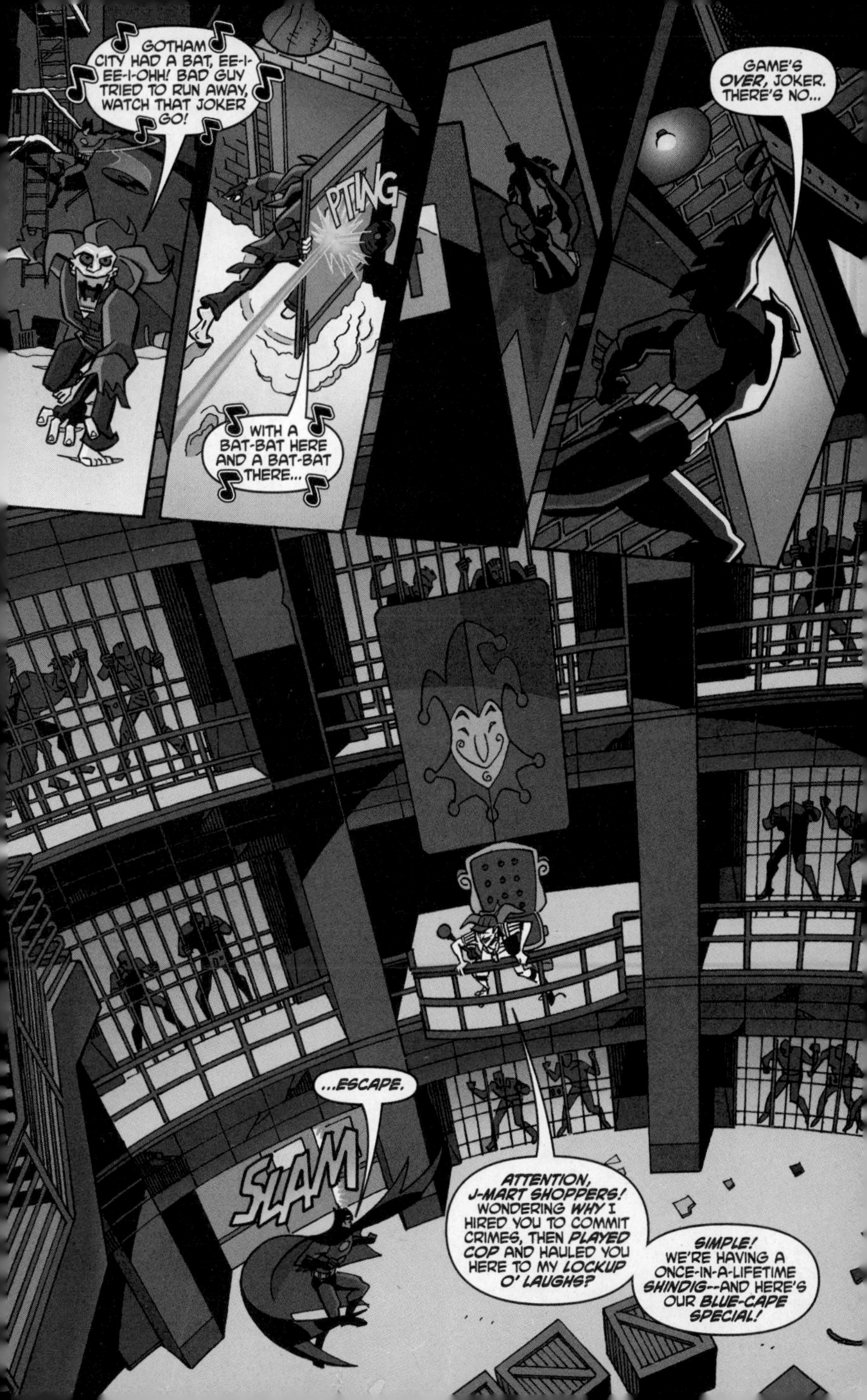
GOTHAM CITY HAD A BAT, EE-I-EE-I-OHH! BAD GUY TRIED TO RUN AWAY, WATCH THAT JOKER GO!
PTING
WITH A BAT-BAT HERE AND A BAT-BAT THERE...
GAME'S OVER, JOKER. THERE'S NO...
...ESCAPE.
SLAM
ATTENTION, J-MART SHOPPERS! WONDERING WHY I HIRED YOU TO COMMIT CRIMES, THEN PLAYED COP AND HAULED YOU HERE TO MY LOCKUP O' LAUGHS?
SIMPLE! WE'RE HAVING A ONCE-IN-A-LIFETIME SHINDIG--AND HERE'S OUR BLUE-CAPE SPECIAL!

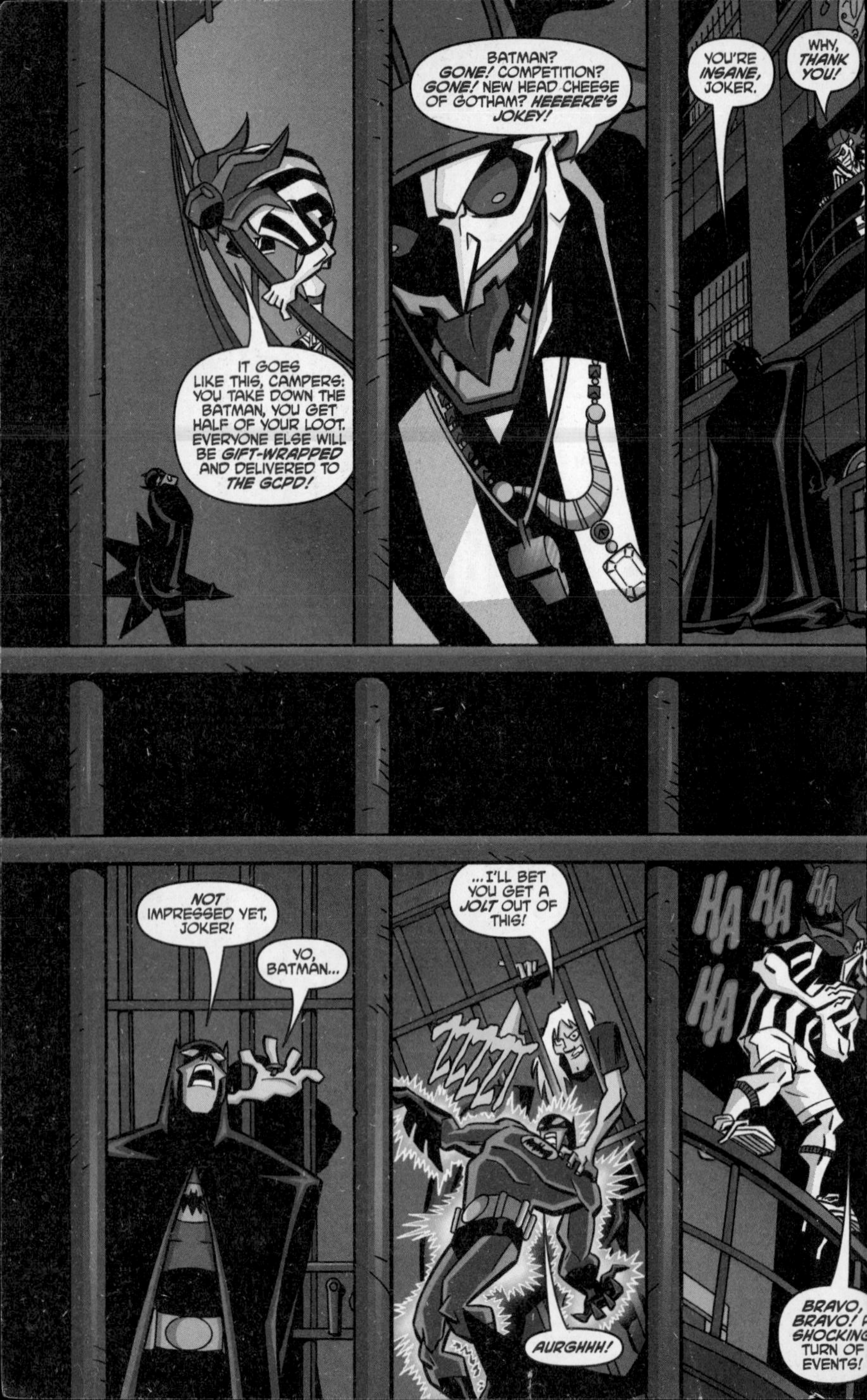
IT GOES LIKE THIS, CAMPERS: YOU TAKE DOWN THE BATMAN, YOU GET HALF OF YOUR LOOT. EVERYONE ELSE WILL BE GIFT-WRAPPED AND DELIVERED TO THE GCPD!
BATMAN? GONE! COMPETITION? GONE! NEW HEAD CHEESE OF GOTHAM? HEEEERE'S JOKEY!
YOU'RE INSANE, JOKER.
WHY, THANK YOU!
NOT IMPRESSED YET, JOKER!
YO, BATMAN...
...I'LL BET YOU GET A JOLT OUT OF THIS!
ZZZZT
AURGHHH!
HA HA HA HA HA
BRAVO, BRAVO! SHOCKING TURN OF EVENTS!

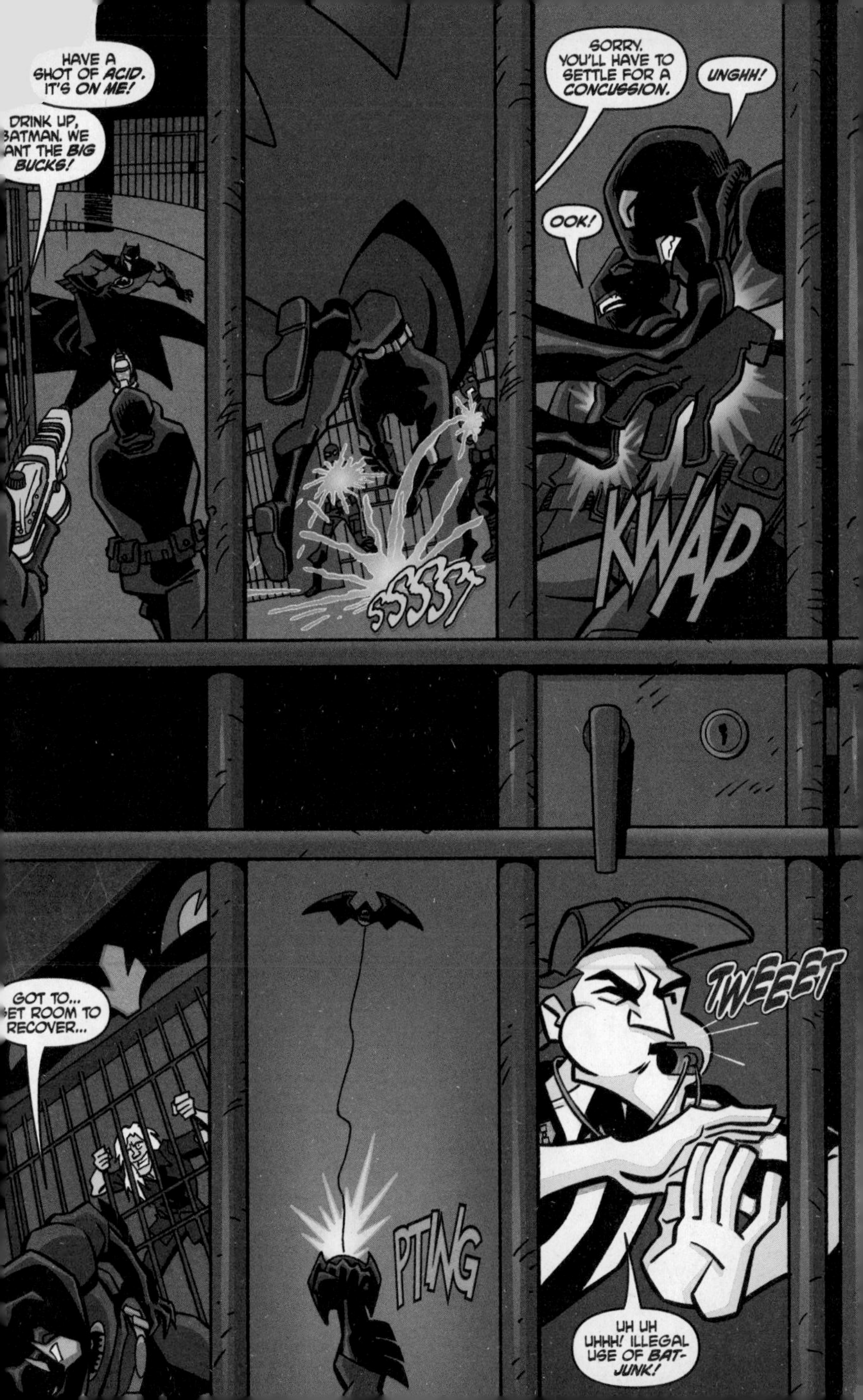
HAVE A SHOT OF ACID. IT'S ON ME!
DRINK UP, BATMAN. WE ANT THE BIG BUCKS!
SSSSST
SORRY. YOU'LL HAVE TO SETTLE FOR A CONCUSSION.
UNGHH!
OOK!
KWAP
GOT TO... ET ROOM TO RECOVER...
PTING
TWEEET
UH UH UHHH! ILLEGAL USE OF BAT-JUNK!

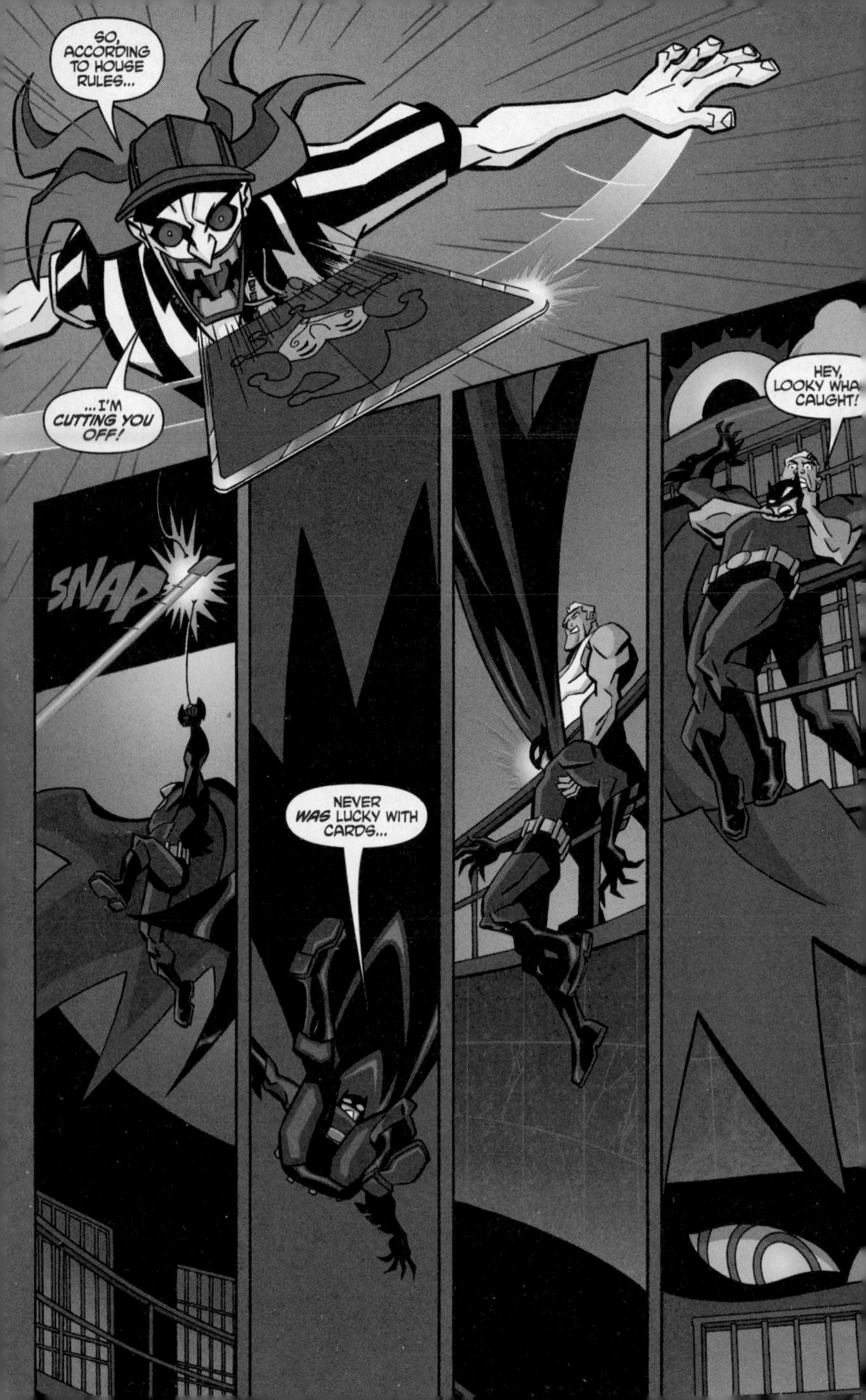
SO, ACCORDING TO HOUSE RULES...
...I'M CUTTING YOU OFF!
SNAP
NEVER WAS LUCKY WITH CARDS...
HEY, LOOKY WHA CAUGHT!

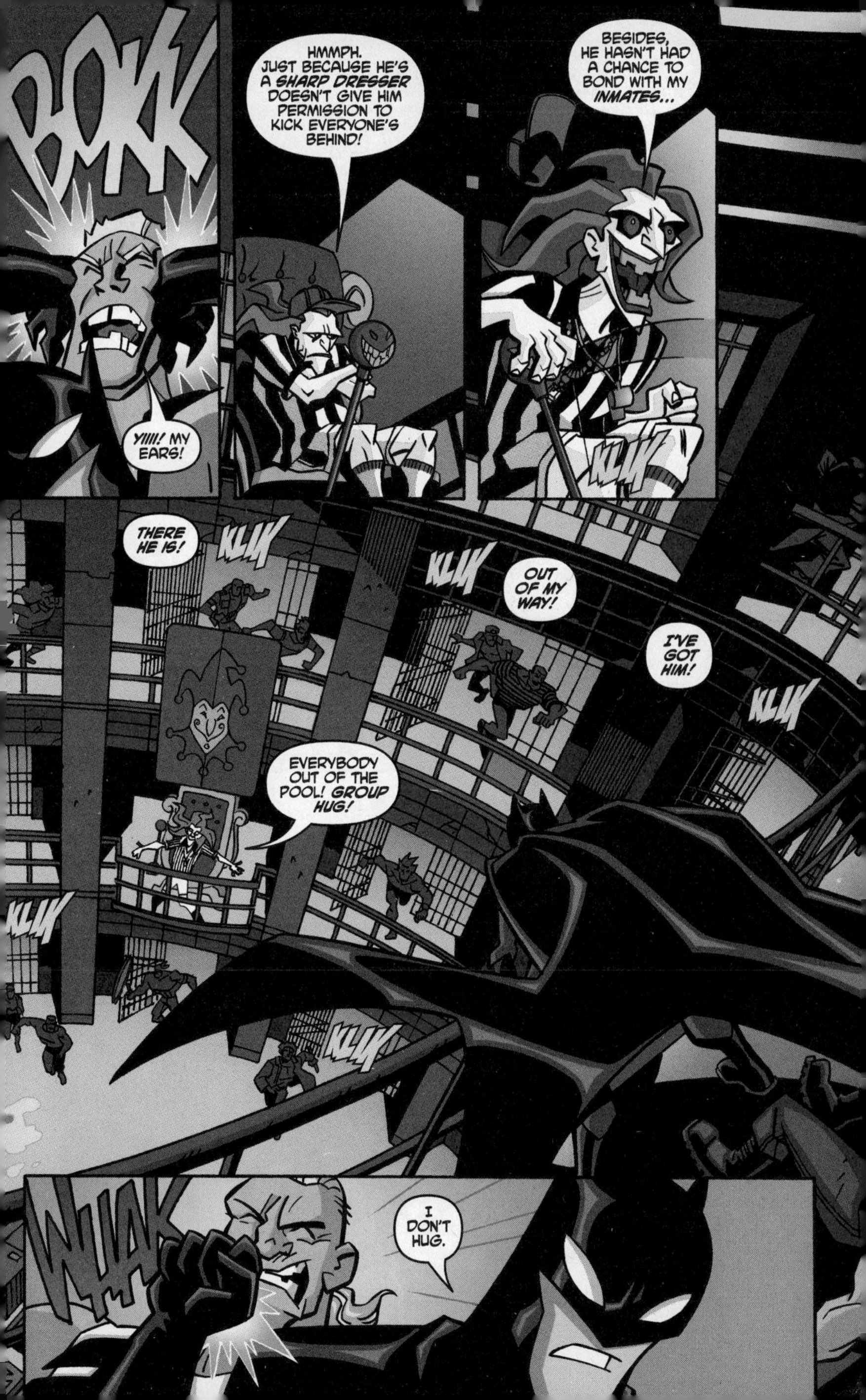
BOOM
YIIII! MY EARS!
HMMPH. JUST BECAUSE HE'S A SHARP DRESSER DOESN'T GIVE HIM PERMISSION TO KICK EVERYONE'S BEHIND!
BESIDES, HE HASN'T HAD A CHANCE TO BOND WITH MY INMATES...
KLIK
THERE HE IS!
KLIK
KLIK
OUT OF MY WAY!
I'VE GOT HIM!
KLIK
EVERYBODY OUT OF THE POOL! GROUP HUG!
KLIK
KLIK
WHAK
I DON'T HUG.

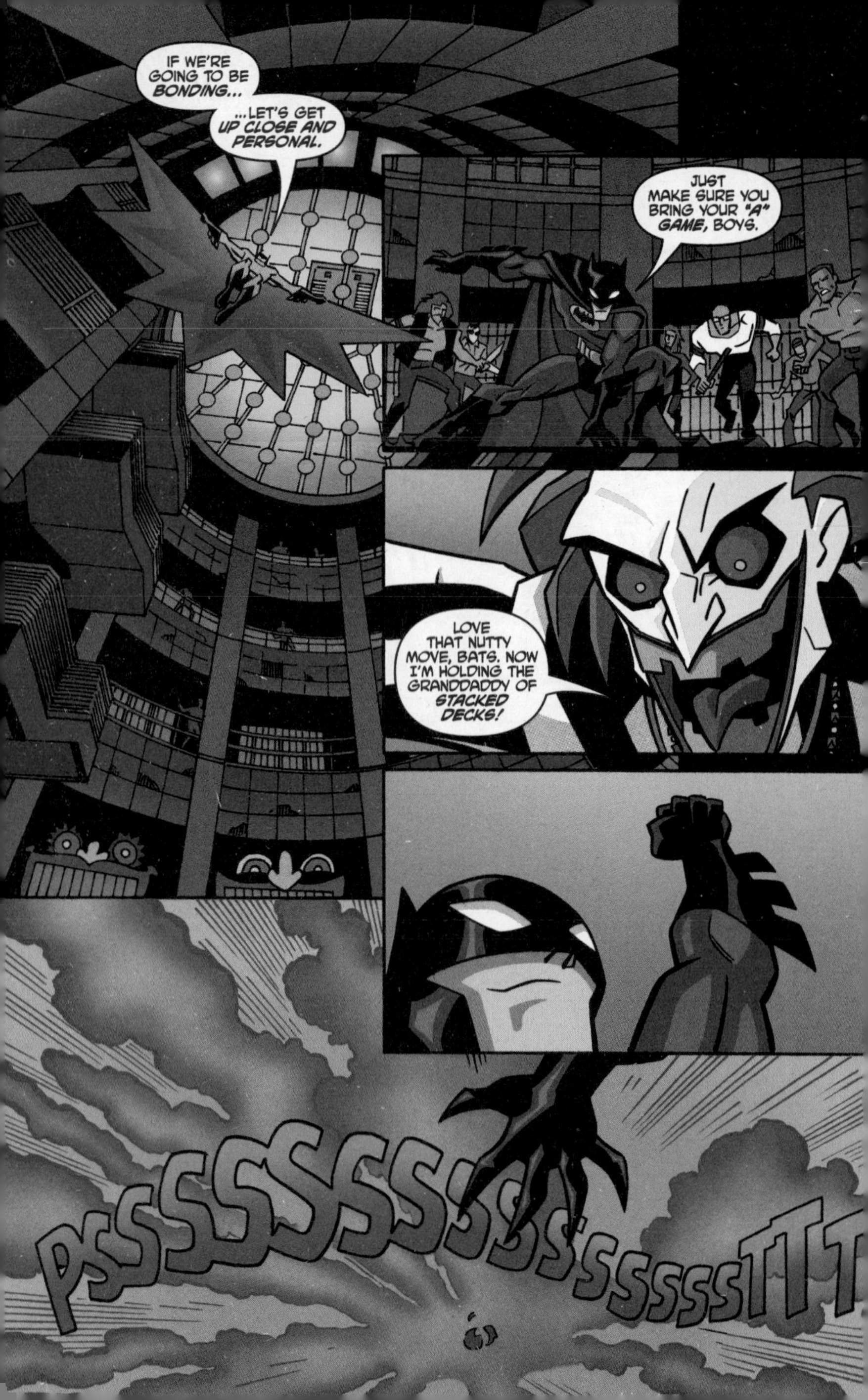
IF WE'RE GOING TO BE BONDING...
...LET'S GET UP CLOSE AND PERSONAL.
JUST MAKE SURE YOU BRING YOUR "A" GAME, BOYS.
LOVE THAT NUTTY MOVE, BATS. NOW I'M HOLDING THE GRANDDADDY OF STACKED DECKS!
PSSSSSSSSSSSSSSSSTTT

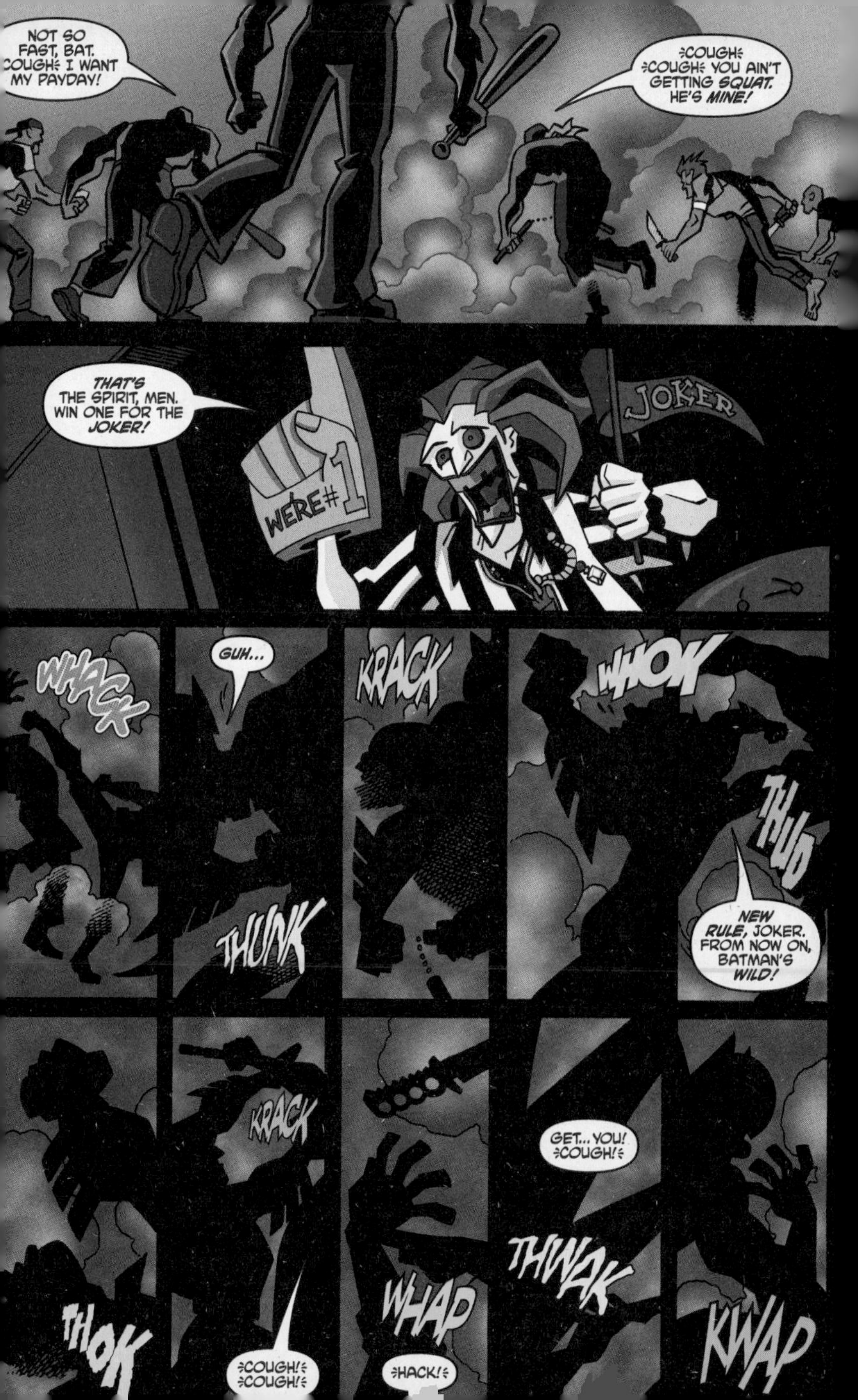
NOT SO FAST, BAT. ⁝COUGH⁝ I WANT MY PAYDAY!
⁝COUGH⁝ ⁝COUGH⁝ YOU AIN'T GETTING SQUAT. HE'S MINE!
THAT'S THE SPIRIT, MEN. WIN ONE FOR THE JOKER!
JOKER
WE'RE #1
WHACK
GUH...
THUNK
KRACK
WHOK
THUD
NEW RULE, JOKER. FROM NOW ON, BATMAN'S WILD!
KRACK
GET... YOU! ⁝COUGH!⁝
THOK
⁝COUGH!⁝ ⁝COUGH!⁝
WHAP
⁝HACK!⁝
THWAK
KWAP

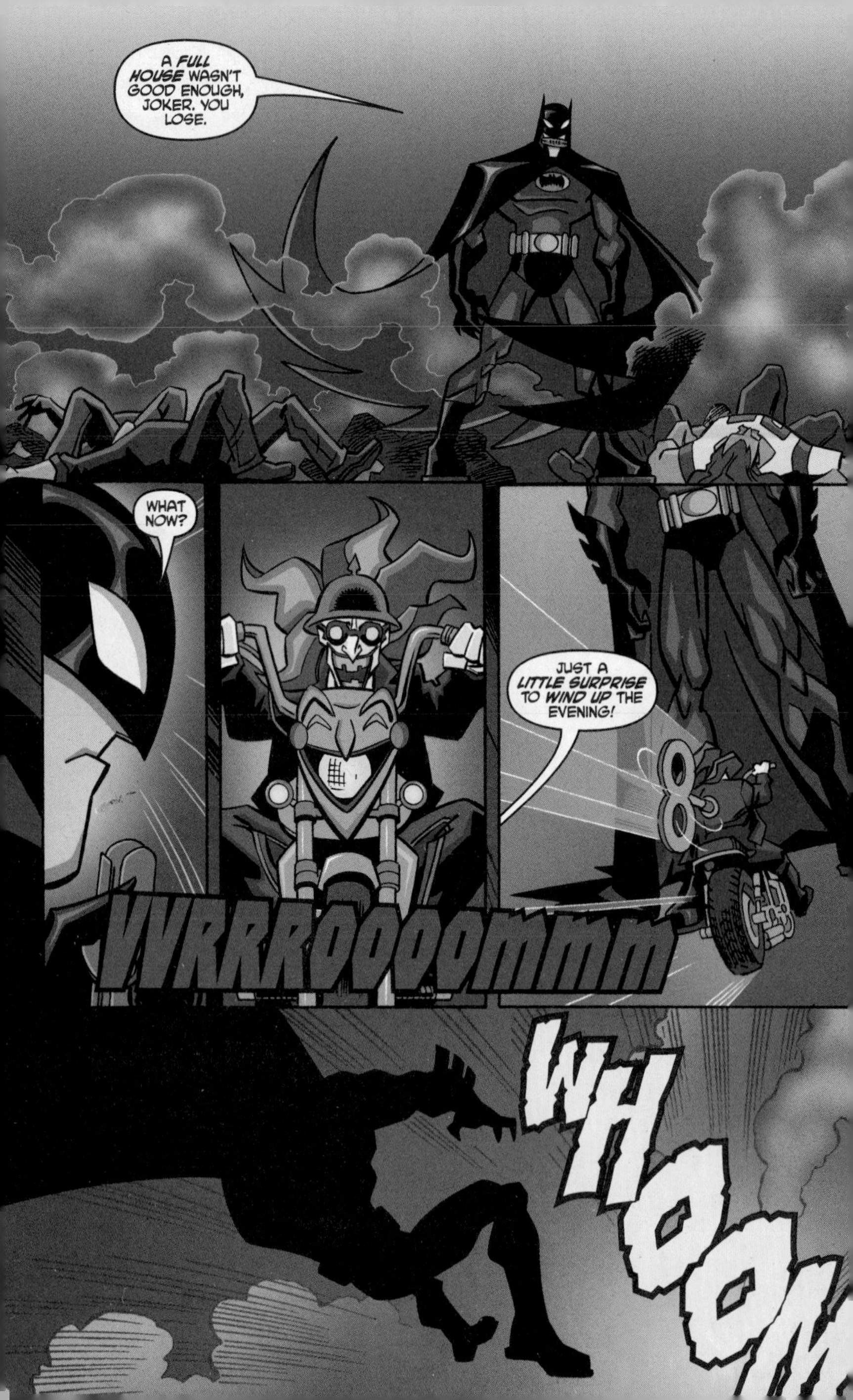
A FULL HOUSE WASN'T GOOD ENOUGH, JOKER. YOU LOSE.
WHAT NOW?
JUST A LITTLE SURPRISE TO WIND UP THE EVENING!
VVRRROOOOMMMM
WHOOM

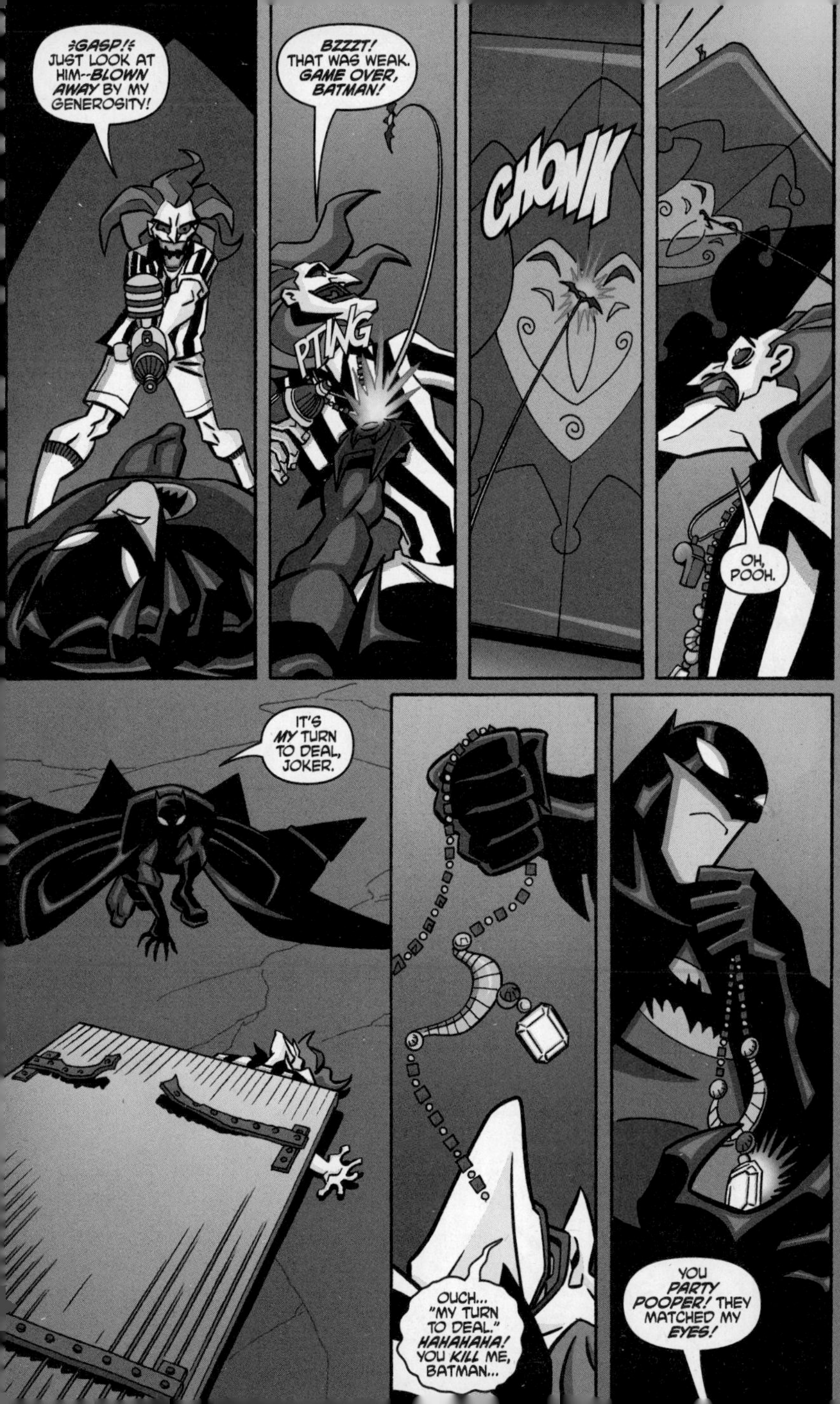
GASP! JUST LOOK AT HIM--BLOWN AWAY BY MY GENEROSITY!
BZZZT! THAT WAS WEAK. GAME OVER, BATMAN!
PTING
CHONK
OH, POOH.
IT'S MY TURN TO DEAL, JOKER.
OUCH... "MY TURN TO DEAL." HAHAHAHA! YOU KILL ME, BATMAN...
YOU PARTY POOPER! THEY MATCHED MY EYES!

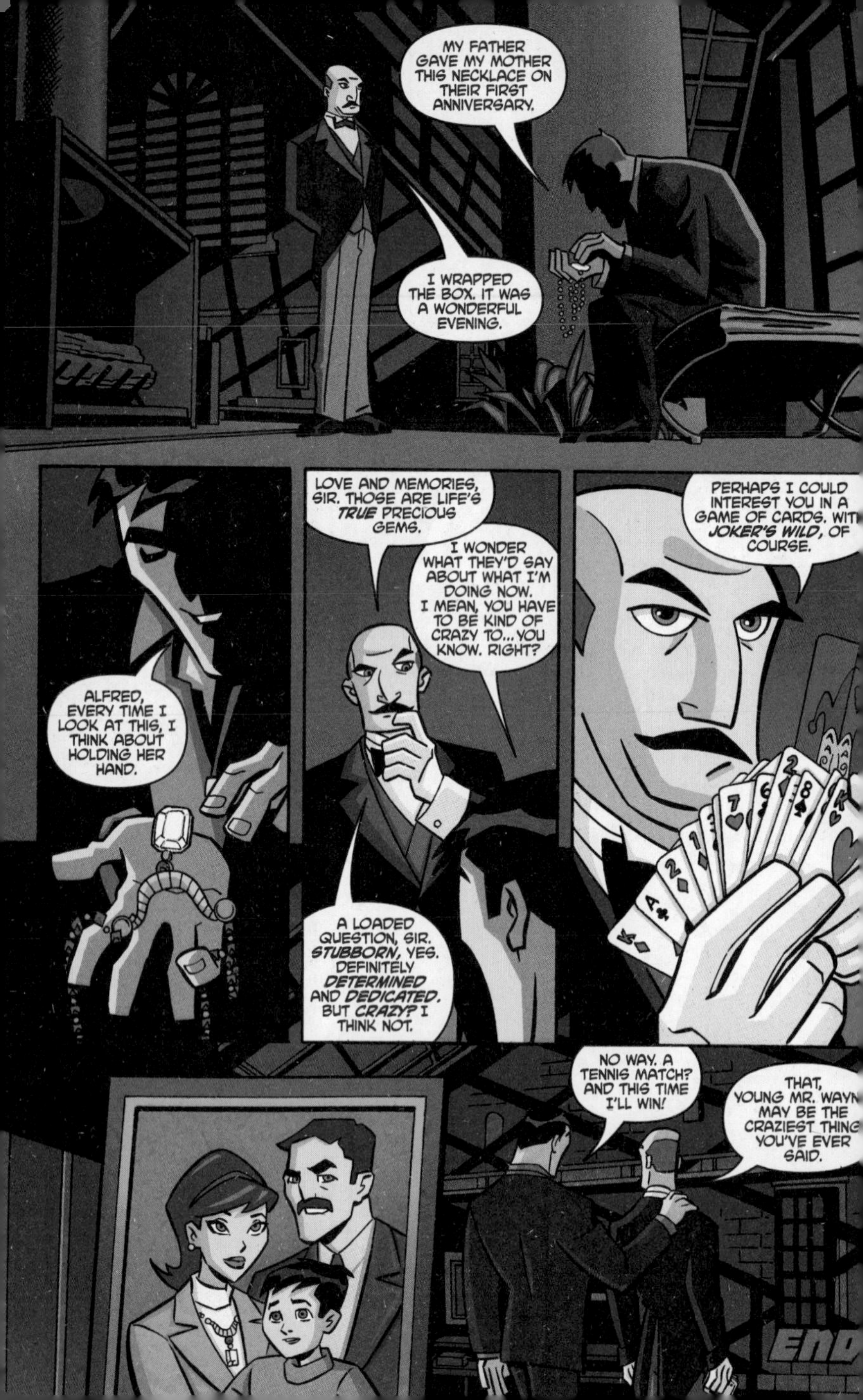
MY FATHER GAVE MY MOTHER THIS NECKLACE ON THEIR FIRST ANNIVERSARY.
I WRAPPED THE BOX. IT WAS A WONDERFUL EVENING.
ALFRED, EVERY TIME I LOOK AT THIS, I THINK ABOUT HOLDING HER HAND.
LOVE AND MEMORIES, SIR. THOSE ARE LIFE'S TRUE PRECIOUS GEMS.
I WONDER WHAT THEY'D SAY ABOUT WHAT I'M DOING NOW. I MEAN, YOU HAVE TO BE KIND OF CRAZY TO... YOU KNOW. RIGHT?
A LOADED QUESTION, SIR. STUBBORN, YES. DEFINITELY DETERMINED AND DEDICATED. BUT CRAZY? I THINK NOT.
PERHAPS I COULD INTEREST YOU IN A GAME OF CARDS. WIT JOKER'S WILD, OF COURSE.
NO WAY. A TENNIS MATCH? AND THIS TIME I'LL WIN!
THAT, YOUNG MR. WAYN MAY BE THE CRAZIEST THING YOU'VE EVER SAID.
END

WITHOUT A CHANCE

LL MATHENY, WRITER
CHRISTOPHER JONES, PENCILLER
TERRY BEATTY, INKER
JARED K. FLETCHER, LETTERER

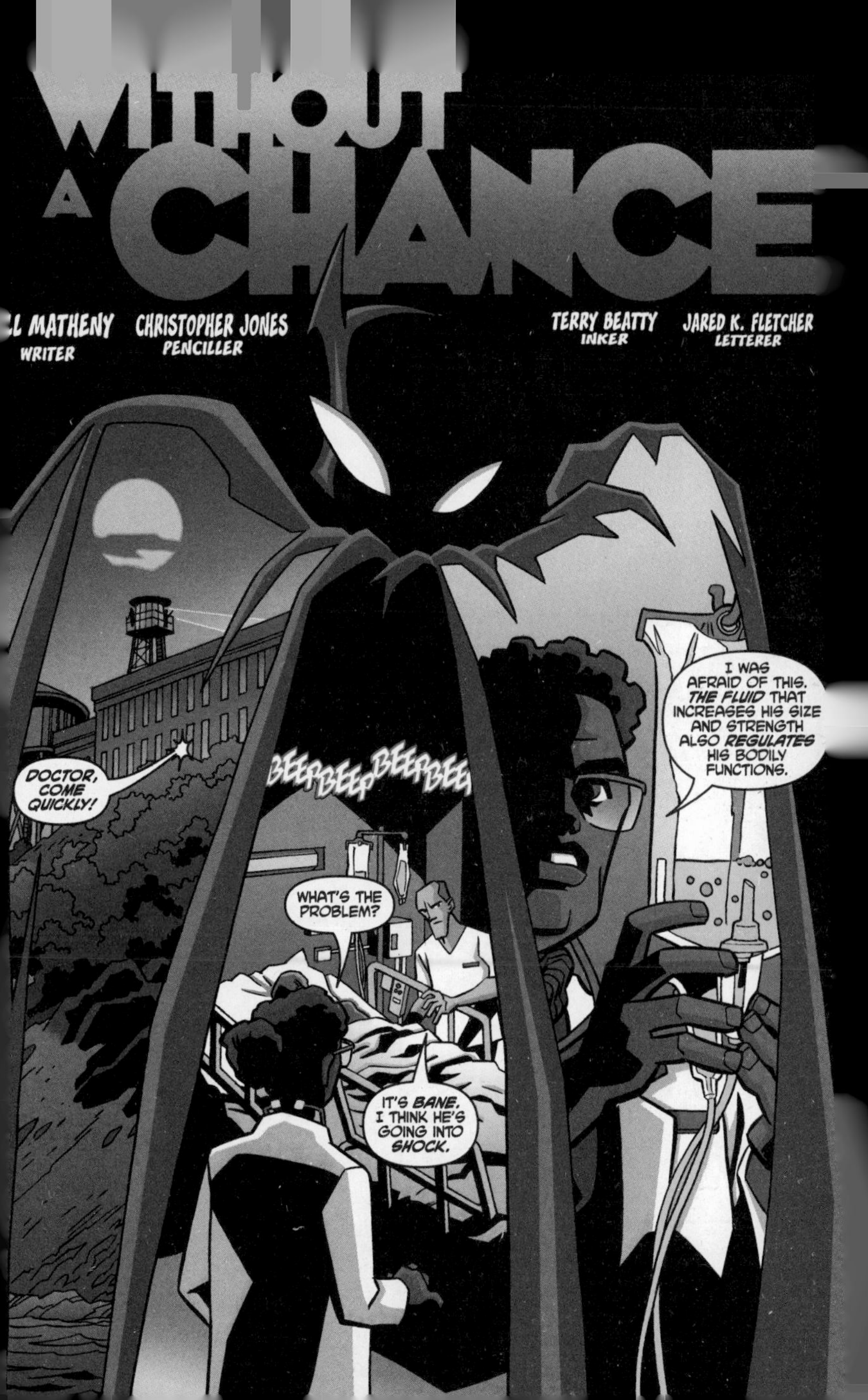

DOCTOR, COME QUICKLY!
BEEPBEEPBEEPBEEP
WHAT'S THE PROBLEM?
IT'S BANE. I THINK HE'S GOING INTO SHOCK.
I WAS AFRAID OF THIS. THE FLUID THAT INCREASES HIS SIZE AND STRENGTH ALSO REGULATES HIS BODILY FUNCTIONS.

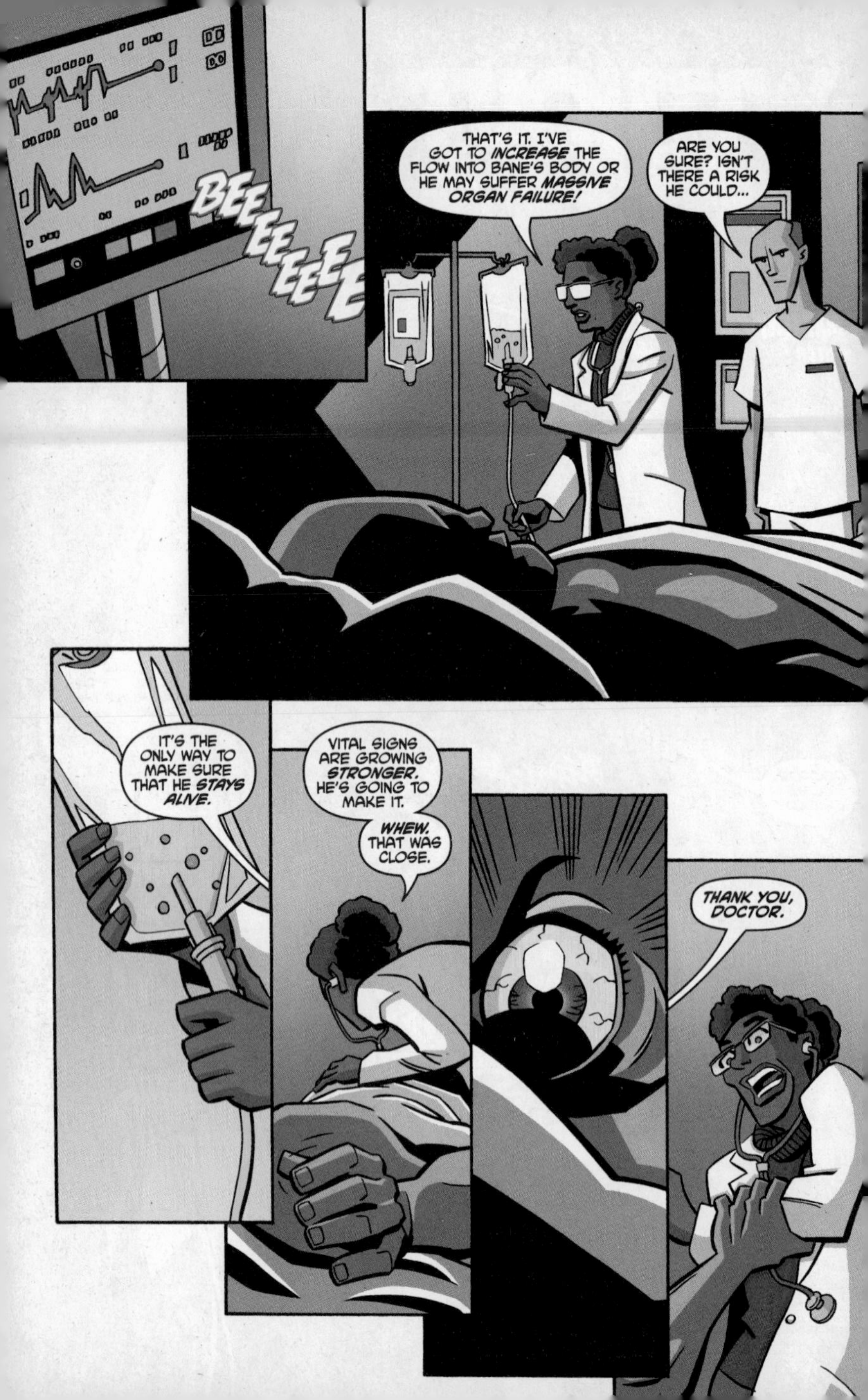
BEEEEEEEE
THAT'S IT. I'VE GOT TO INCREASE THE FLOW INTO BANE'S BODY OR HE MAY SUFFER MASSIVE ORGAN FAILURE!
ARE YOU SURE? ISN'T THERE A RISK HE COULD...
IT'S THE ONLY WAY TO MAKE SURE THAT HE STAYS ALIVE.
VITAL SIGNS ARE GROWING STRONGER. HE'S GOING TO MAKE IT.
WHEW. THAT WAS CLOSE.
THANK YOU, DOCTOR.

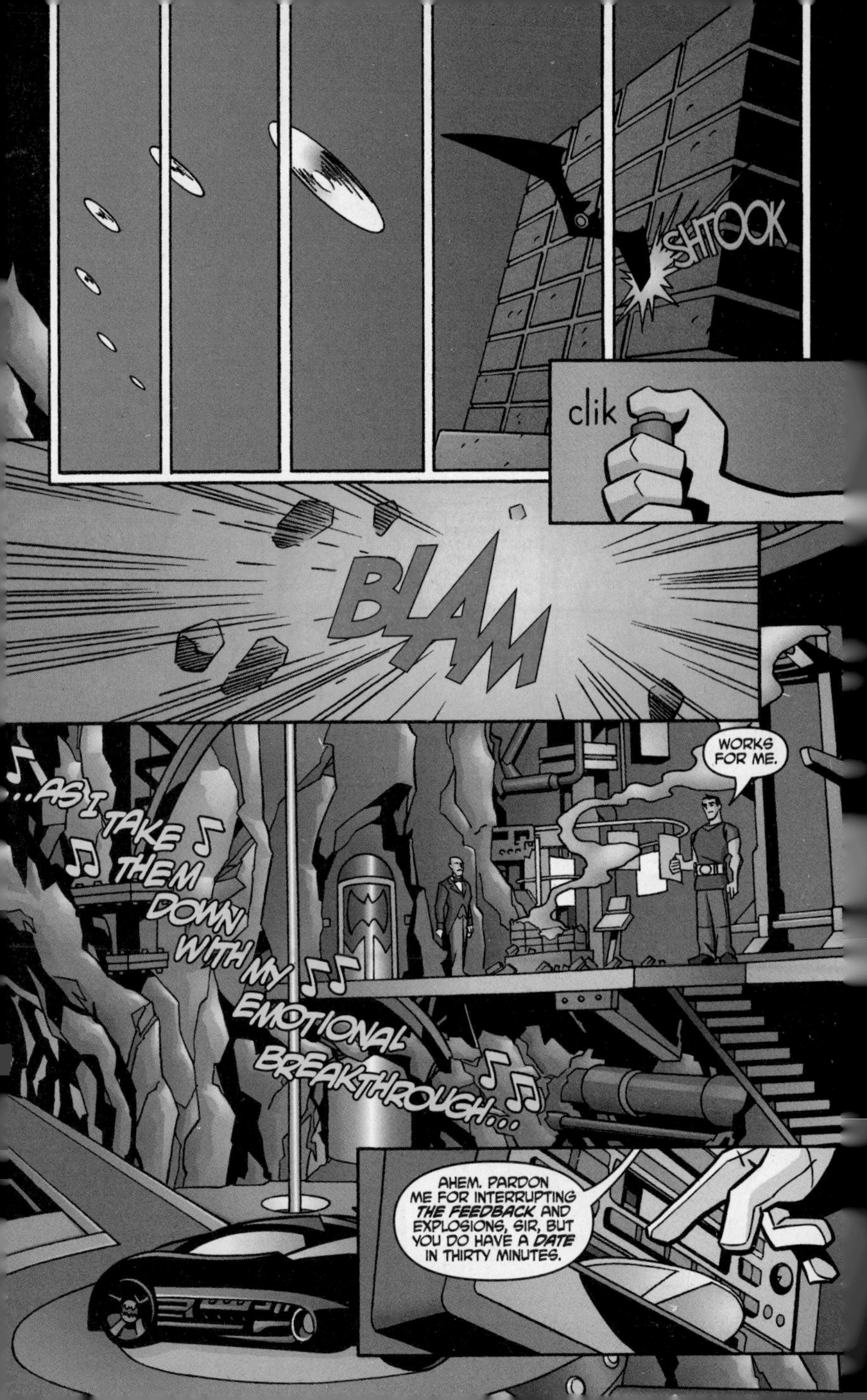
SHTOOK
clik
BLAM
♫ ...AS I TAKE ♫ ♫ THEM DOWN WITH MY ♫♫ EMOTIONAL BREAKTHROUGH... ♫♫
WORKS FOR ME.
AHEM. PARDON ME FOR INTERRUPTING *THE FEEDBACK* AND EXPLOSIONS, SIR, BUT YOU DO HAVE A *DATE* IN THIRTY MINUTES.

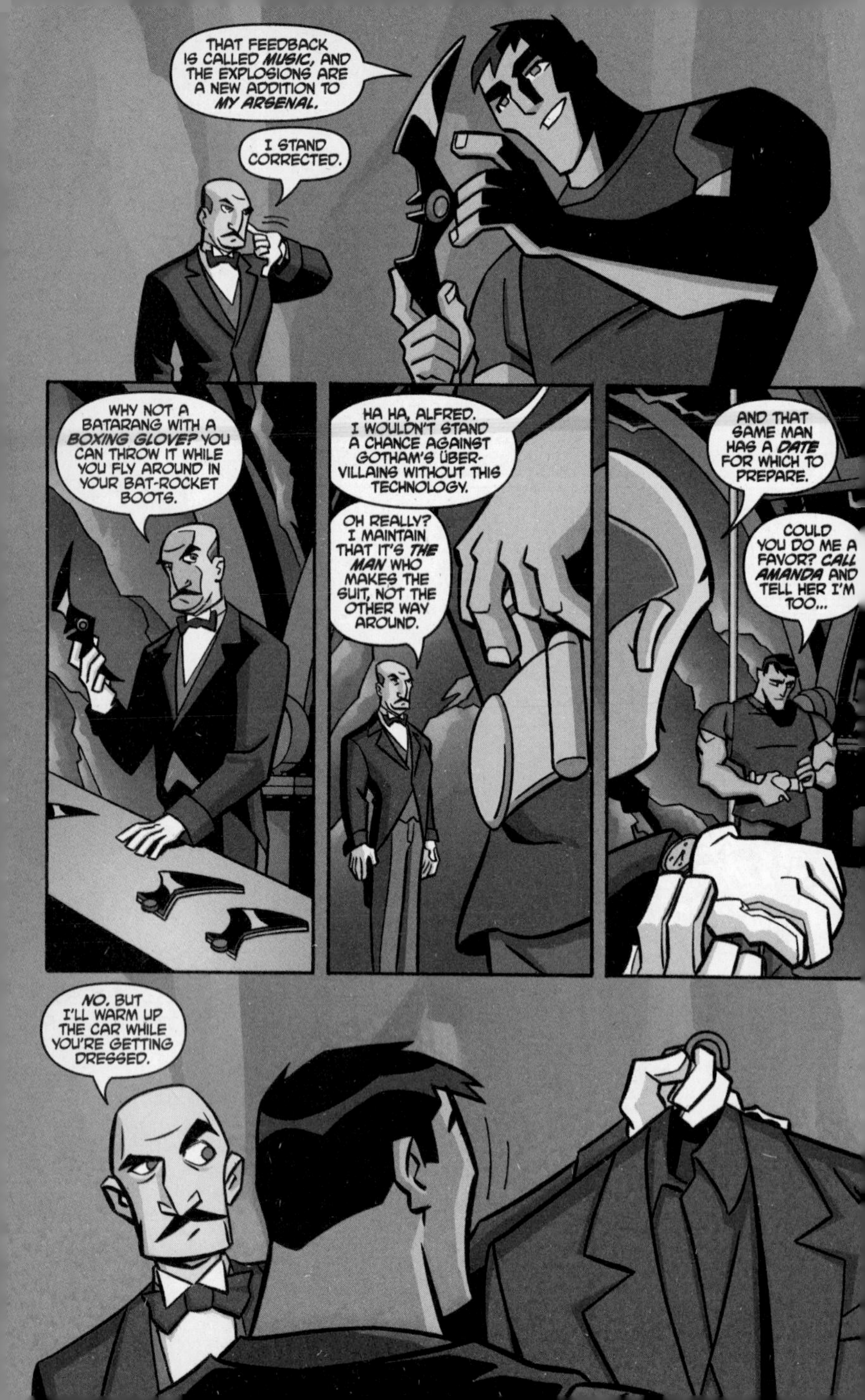
THAT FEEDBACK IS CALLED *MUSIC,* AND THE EXPLOSIONS ARE A NEW ADDITION TO *MY ARSENAL.*
I STAND CORRECTED.
WHY NOT A BATARANG WITH A *BOXING GLOVE?* YOU CAN THROW IT WHILE YOU FLY AROUND IN YOUR BAT-ROCKET BOOTS.
HA HA, ALFRED. I WOULDN'T STAND A CHANCE AGAINST GOTHAM'S ÜBER-VILLAINS WITHOUT THIS TECHNOLOGY.
OH REALLY? I MAINTAIN THAT IT'S *THE MAN* WHO MAKES THE SUIT, NOT THE OTHER WAY AROUND.
AND THAT SAME MAN HAS A *DATE* FOR WHICH TO PREPARE.
COULD YOU DO ME A FAVOR? *CALL AMANDA* AND TELL HER I'M TOO...
NO. BUT I'LL WARM UP THE CAR WHILE YOU'RE GETTING DRESSED.

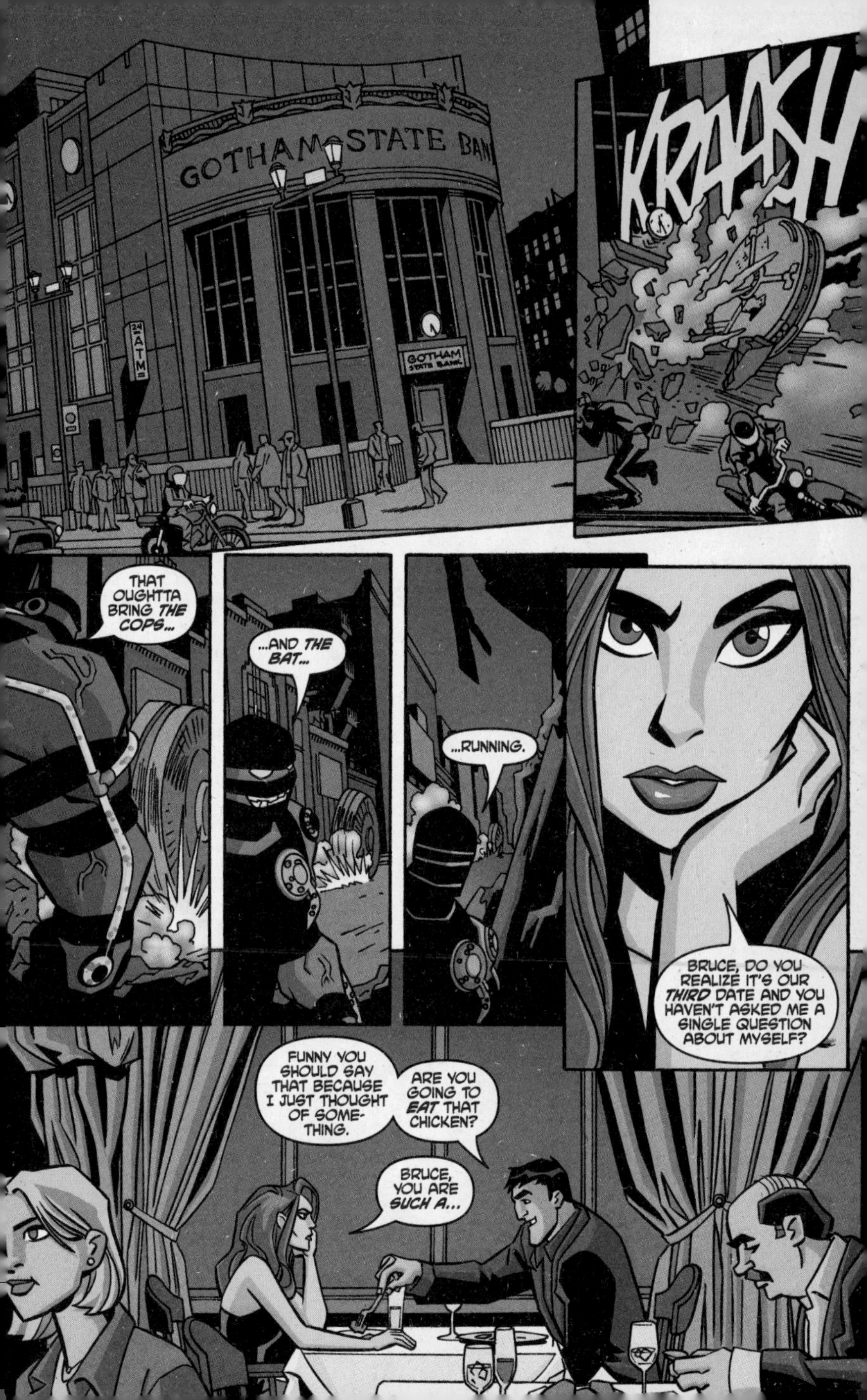
GOTHAM STATE BAN
24 ATM
GOTHAM STATE BANK
KRAASH!
THAT OUGHTTA BRING THE COPS...
...AND THE BAT...
...RUNNING.
BRUCE, DO YOU REALIZE IT'S OUR THIRD DATE AND YOU HAVEN'T ASKED ME A SINGLE QUESTION ABOUT MYSELF?
FUNNY YOU SHOULD SAY THAT BECAUSE I JUST THOUGHT OF SOME-THING.
ARE YOU GOING TO EAT THAT CHICKEN?
BRUCE, YOU ARE SUCH A...

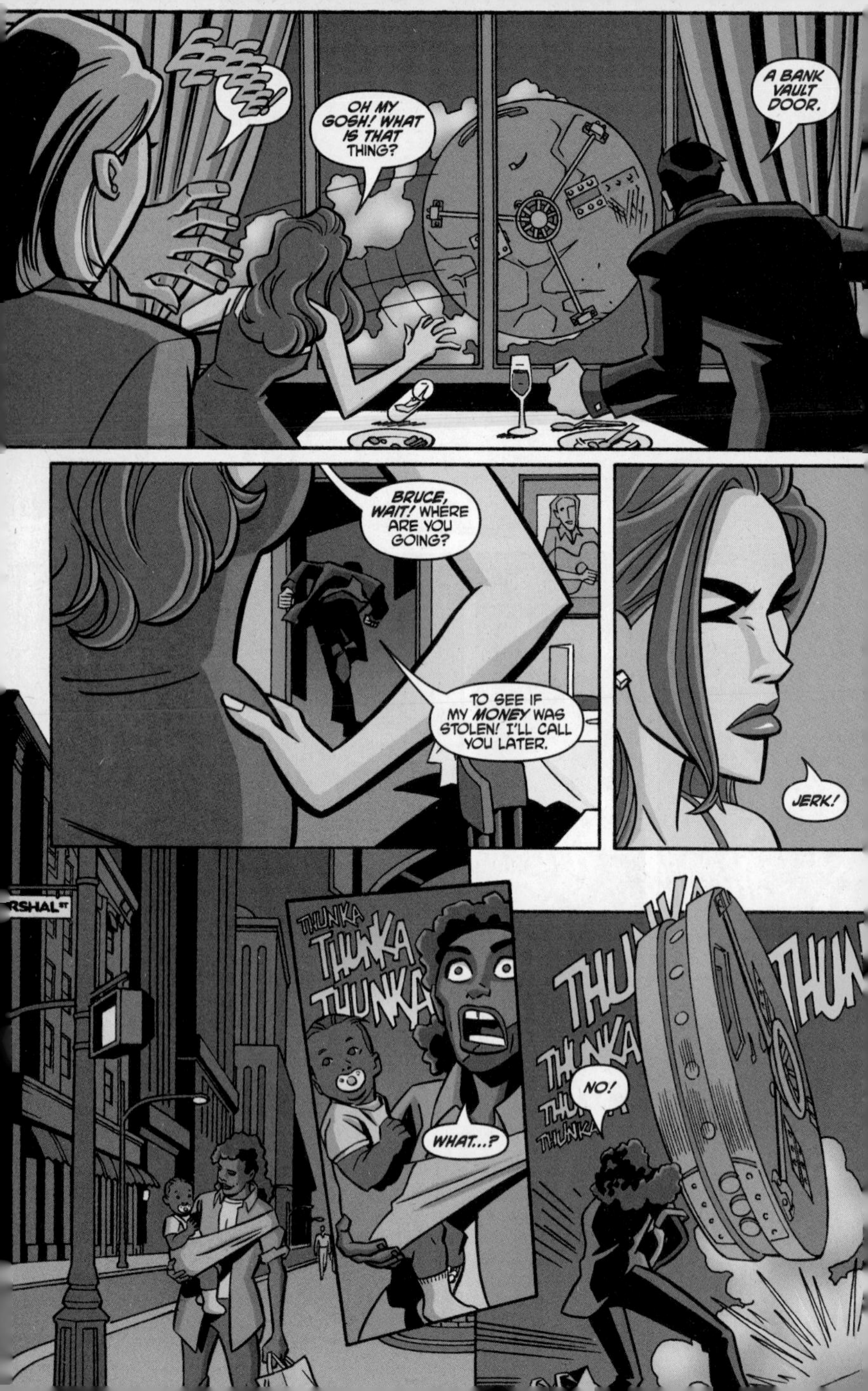
EEEEEE!
OH MY GOSH! WHAT IS THAT THING?
A BANK VAULT DOOR.
BRUCE, WAIT! WHERE ARE YOU GOING?
TO SEE IF MY MONEY WAS STOLEN! I'LL CALL YOU LATER.
JERK!
RSHAL ST
THUNKA THUNKA THUNKA
WHAT...?
THUNKA THUNKA THUNKA THUNKA
NO!

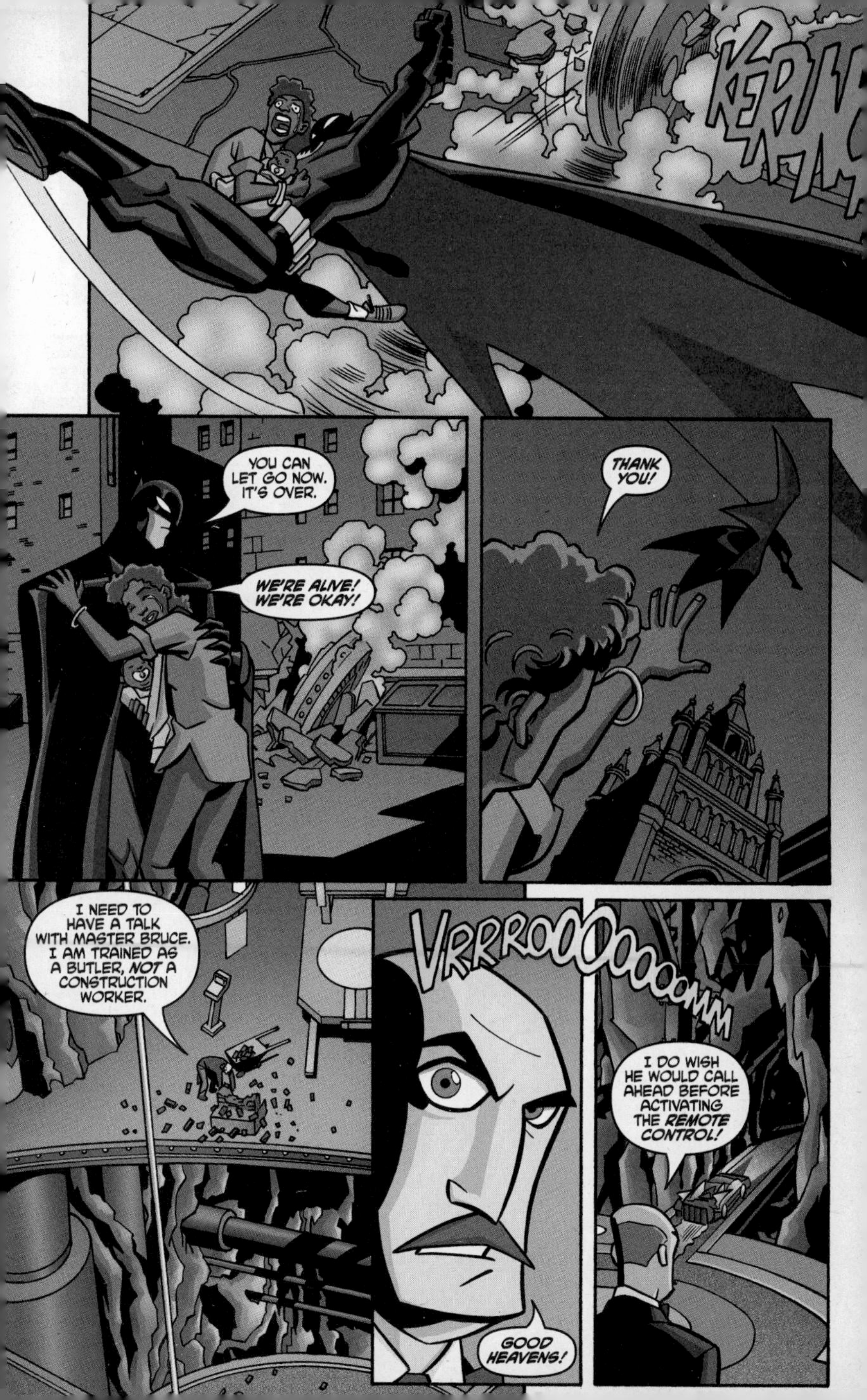
YOU CAN LET GO NOW. IT'S OVER.
WE'RE ALIVE! WE'RE OKAY!
THANK YOU!
I NEED TO HAVE A TALK WITH MASTER BRUCE. I AM TRAINED AS A BUTLER, NOT A CONSTRUCTION WORKER.
VRRROOOOOOOOOMM
GOOD HEAVENS!
I DO WISH HE WOULD CALL AHEAD BEFORE ACTIVATING THE REMOTE CONTROL!

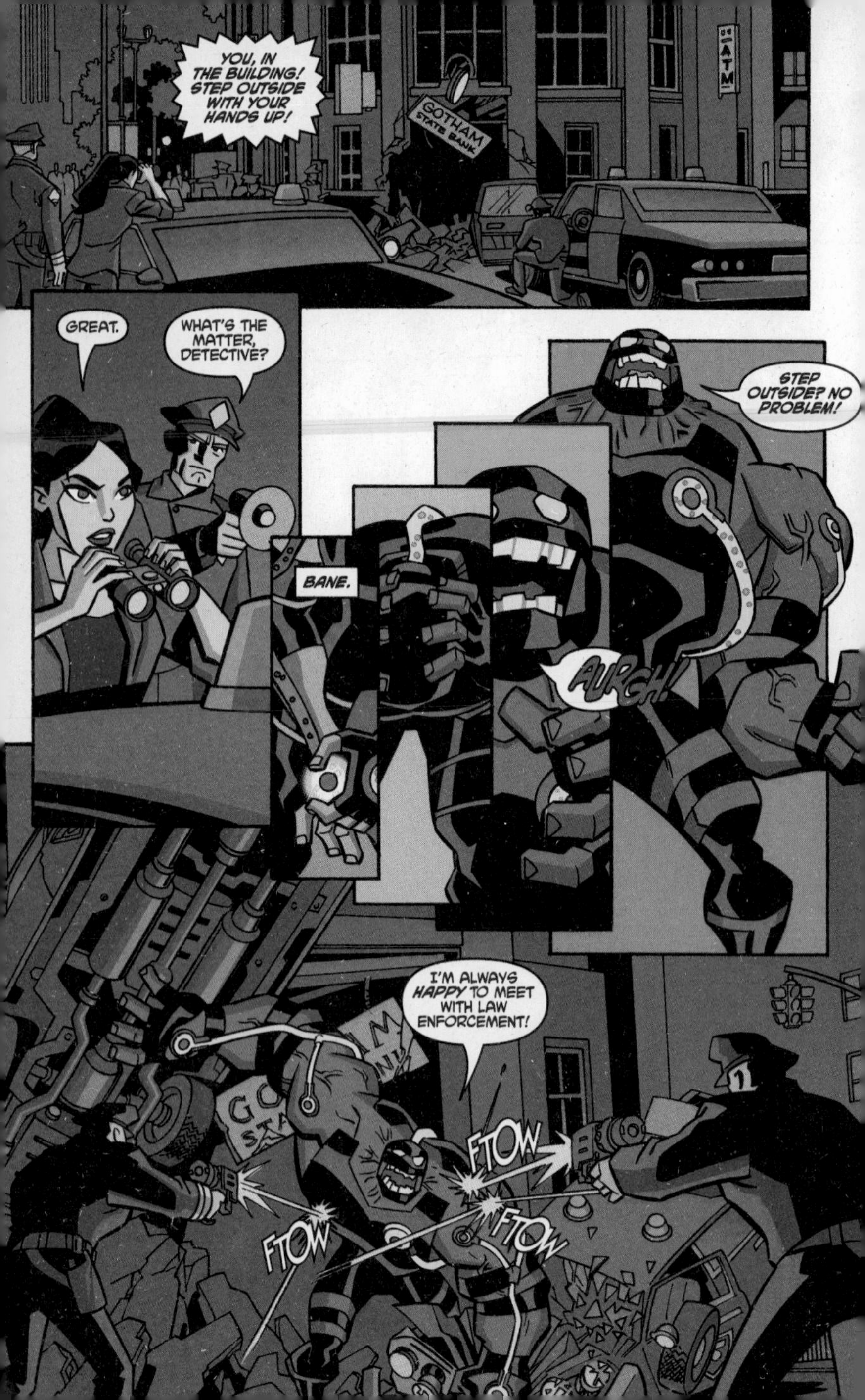
YOU, IN THE BUILDING! STEP OUTSIDE WITH YOUR HANDS UP!
GOTHAM STATE BANK
ATM
GREAT.
WHAT'S THE MATTER, DETECTIVE?
BANE.
STEP OUTSIDE? NO PROBLEM!
AURGH!
I'M ALWAYS HAPPY TO MEET WITH LAW ENFORCEMENT!
FTOW
FTOW
FTOW

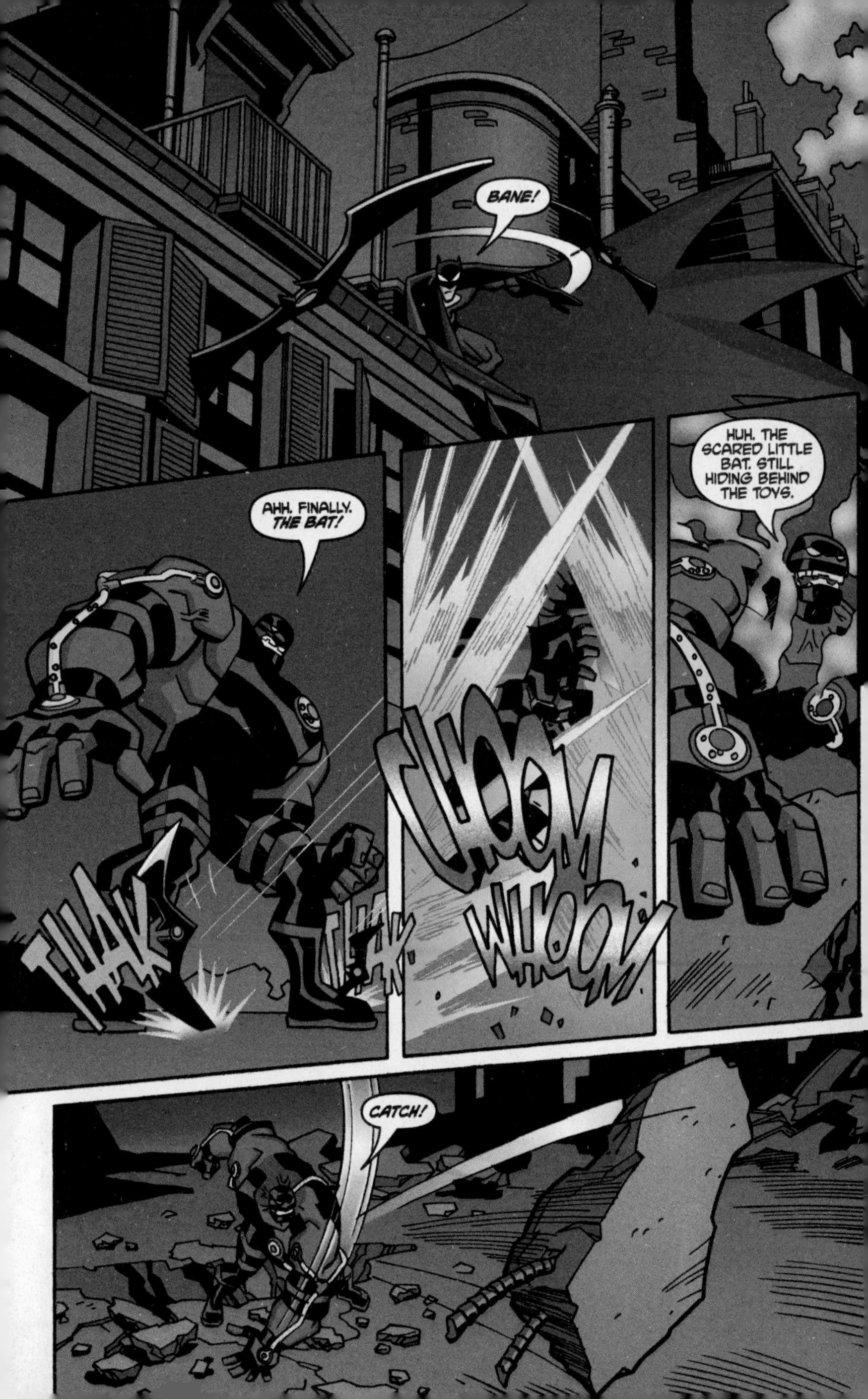

BANE!
AHH. FINALLY. THE BAT!
THAK
THAK
CHOOM
WHOOM
HUH. THE SCARED LITTLE BAT. STILL HIDING BEHIND THE TOYS.
CATCH!

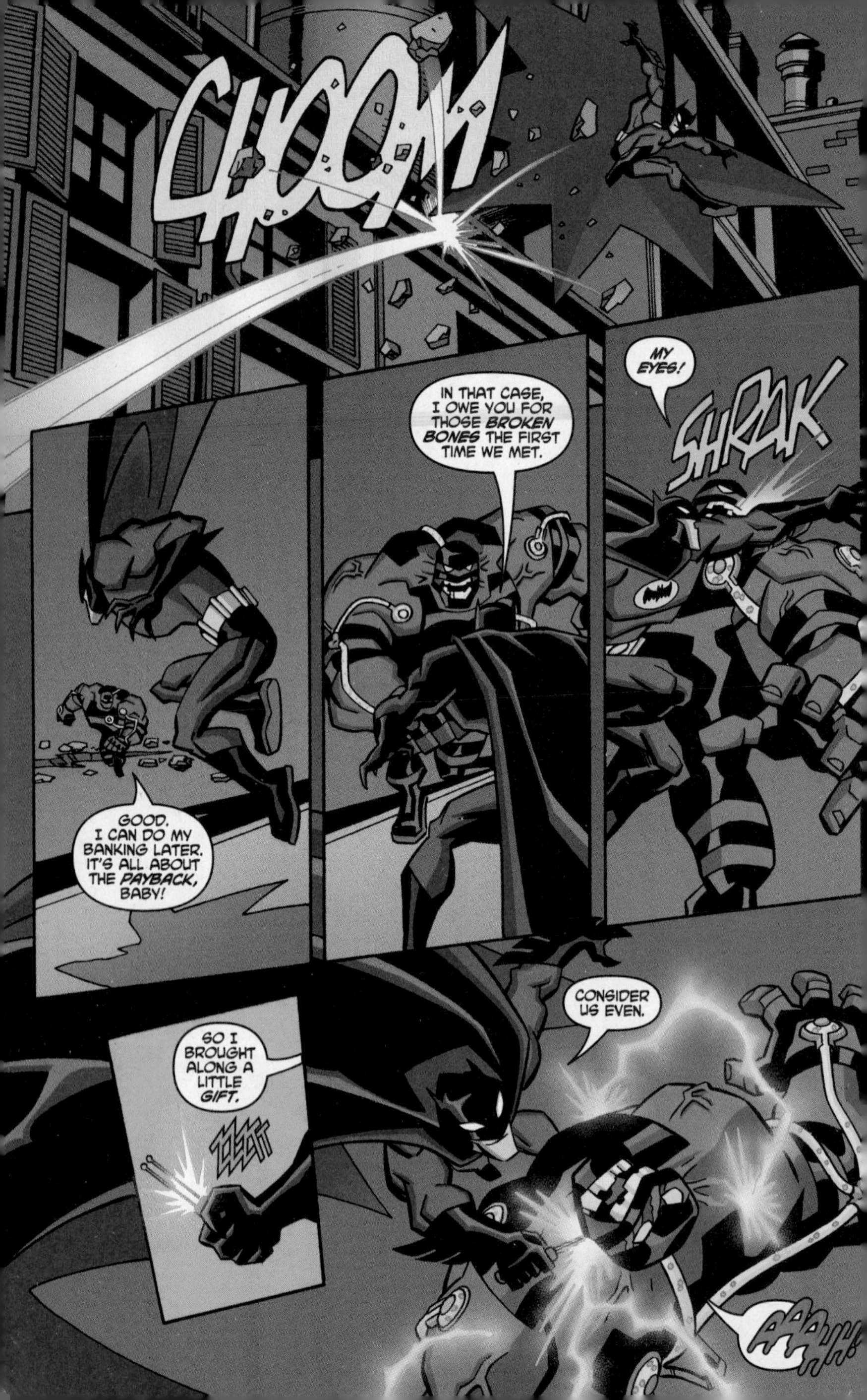
CHOOM
GOOD. I CAN DO MY BANKING LATER. IT'S ALL ABOUT THE PAYBACK, BABY!
IN THAT CASE, I OWE YOU FOR THOSE BROKEN BONES THE FIRST TIME WE MET.
MY EYES!
SHRAK
SO I BROUGHT ALONG A LITTLE GIFT.
CONSIDER US EVEN.
AAAHH!

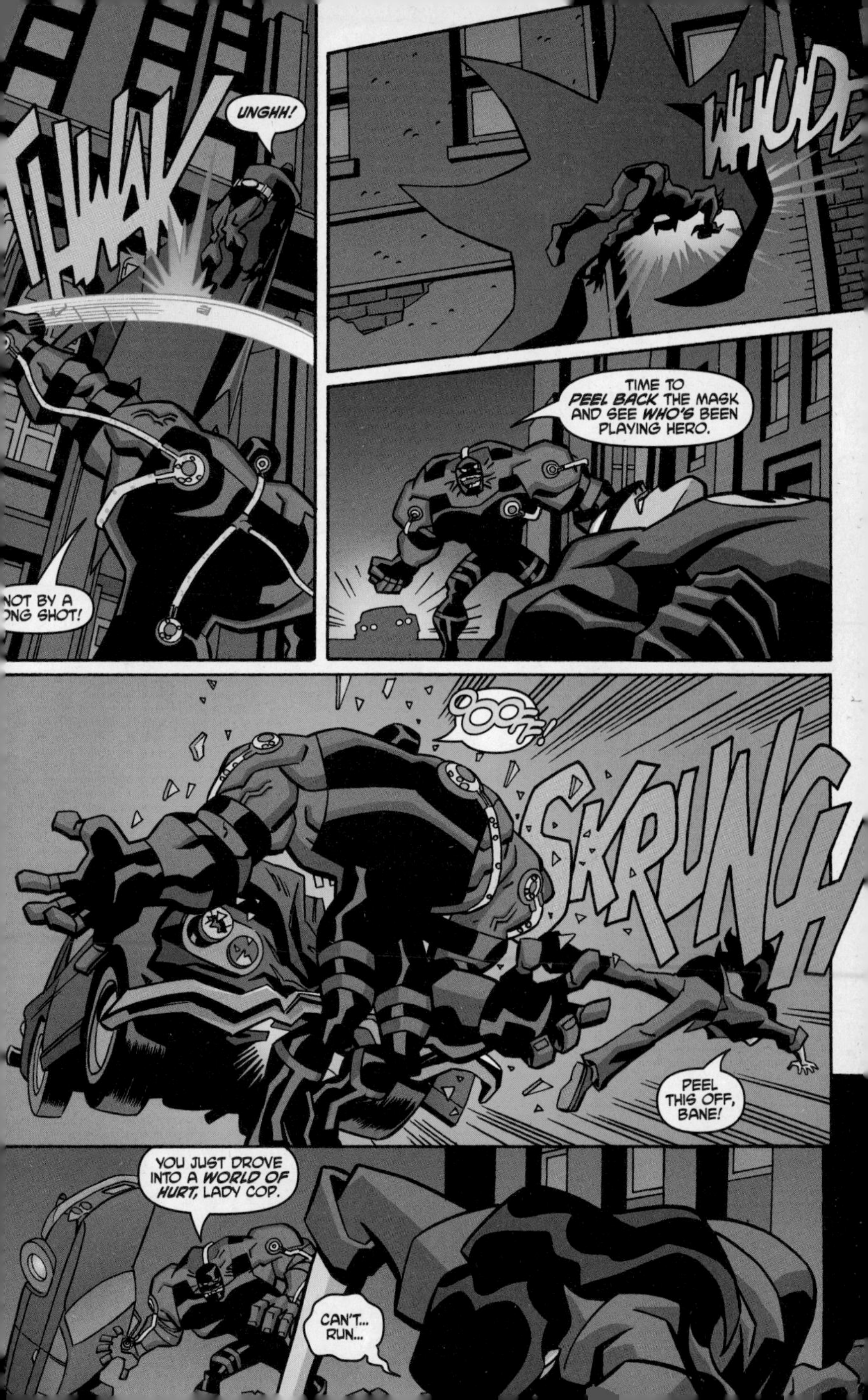
THWAK
UNGHH!
NOT BY A
ONG SHOT!
WHUD
TIME TO PEEL BACK THE MASK AND SEE WHO'S BEEN PLAYING HERO.
OOOF!
SKRUNCH
PEEL THIS OFF, BANE!
YOU JUST DROVE INTO A WORLD OF HURT, LADY COP.
CAN'T... RUN...

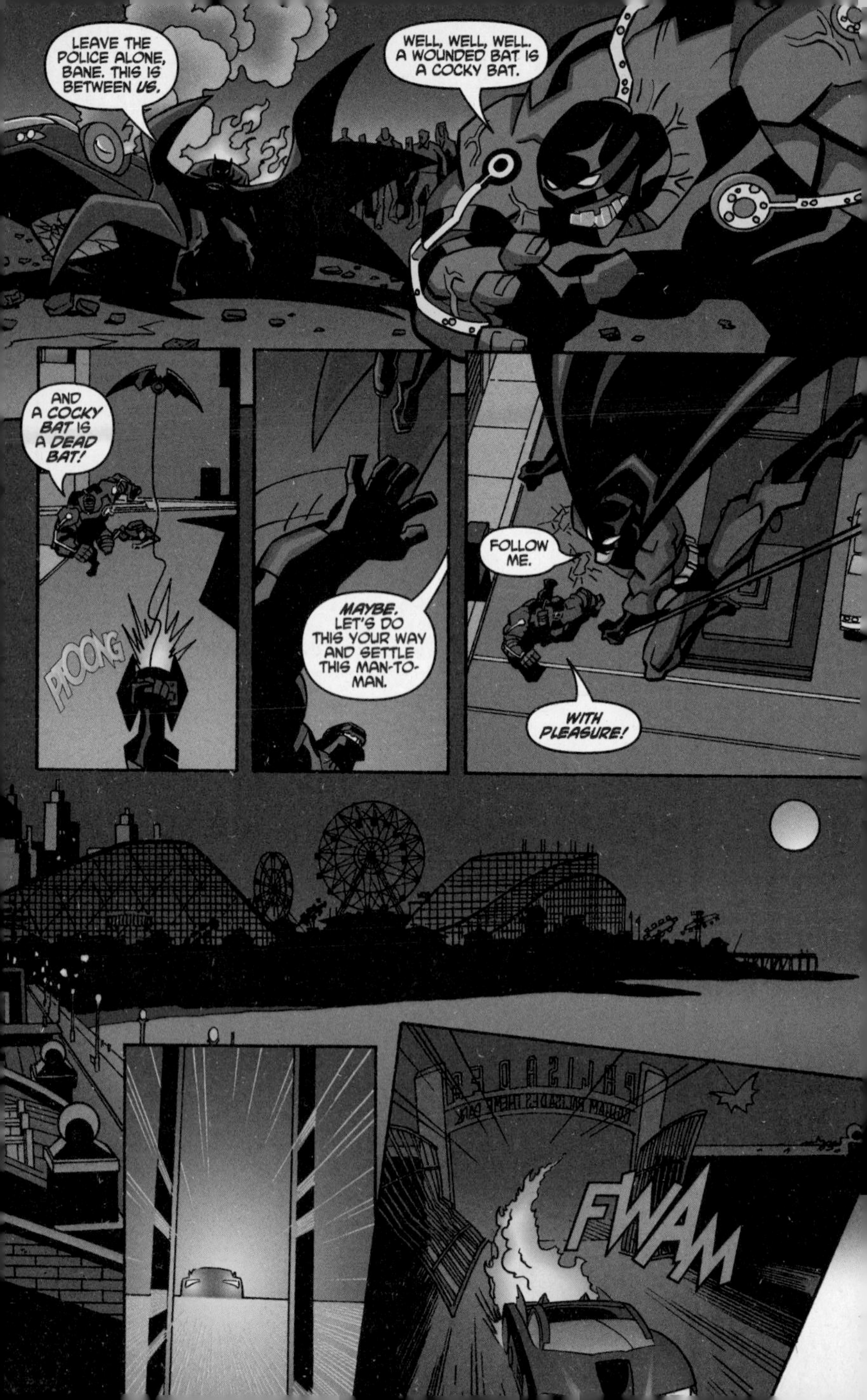
LEAVE THE POLICE ALONE, BANE. THIS IS BETWEEN US.
WELL, WELL, WELL. A WOUNDED BAT IS A COCKY BAT.
AND A COCKY BAT IS A DEAD BAT!
PTOOONG
MAYBE. LET'S DO THIS YOUR WAY AND SETTLE THIS MAN-TO-MAN.
FOLLOW ME.
WITH PLEASURE!
FWAM

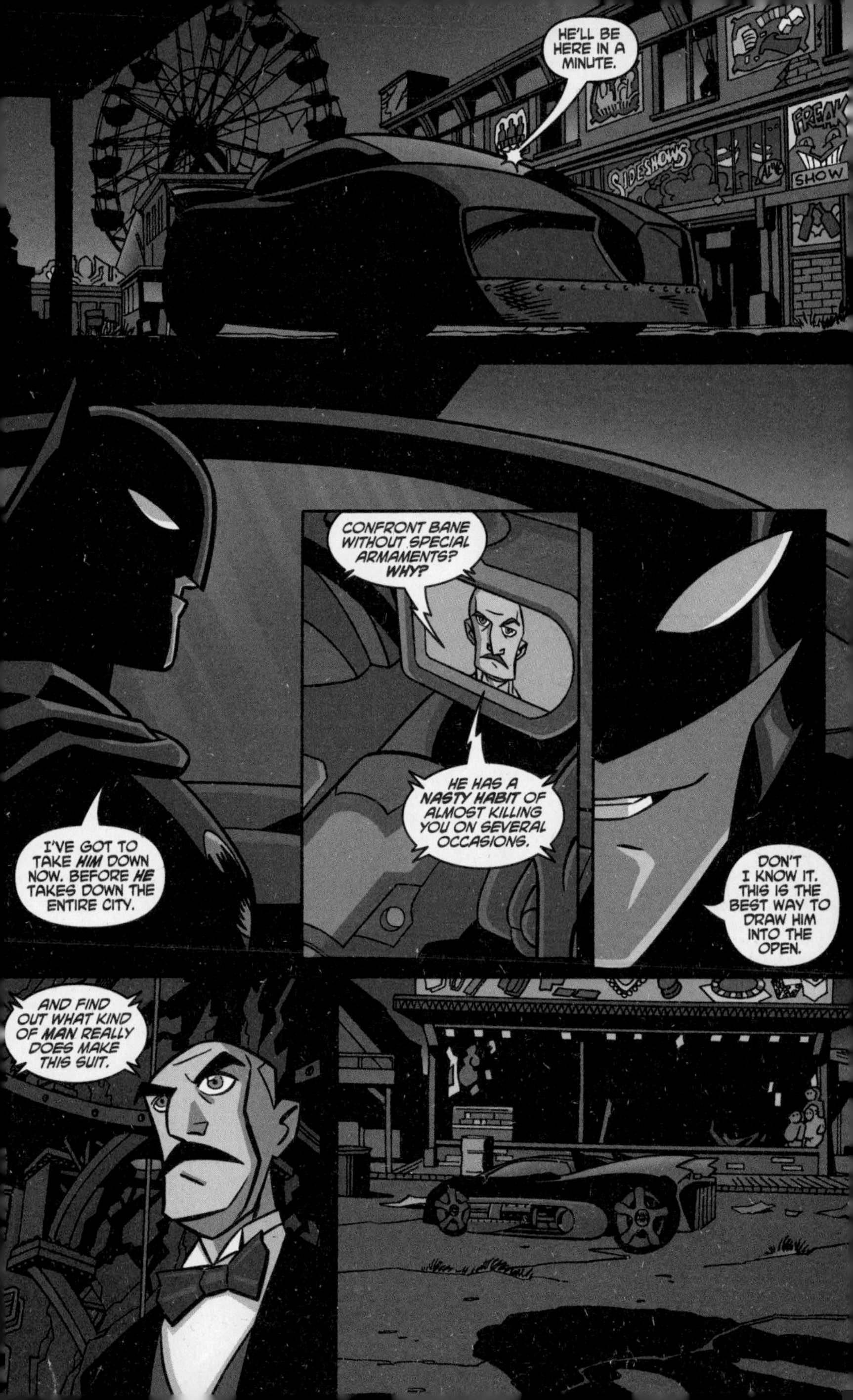
HE'LL BE HERE IN A MINUTE.
I'VE GOT TO TAKE HIM DOWN NOW. BEFORE HE TAKES DOWN THE ENTIRE CITY.
CONFRONT BANE WITHOUT SPECIAL ARMAMENTS? WHY?
HE HAS A NASTY HABIT OF ALMOST KILLING YOU ON SEVERAL OCCASIONS.
DON'T I KNOW IT. THIS IS THE BEST WAY TO DRAW HIM INTO THE OPEN.
AND FIND OUT WHAT KIND OF MAN REALLY DOES MAKE THIS SUIT.
SIDESHOWS
FREAK SHOW
ALIVE

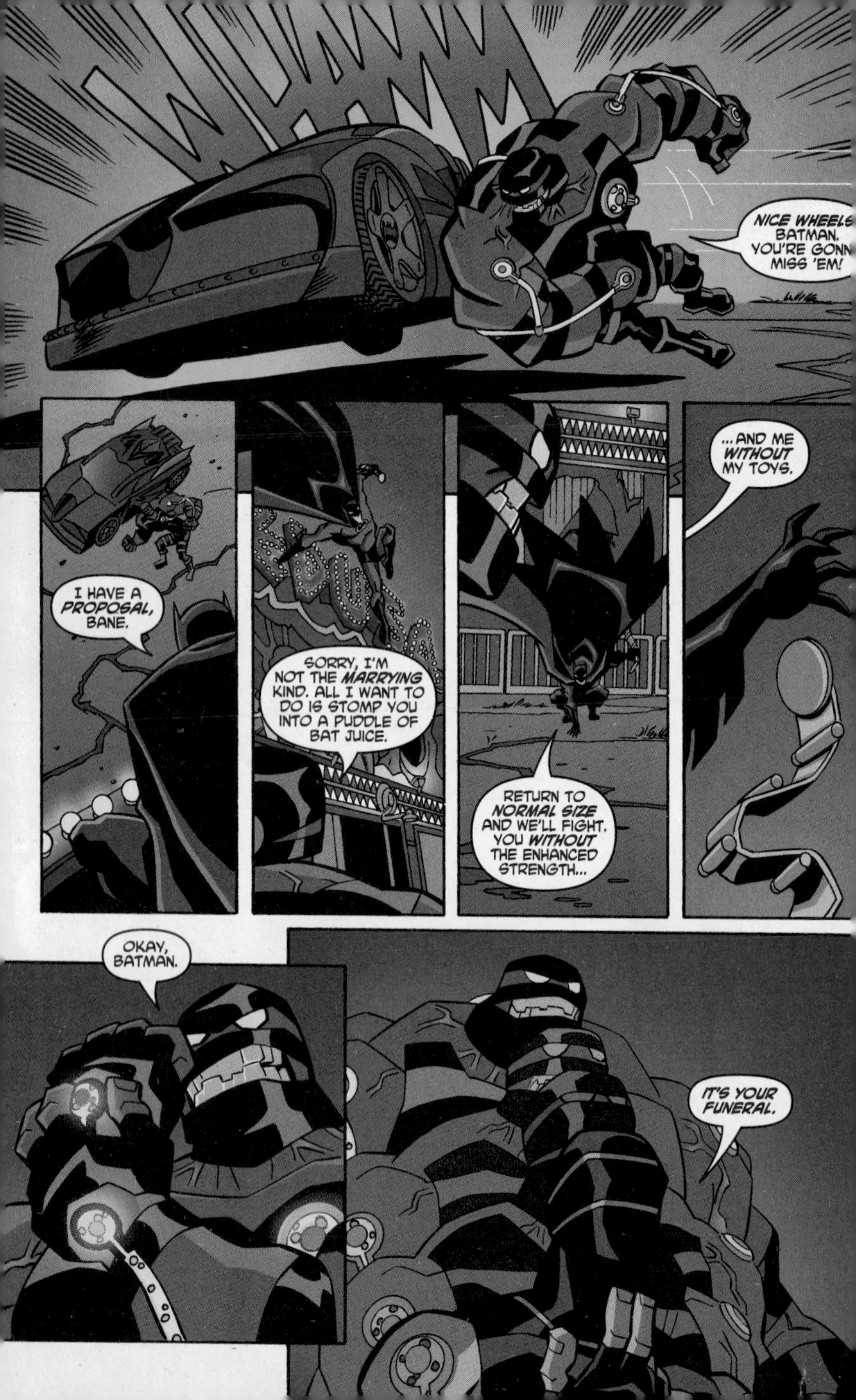
WHUMMM
NICE WHEELS BATMAN. YOU'RE GONN MISS 'EM!
I HAVE A PROPOSAL, BANE.
SORRY, I'M NOT THE MARRYING KIND. ALL I WANT TO DO IS STOMP YOU INTO A PUDDLE OF BAT JUICE.
RETURN TO NORMAL SIZE AND WE'LL FIGHT. YOU WITHOUT THE ENHANCED STRENGTH...
...AND ME WITHOUT MY TOYS.
OKAY, BATMAN.
IT'S YOUR FUNERAL.

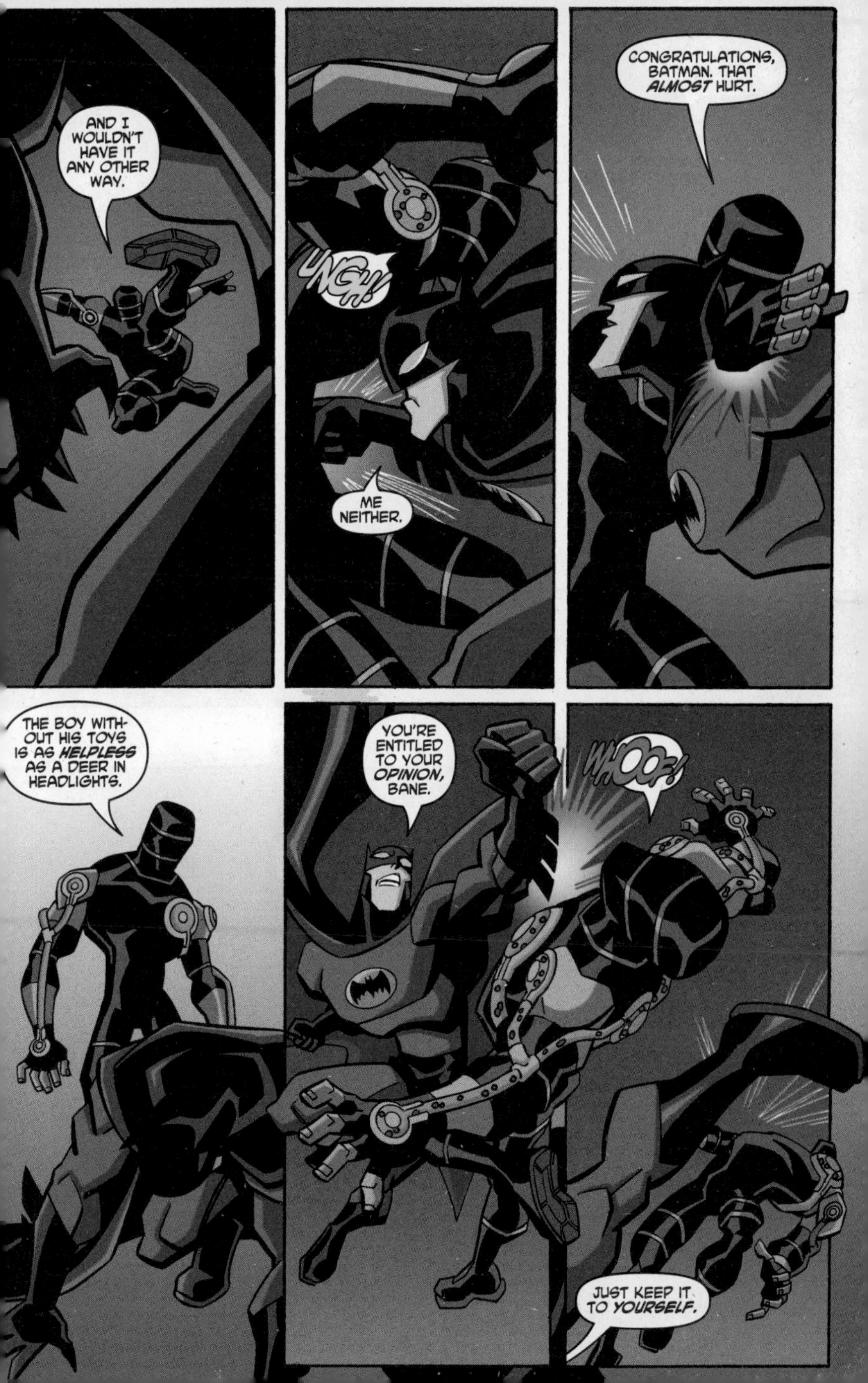
AND I WOULDN'T HAVE IT ANY OTHER WAY.
UNGH!
ME NEITHER.
CONGRATULATIONS, BATMAN. THAT *ALMOST* HURT.
THE BOY WITH-OUT HIS TOYS IS AS *HELPLESS* AS A DEER IN HEADLIGHTS.
YOU'RE ENTITLED TO YOUR *OPINION,* BANE.
WHOOF!
JUST KEEP IT TO *YOURSELF.*

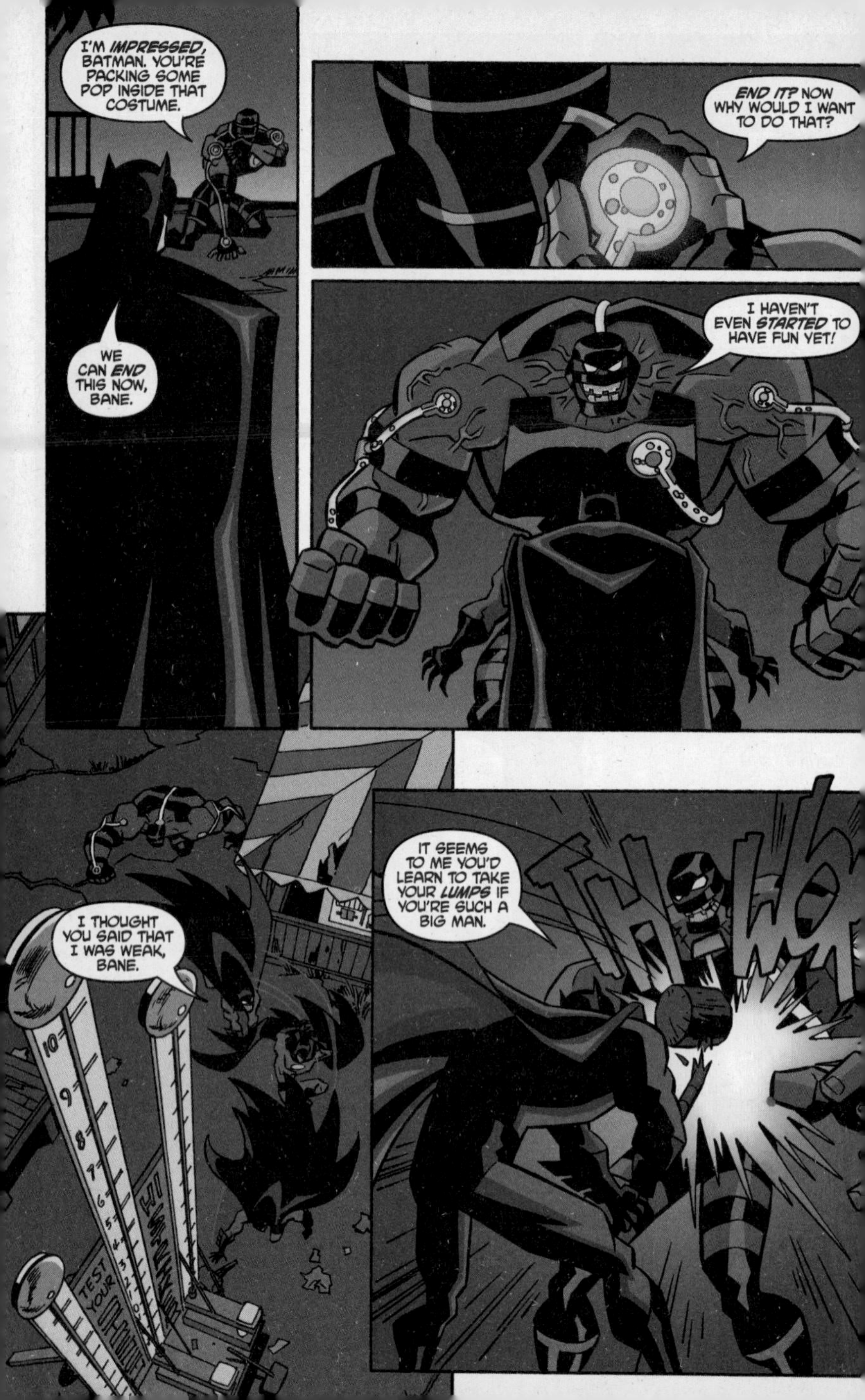
I'M *IMPRESSED*, BATMAN. YOU'RE PACKING SOME POP INSIDE THAT COSTUME.
WE CAN *END* THIS NOW, BANE.
END IT? NOW WHY WOULD I WANT TO DO THAT?
I HAVEN'T EVEN *STARTED* TO HAVE FUN YET!
I THOUGHT YOU SAID THAT I WAS WEAK, BANE.
TEST YOUR
IT SEEMS TO ME YOU'D LEARN TO TAKE YOUR *LUMPS* IF YOU'RE SUCH A BIG MAN.

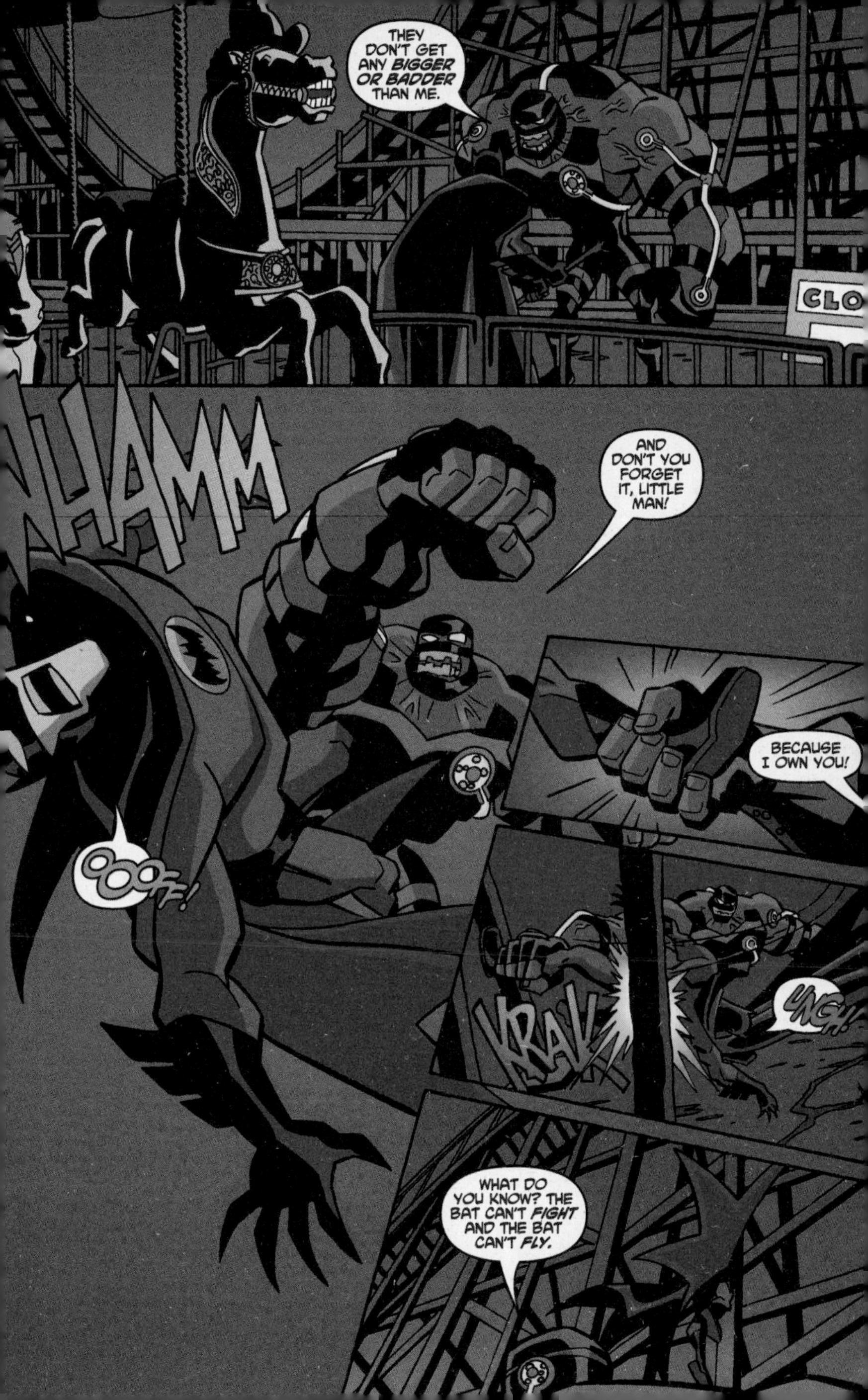

THEY DON'T GET ANY *BIGGER* OR *BADDER* THAN ME.
CLO
WHAMM
AND DON'T YOU FORGET IT, LITTLE MAN!
OOOFF!
BECAUSE I OWN YOU!
KRAK
UNGH!
WHAT DO YOU KNOW? THE BAT CAN'T *FIGHT* AND THE BAT CAN'T *FLY*.

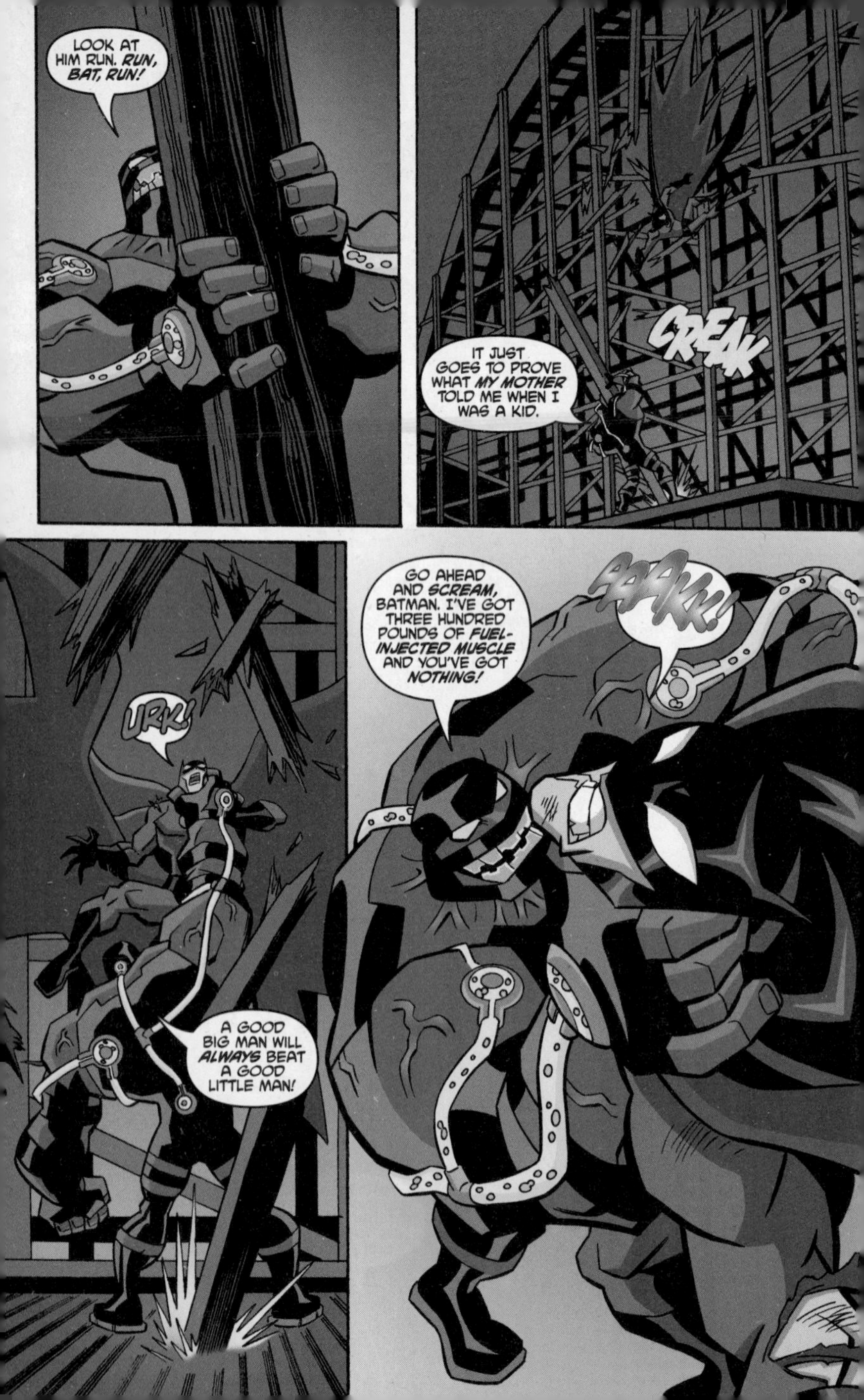
LOOK AT HIM RUN. RUN, BAT, RUN!
IT JUST GOES TO PROVE WHAT MY MOTHER TOLD ME WHEN I WAS A KID.
CREAK
URK!
A GOOD BIG MAN WILL ALWAYS BEAT A GOOD LITTLE MAN!
GO AHEAD AND SCREAM, BATMAN. I'VE GOT THREE HUNDRED POUNDS OF FUEL-INJECTED MUSCLE AND YOU'VE GOT NOTHING!

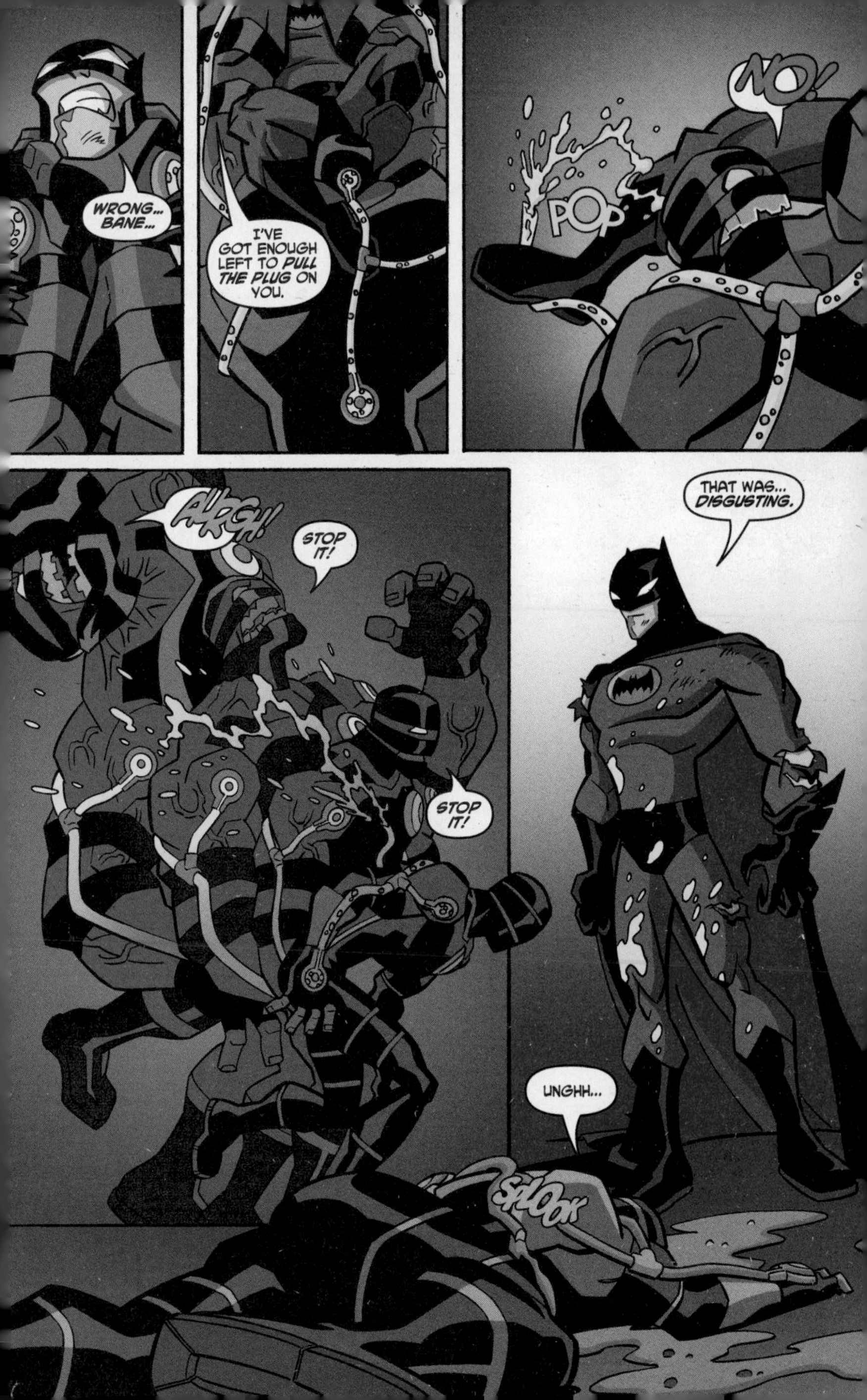
WRONG... BANE...
I'VE GOT ENOUGH LEFT TO PULL THE PLUG ON YOU.
NO!
POP
ARRGH!
STOP IT!
STOP IT!
THAT WAS... DISGUSTING.
UNGHH...
SPLOOK

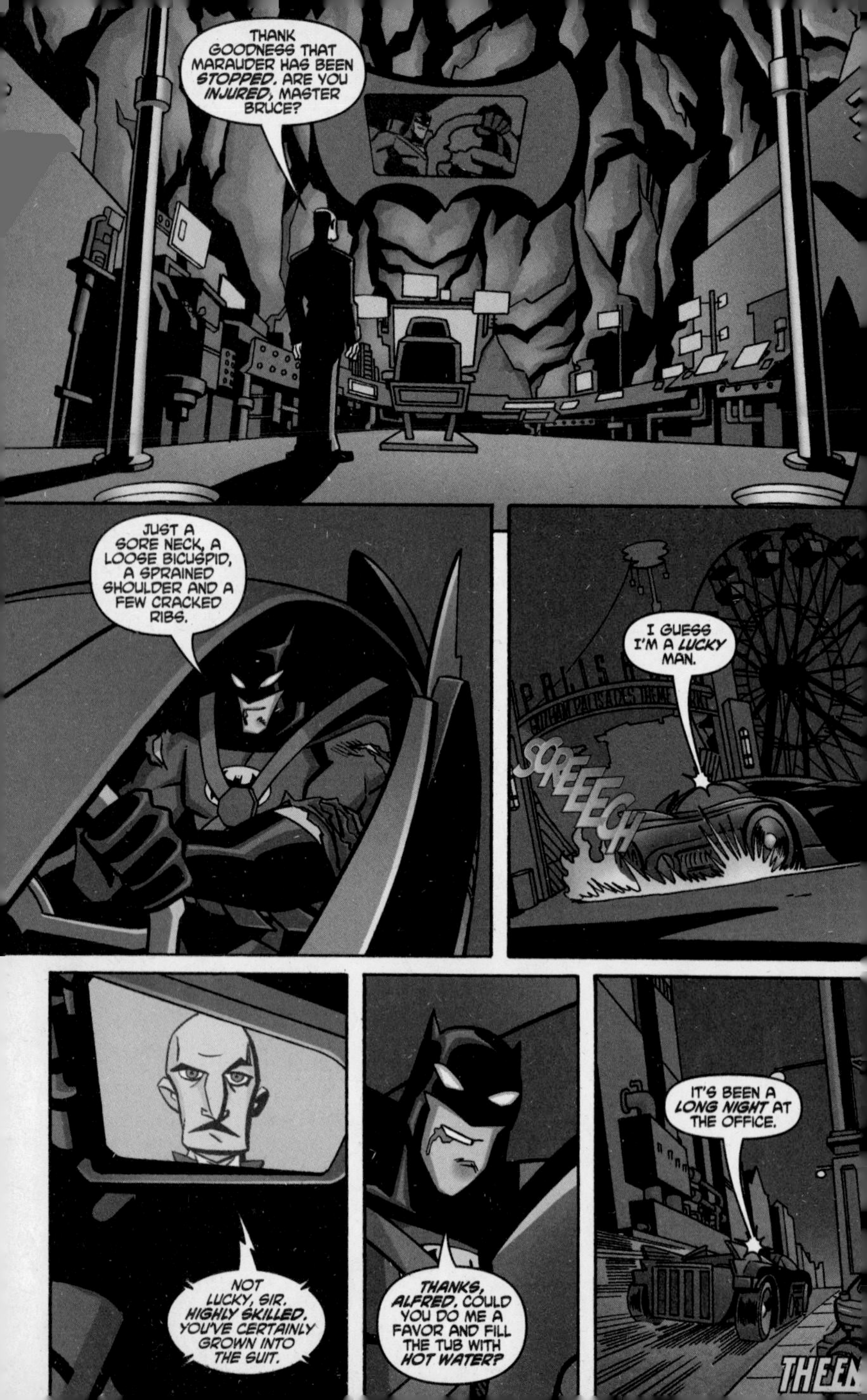
THANK GOODNESS THAT MARAUDER HAS BEEN *STOPPED*. ARE YOU *INJURED*, MASTER BRUCE?
JUST A SORE NECK, A LOOSE BICUSPID, A SPRAINED SHOULDER AND A FEW CRACKED RIBS.
I GUESS I'M A *LUCKY* MAN.
SCREEEECH
NOT LUCKY, SIR. *HIGHLY SKILLED*. YOU'VE CERTAINLY GROWN INTO THE SUIT.
THANKS, ALFRED. COULD YOU DO ME A FAVOR AND FILL THE TUB WITH *HOT WATER?*
IT'S BEEN A *LONG NIGHT* AT THE OFFICE.
THE EN

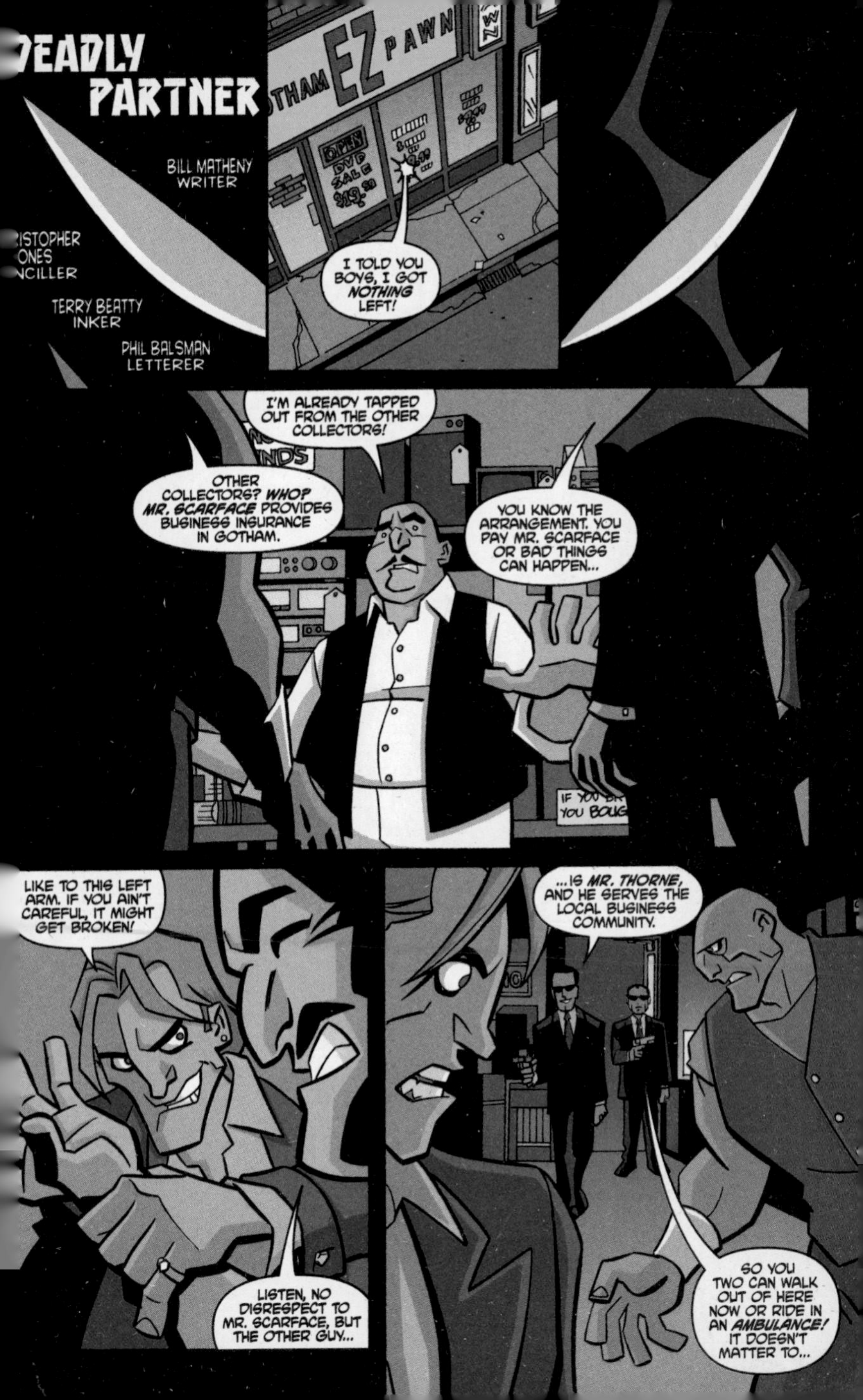
DEADLY PARTNER
BILL MATHENY WRITER
RISTOPHER ONES NCILLER
TERRY BEATTY INKER
PHIL BALSMAN LETTERER
GOTHAM EZ PAWN
OPEN DVD SALE $19.99
I TOLD YOU BOYS, I GOT NOTHING LEFT!
I'M ALREADY TAPPED OUT FROM THE OTHER COLLECTORS!
OTHER COLLECTORS? WHO? MR. SCARFACE PROVIDES BUSINESS INSURANCE IN GOTHAM.
YOU KNOW THE ARRANGEMENT. YOU PAY MR. SCARFACE OR BAD THINGS CAN HAPPEN...
LIKE TO THIS LEFT ARM. IF YOU AIN'T CAREFUL, IT MIGHT GET BROKEN!
LISTEN, NO DISRESPECT TO MR. SCARFACE, BUT THE OTHER GUY...
...IS MR. THORNE, AND HE SERVES THE LOCAL BUSINESS COMMUNITY.
SO YOU TWO CAN WALK OUT OF HERE NOW OR RIDE IN AN AMBULANCE! IT DOESN'T MATTER TO...

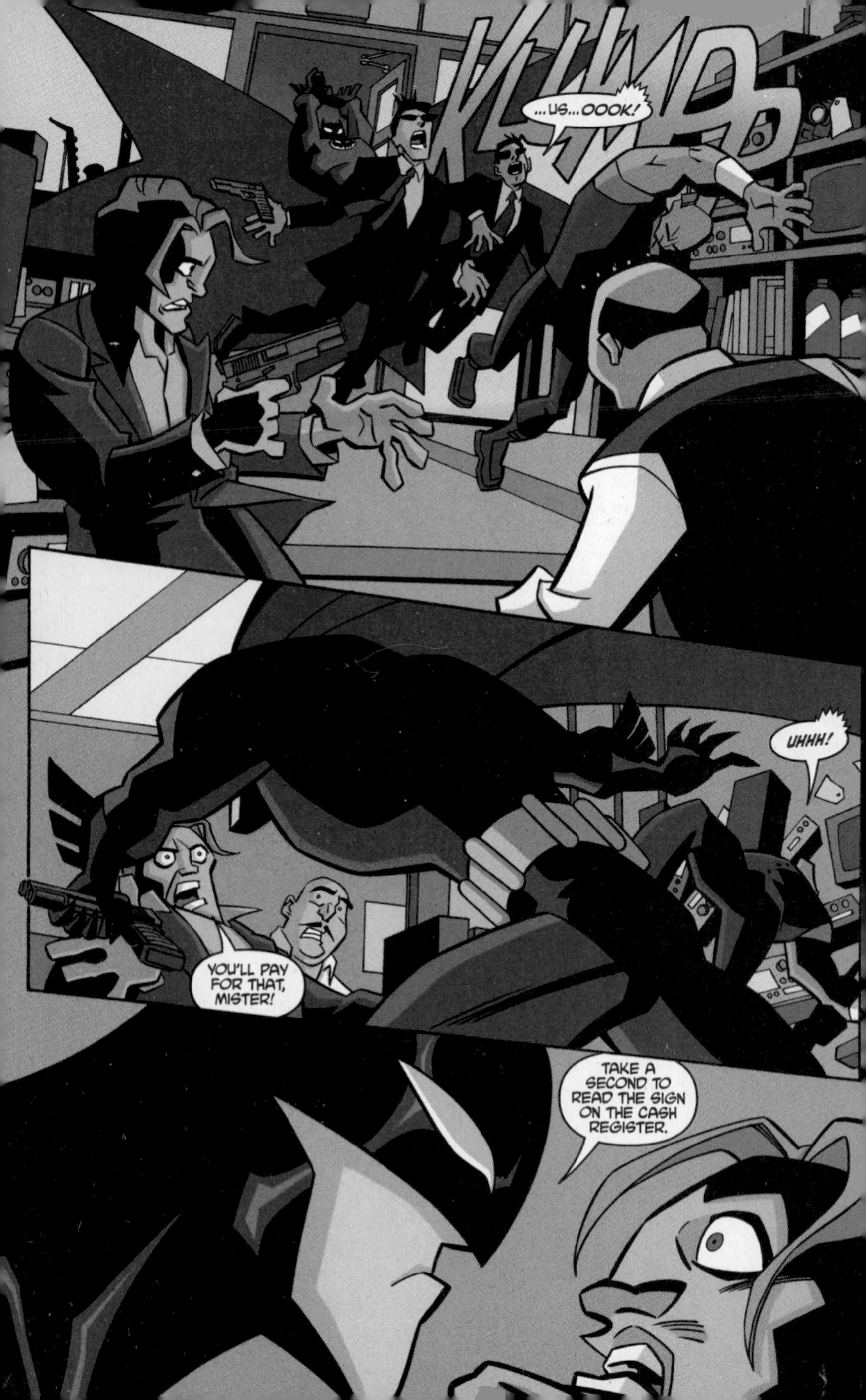
...US...OOOK!
UHHH!
YOU'LL PAY FOR THAT, MISTER!
TAKE A SECOND TO READ THE SIGN ON THE CASH REGISTER.

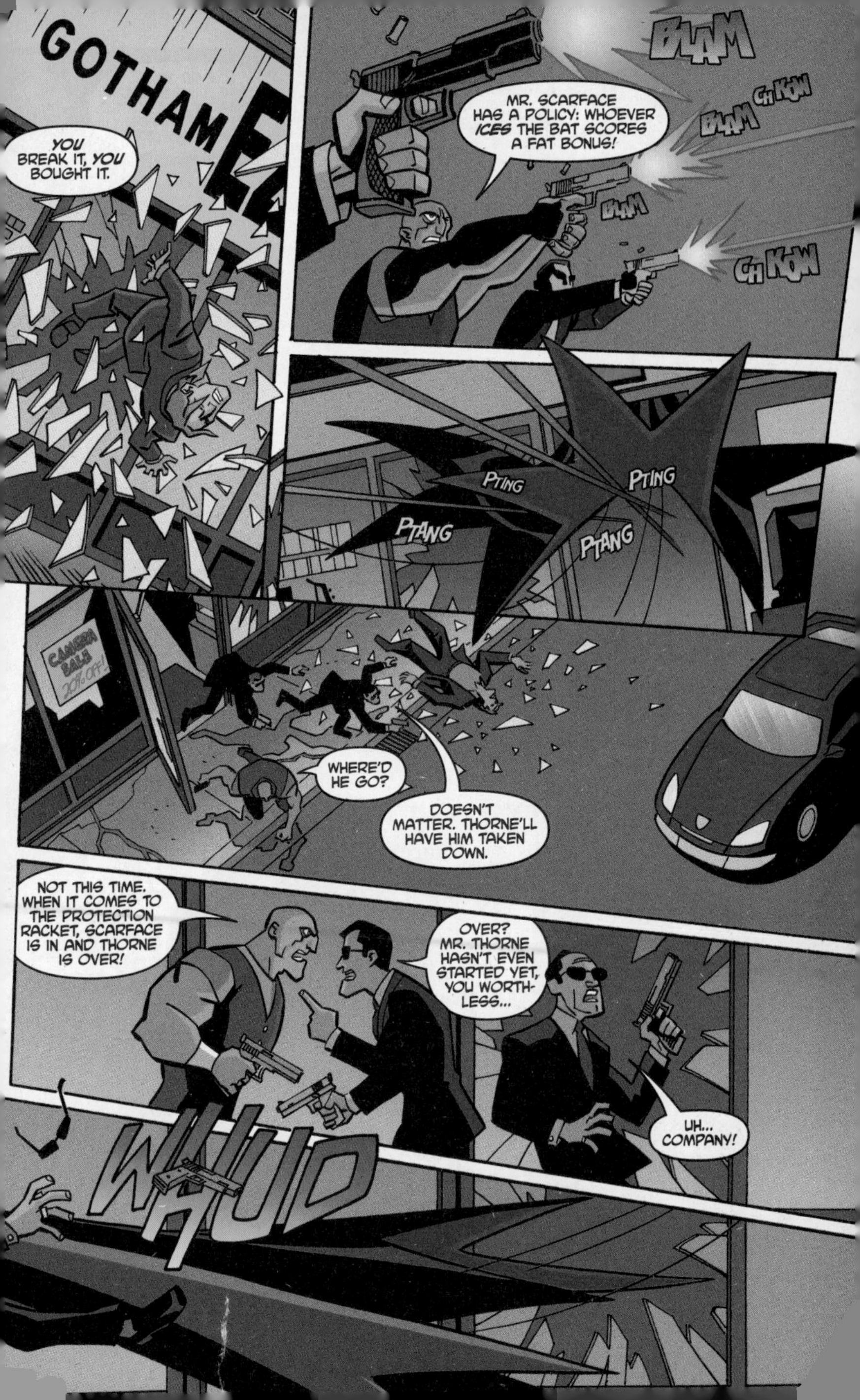
GOTHAM
YOU BREAK IT, YOU BOUGHT IT.
BLAM
MR. SCARFACE HAS A POLICY: WHOEVER ICES THE BAT SCORES A FAT BONUS!
BLAM CH KOW
BLAM
CH KOW
PTING
PTING
PTANG
PTANG
CAMERA SALE 20% OFF!
WHERE'D HE GO?
DOESN'T MATTER. THORNE'LL HAVE HIM TAKEN DOWN.
NOT THIS TIME. WHEN IT COMES TO THE PROTECTION RACKET, SCARFACE IS IN AND THORNE IS OVER!
OVER? MR. THORNE HASN'T EVEN STARTED YET, YOU WORTHLESS...
UH... COMPANY!
WHUD

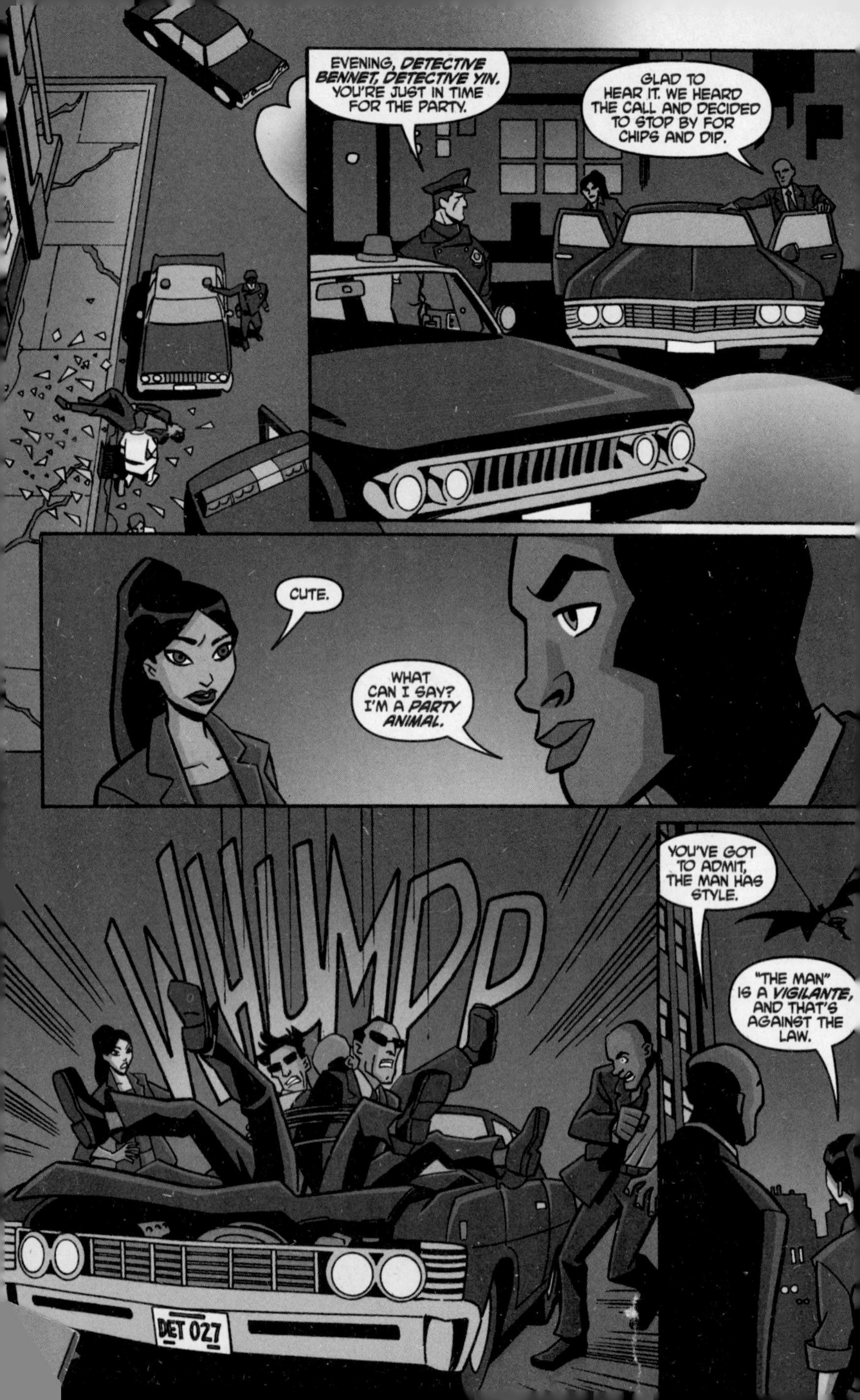
EVENING, *DETECTIVE BENNET, DETECTIVE YIN.* YOU'RE JUST IN TIME FOR THE PARTY.
GLAD TO HEAR IT. WE HEARD THE CALL AND DECIDED TO STOP BY FOR CHIPS AND DIP.
CUTE.
WHAT CAN I SAY? I'M A *PARTY ANIMAL.*
WHUMP
YOU'VE GOT TO ADMIT, THE MAN HAS STYLE.
"THE MAN" IS A *VIGILANTE,* AND THAT'S AGAINST THE LAW.
DET 027

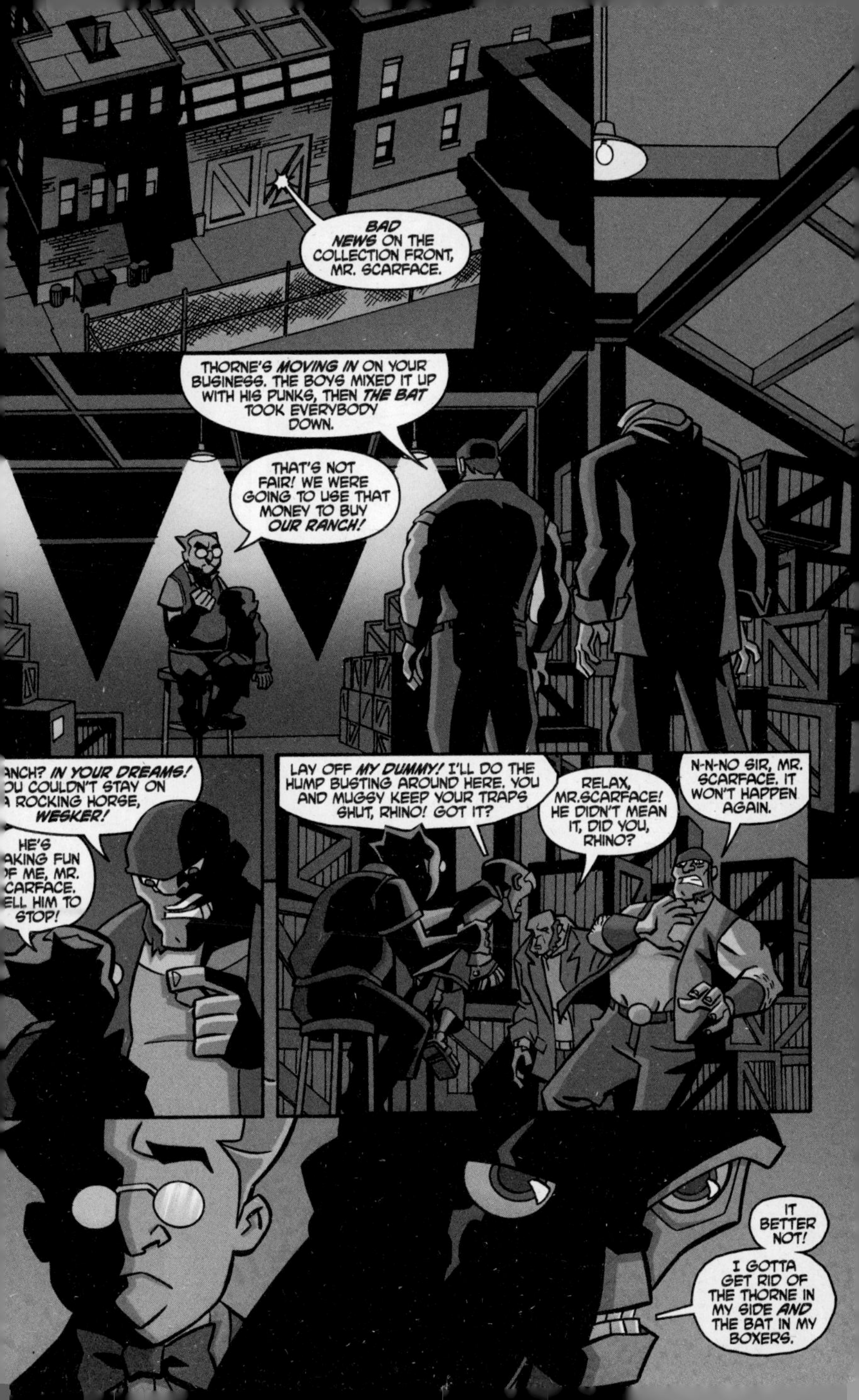
BAD NEWS ON THE COLLECTION FRONT, MR. SCARFACE.
THORNE'S MOVING IN ON YOUR BUSINESS. THE BOYS MIXED IT UP WITH HIS PUNKS, THEN THE BAT TOOK EVERYBODY DOWN.
THAT'S NOT FAIR! WE WERE GOING TO USE THAT MONEY TO BUY OUR RANCH!
ANCH? IN YOUR DREAMS! OU COULDN'T STAY ON A ROCKING HORSE, WESKER!
HE'S AKING FUN OF ME, MR. CARFACE. ELL HIM TO STOP!
LAY OFF MY DUMMY! I'LL DO THE HUMP BUSTING AROUND HERE. YOU AND MUGSY KEEP YOUR TRAPS SHUT, RHINO! GOT IT?
RELAX, MR.SCARFACE! HE DIDN'T MEAN IT, DID YOU, RHINO?
N-N-NO SIR, MR. SCARFACE. IT WON'T HAPPEN AGAIN.
IT BETTER NOT!
I GOTTA GET RID OF THE THORNE IN MY SIDE AND THE BAT IN MY BOXERS.

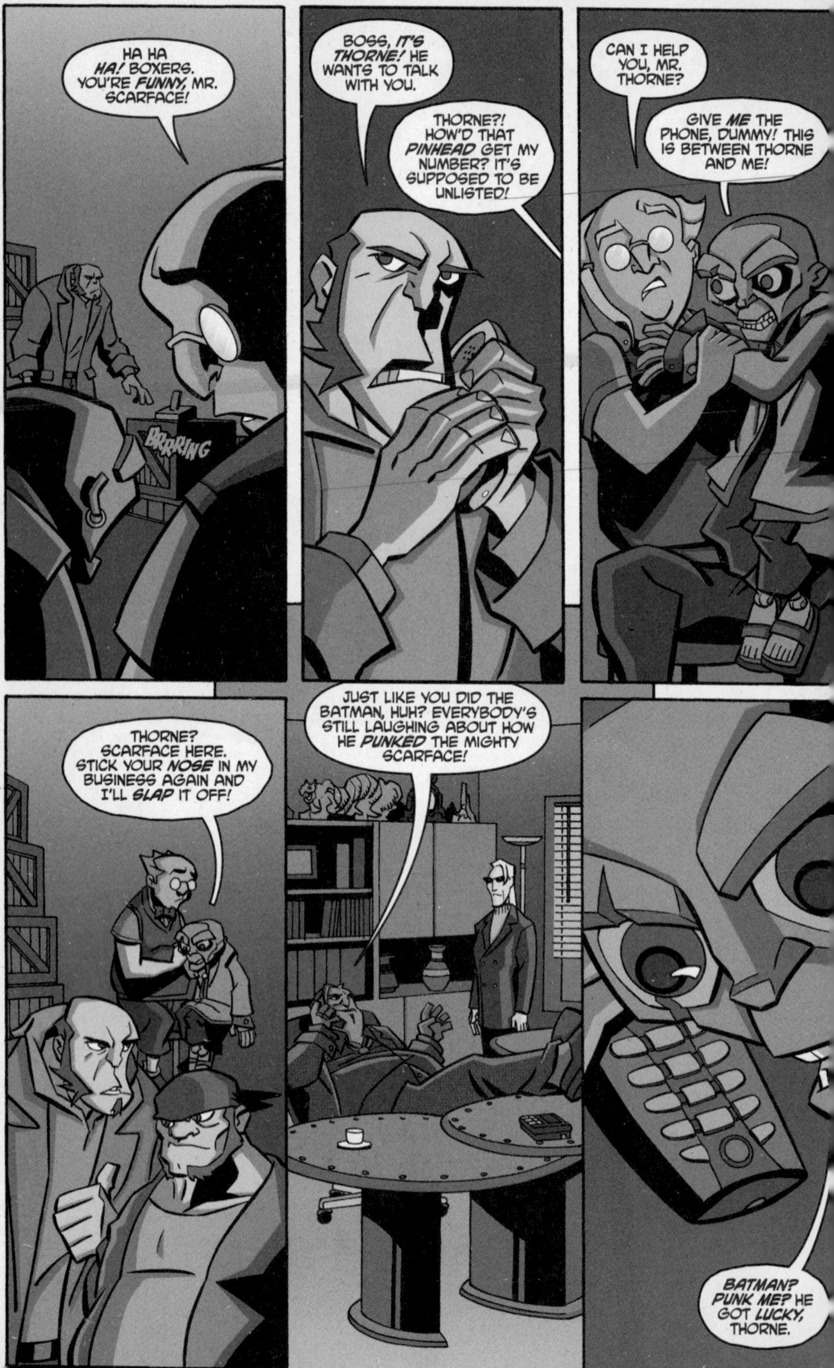
HA HA HA! BOXERS. YOU'RE FUNNY, MR. SCARFACE!
BRRRING
BOSS, IT'S THORNE! HE WANTS TO TALK WITH YOU.
THORNE?! HOW'D THAT PINHEAD GET MY NUMBER? IT'S SUPPOSED TO BE UNLISTED!
CAN I HELP YOU, MR. THORNE?
GIVE ME THE PHONE, DUMMY! THIS IS BETWEEN THORNE AND ME!
THORNE? SCARFACE HERE. STICK YOUR NOSE IN MY BUSINESS AGAIN AND I'LL SLAP IT OFF!
JUST LIKE YOU DID THE BATMAN, HUH? EVERYBODY'S STILL LAUGHING ABOUT HOW HE PUNKED THE MIGHTY SCARFACE!
BATMAN? PUNK ME? HE GOT LUCKY, THORNE.

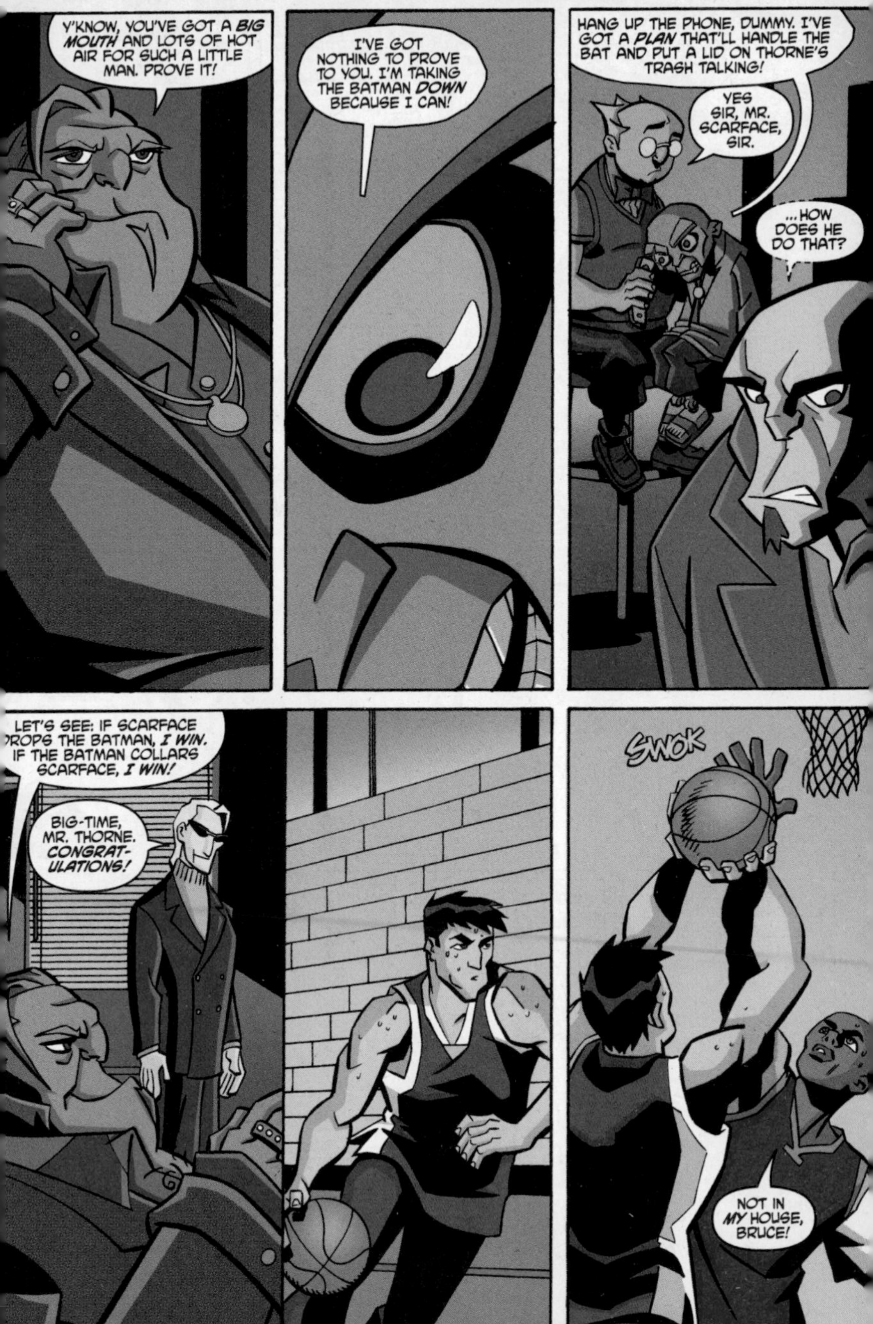
Y'KNOW, YOU'VE GOT A *BIG MOUTH* AND LOTS OF HOT AIR FOR SUCH A LITTLE MAN. PROVE IT!
I'VE GOT NOTHING TO PROVE TO YOU. I'M TAKING THE BATMAN *DOWN* BECAUSE I CAN!
HANG UP THE PHONE, DUMMY. I'VE GOT A *PLAN* THAT'LL HANDLE THE BAT AND PUT A LID ON THORNE'S TRASH TALKING!
YES SIR, MR. SCARFACE, SIR.
...HOW DOES HE DO THAT?
LET'S SEE: IF SCARFACE DROPS THE BATMAN, *I WIN.* IF THE BATMAN COLLARS SCARFACE, *I WIN!*
BIG-TIME, MR. THORNE. *CONGRATULATIONS!*
SWOK
NOT IN *MY* HOUSE, BRUCE!

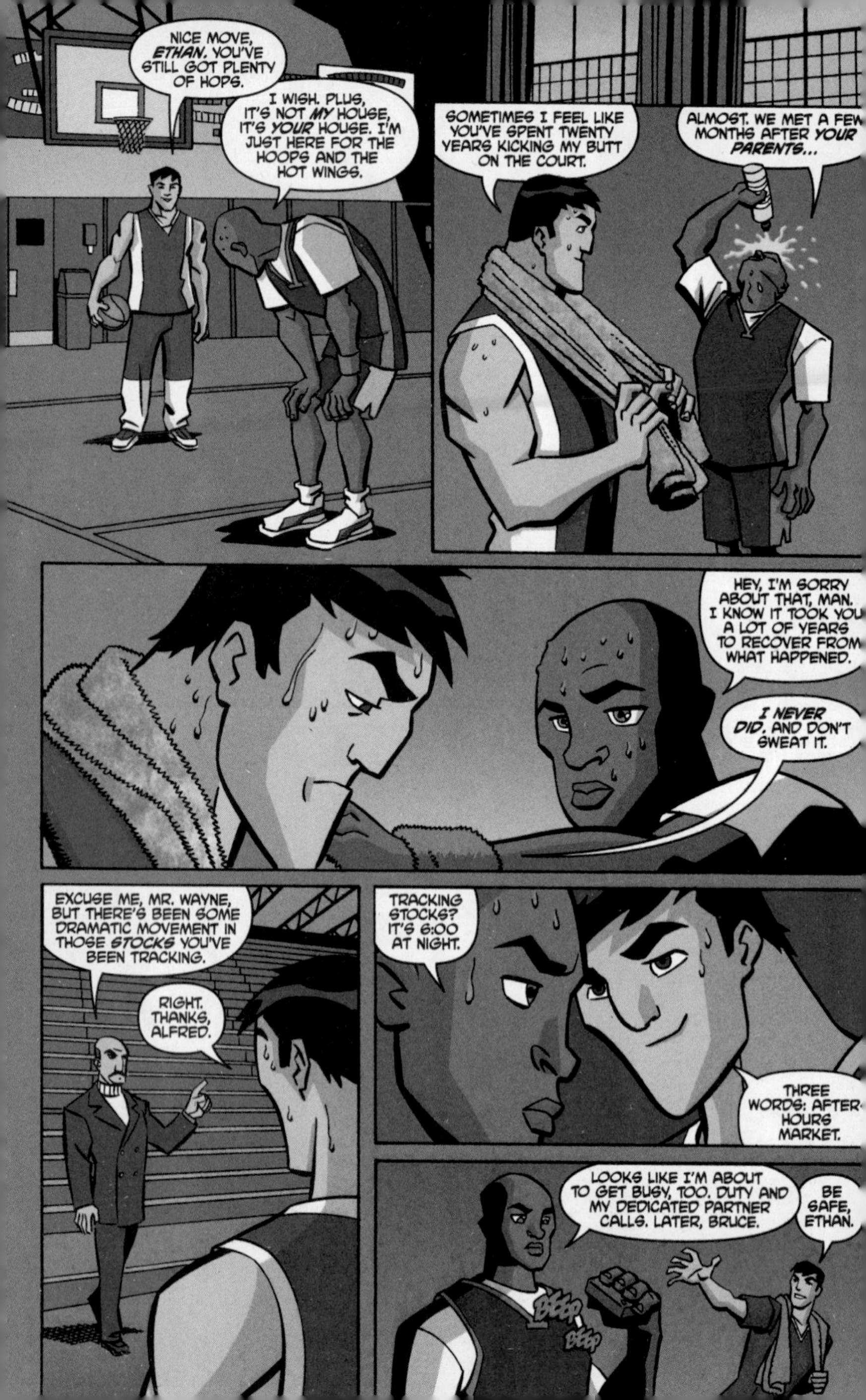
NICE MOVE, ETHAN. YOU'VE STILL GOT PLENTY OF HOPS.
I WISH. PLUS, IT'S NOT MY HOUSE, IT'S YOUR HOUSE. I'M JUST HERE FOR THE HOOPS AND THE HOT WINGS.
SOMETIMES I FEEL LIKE YOU'VE SPENT TWENTY YEARS KICKING MY BUTT ON THE COURT.
ALMOST. WE MET A FEW MONTHS AFTER YOUR PARENTS...
HEY, I'M SORRY ABOUT THAT, MAN. I KNOW IT TOOK YOU A LOT OF YEARS TO RECOVER FROM WHAT HAPPENED.
I NEVER DID. AND DON'T SWEAT IT.
EXCUSE ME, MR. WAYNE, BUT THERE'S BEEN SOME DRAMATIC MOVEMENT IN THOSE STOCKS YOU'VE BEEN TRACKING.
RIGHT. THANKS, ALFRED.
TRACKING STOCKS? IT'S 6:00 AT NIGHT.
THREE WORDS: AFTER-HOURS MARKET.
LOOKS LIKE I'M ABOUT TO GET BUSY, TOO. DUTY AND MY DEDICATED PARTNER CALLS. LATER, BRUCE.
BE SAFE, ETHAN.
BEEP
BEEP

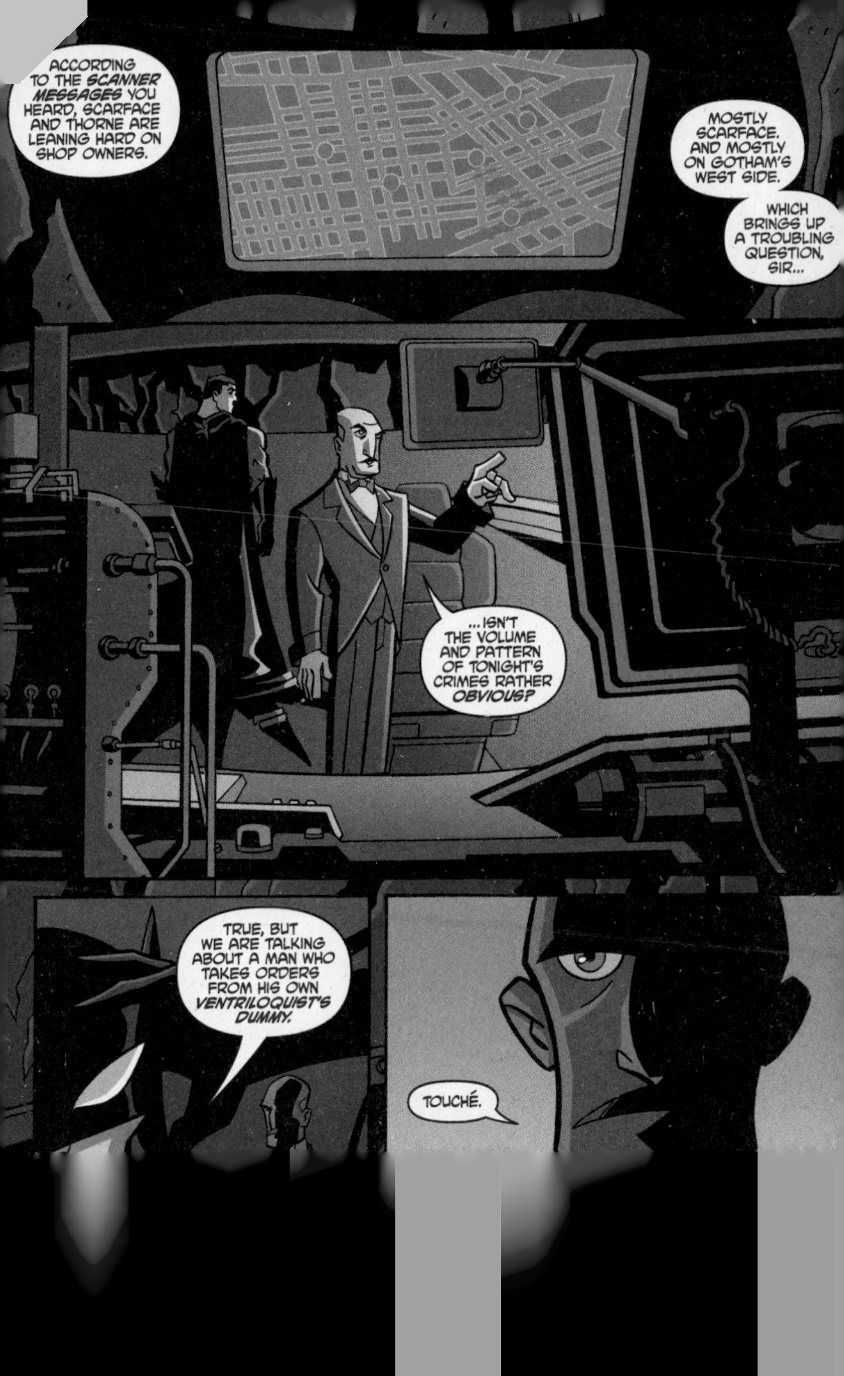
ACCORDING TO THE *SCANNER MESSAGES* YOU HEARD, SCARFACE AND THORNE ARE LEANING HARD ON SHOP OWNERS.
MOSTLY SCARFACE. AND MOSTLY ON GOTHAM'S WEST SIDE.
WHICH BRINGS UP A TROUBLING QUESTION, SIR...
...ISN'T THE VOLUME AND PATTERN OF TONIGHT'S CRIMES RATHER *OBVIOUS?*
TRUE, BUT WE ARE TALKING ABOUT A MAN WHO TAKES ORDERS FROM HIS OWN *VENTRILOQUIST'S DUMMY.*
TOUCHÉ.

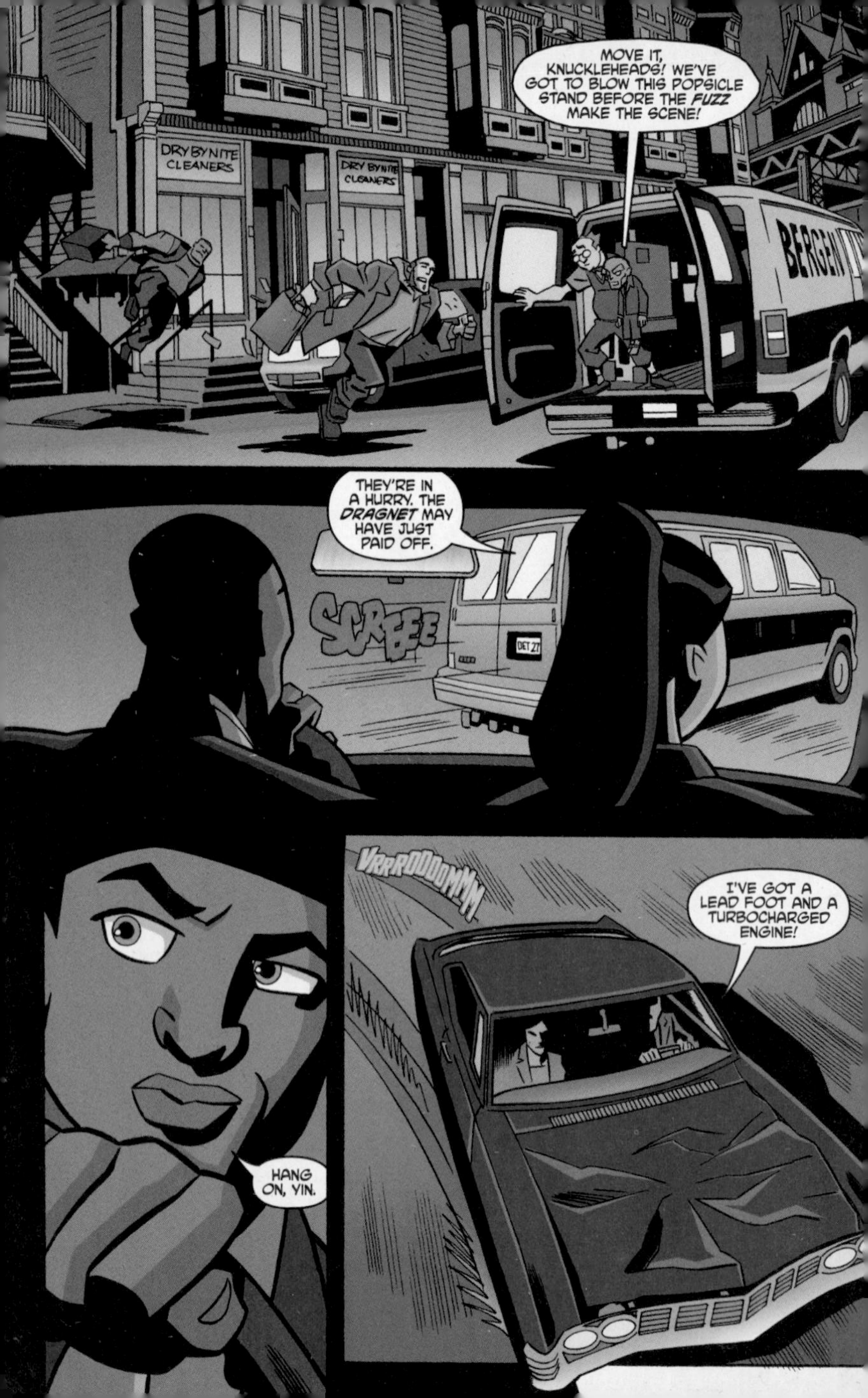
MOVE IT, KNUCKLEHEADS! WE'VE GOT TO BLOW THIS POPSICLE STAND BEFORE THE *FUZZ* MAKE THE SCENE!
DRY BY NITE CLEANERS
DRY BY NITE CLEANERS
BERGEN
THEY'RE IN A HURRY. THE *DRAGNET* MAY HAVE JUST PAID OFF.
SCREEE
DET 27
HANG ON, YIN.
VRRROOOOMMM
I'VE GOT A LEAD FOOT AND A TURBOCHARGED ENGINE!

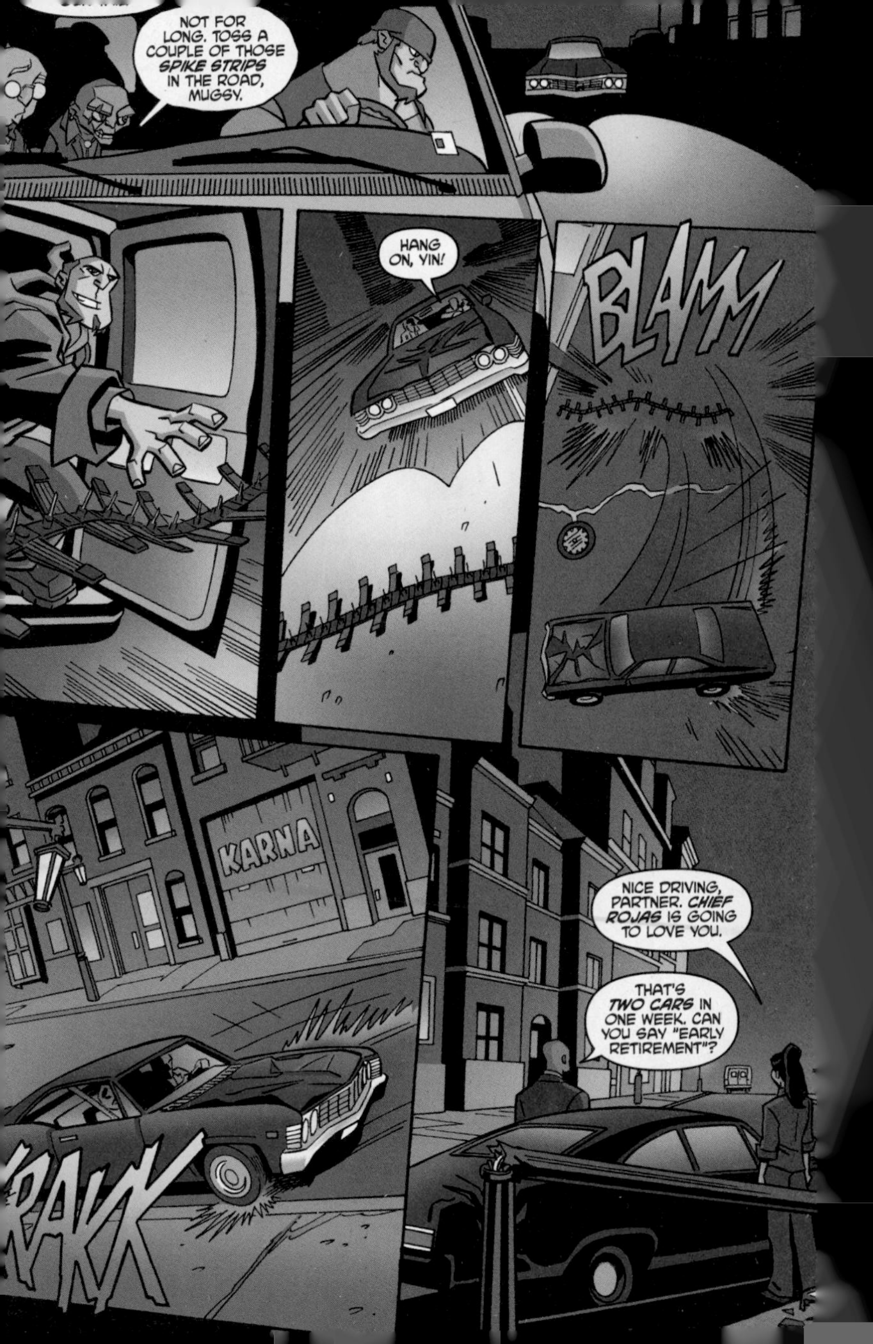
NOT FOR LONG. TOSS A COUPLE OF THOSE SPIKE STRIPS IN THE ROAD, MUGSY.
HANG ON, YIN!
BLAMM
KARNA
NICE DRIVING, PARTNER. CHIEF ROJAS IS GOING TO LOVE YOU.
THAT'S TWO CARS IN ONE WEEK. CAN YOU SAY "EARLY RETIREMENT"?
RAKK

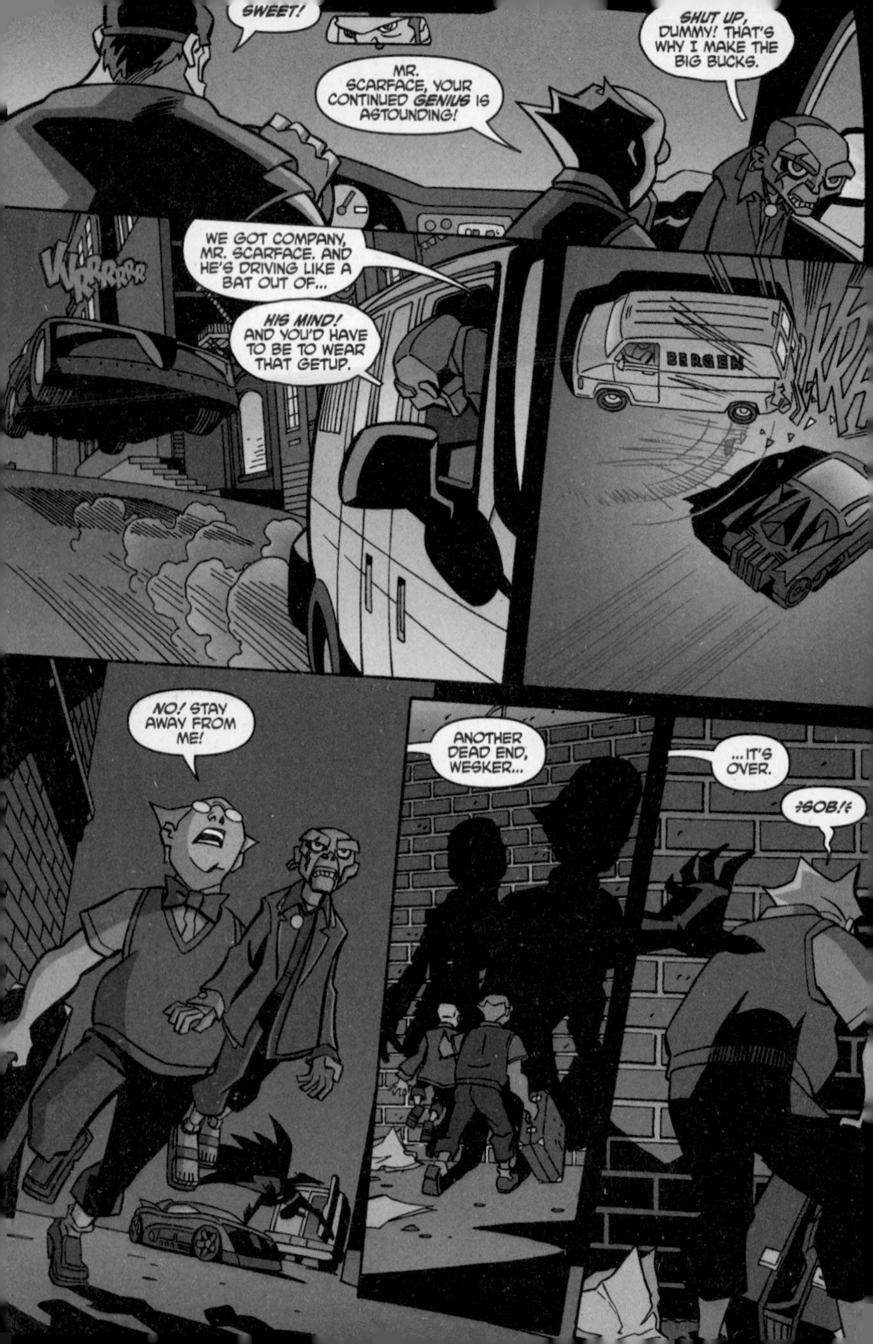
SWEET!
MR. SCARFACE, YOUR CONTINUED GENIUS IS ASTOUNDING!
SHUT UP, DUMMY! THAT'S WHY I MAKE THE BIG BUCKS.
VVRRRRRR
WE GOT COMPANY, MR. SCARFACE. AND HE'S DRIVING LIKE A BAT OUT OF...
HIS MIND! AND YOU'D HAVE TO BE TO WEAR THAT GETUP.
BERGEN
NO! STAY AWAY FROM ME!
ANOTHER DEAD END, WESKER...
...IT'S OVER.
SOB!

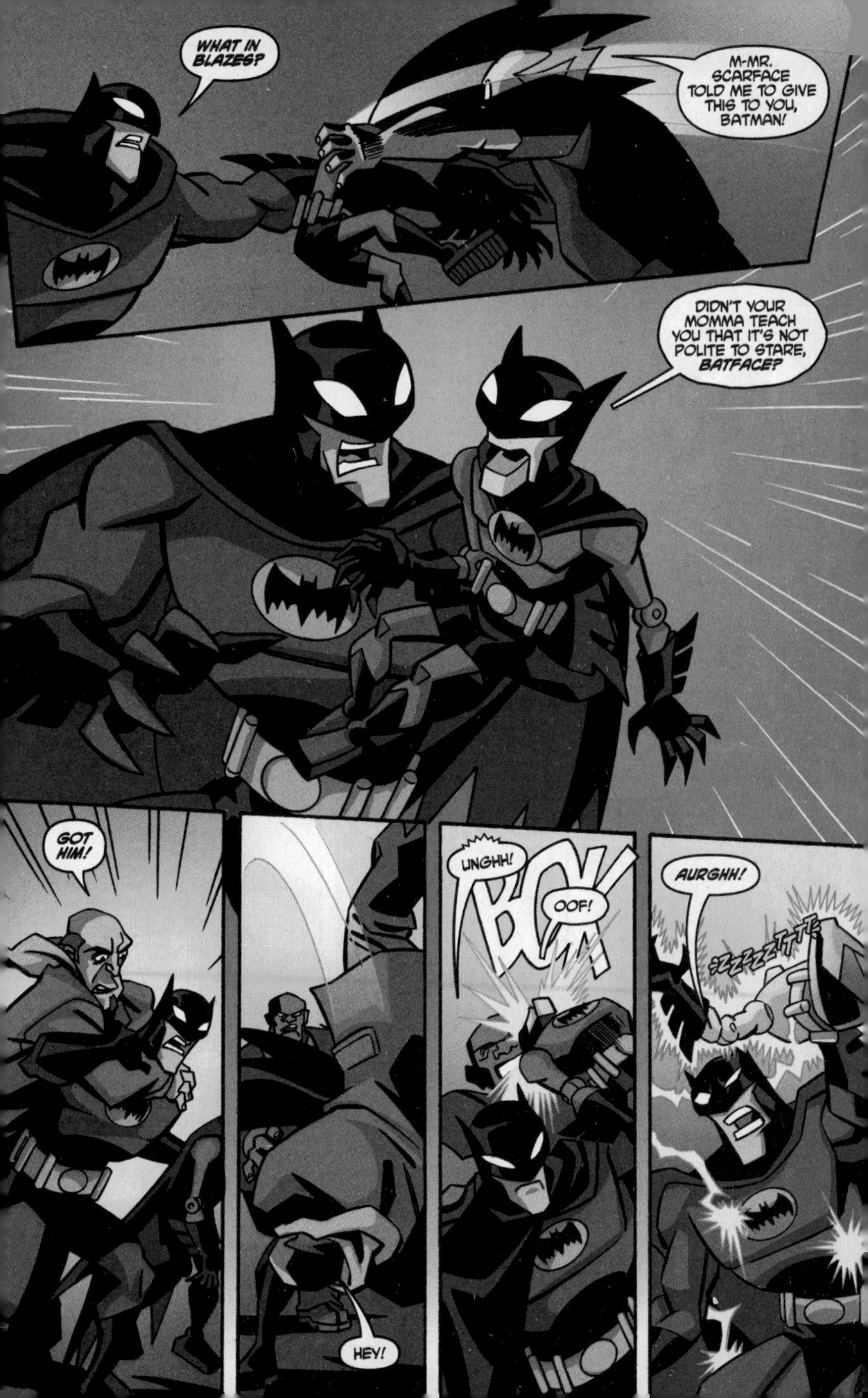
WHAT IN BLAZES?
M-MR. SCARFACE TOLD ME TO GIVE THIS TO YOU, BATMAN!
DIDN'T YOUR MOMMA TEACH YOU THAT IT'S NOT POLITE TO STARE, BATFACE?
GOT HIM!
HEY!
UNGHH!
OOF!
AURGHH!
ZZZZZTTT

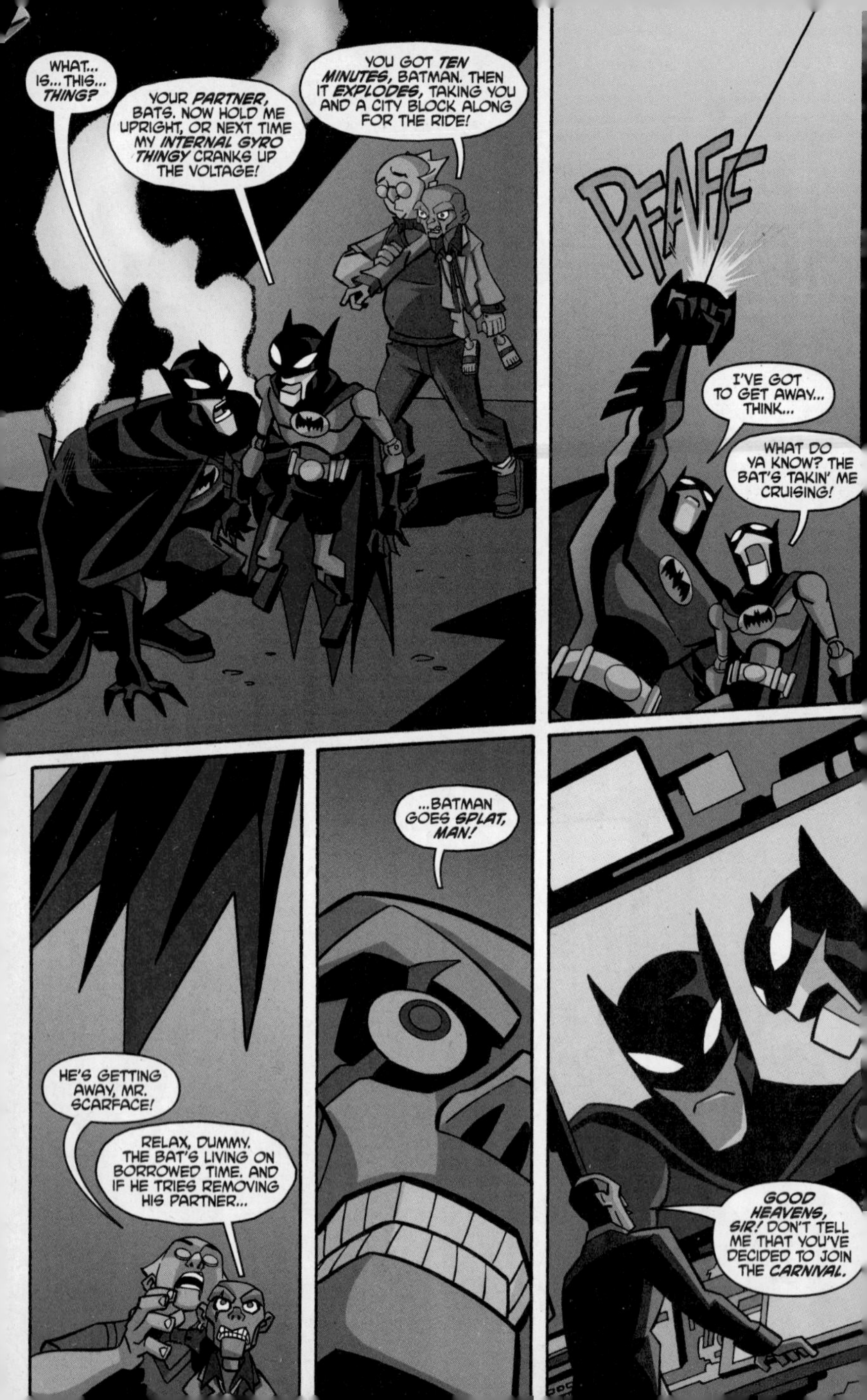
WHAT... IS... THIS... THING?
YOUR PARTNER, BATS. NOW HOLD ME UPRIGHT, OR NEXT TIME MY INTERNAL GYRO THINGY CRANKS UP THE VOLTAGE!
YOU GOT TEN MINUTES, BATMAN. THEN IT EXPLODES, TAKING YOU AND A CITY BLOCK ALONG FOR THE RIDE!
PFAFF
I'VE GOT TO GET AWAY... THINK...
WHAT DO YA KNOW? THE BAT'S TAKIN' ME CRUISING!
HE'S GETTING AWAY, MR. SCARFACE!
RELAX, DUMMY. THE BAT'S LIVING ON BORROWED TIME. AND IF HE TRIES REMOVING HIS PARTNER...
...BATMAN GOES SPLAT, MAN!
GOOD HEAVENS, SIR! DON'T TELL ME THAT YOU'VE DECIDED TO JOIN THE CARNIVAL.

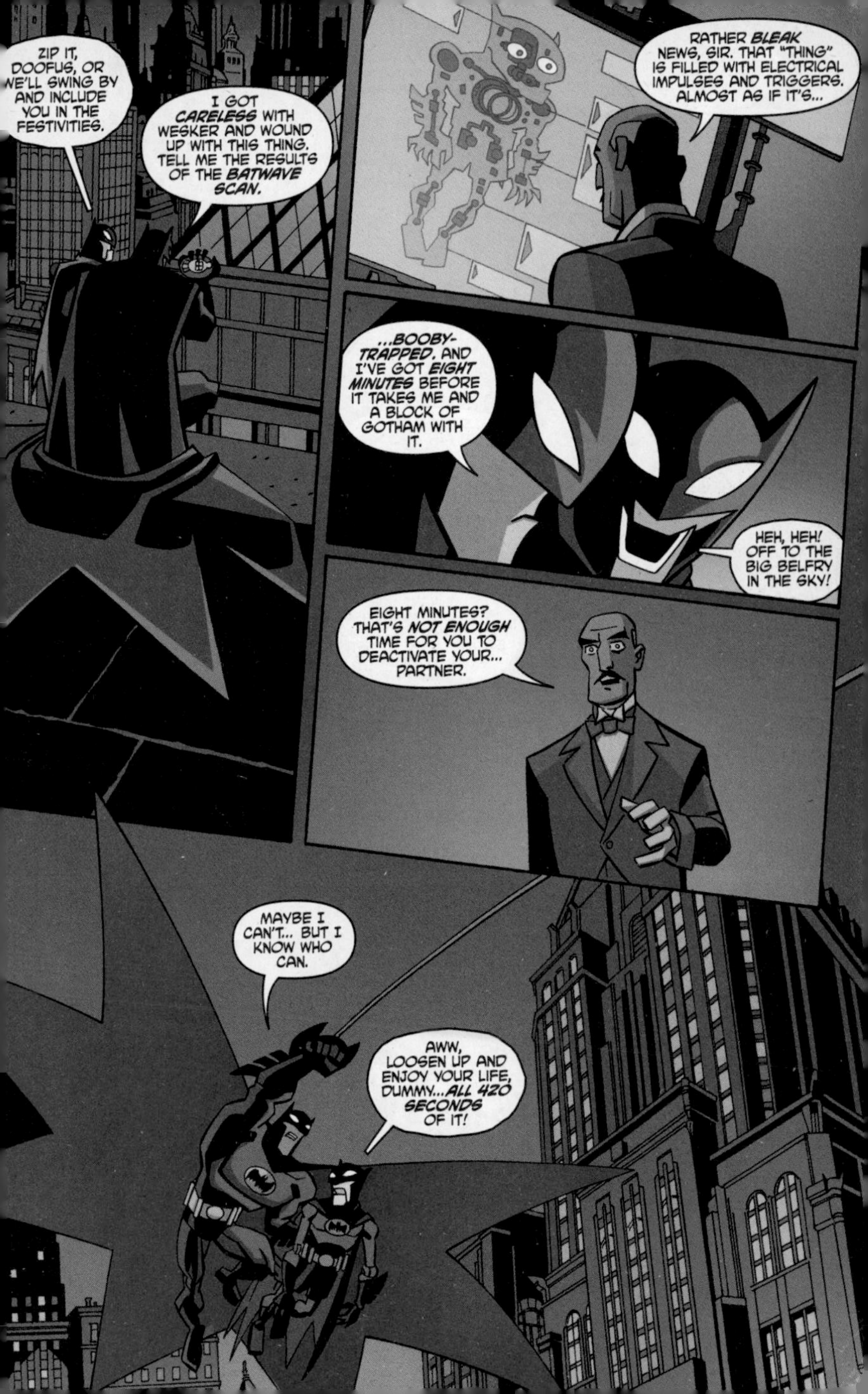

ZIP IT, DOOFUS, OR WE'LL SWING BY AND INCLUDE YOU IN THE FESTIVITIES.
I GOT *CARELESS* WITH WESKER AND WOUND UP WITH THIS THING. TELL ME THE RESULTS OF THE *BATWAVE* SCAN.
RATHER *BLEAK* NEWS, SIR. THAT "THING" IS FILLED WITH ELECTRICAL IMPULSES AND TRIGGERS. ALMOST AS IF IT'S...
...*BOOBY-TRAPPED.* AND I'VE GOT *EIGHT MINUTES* BEFORE IT TAKES ME AND A BLOCK OF GOTHAM WITH IT.
HEH, HEH! OFF TO THE BIG BELFRY IN THE SKY!
EIGHT MINUTES? THAT'S *NOT ENOUGH* TIME FOR YOU TO DEACTIVATE YOUR... PARTNER.
MAYBE I CAN'T... BUT I KNOW WHO CAN.
AWW, LOOSEN UP AND ENJOY YOUR LIFE, DUMMY... *ALL 420 SECONDS* OF IT!

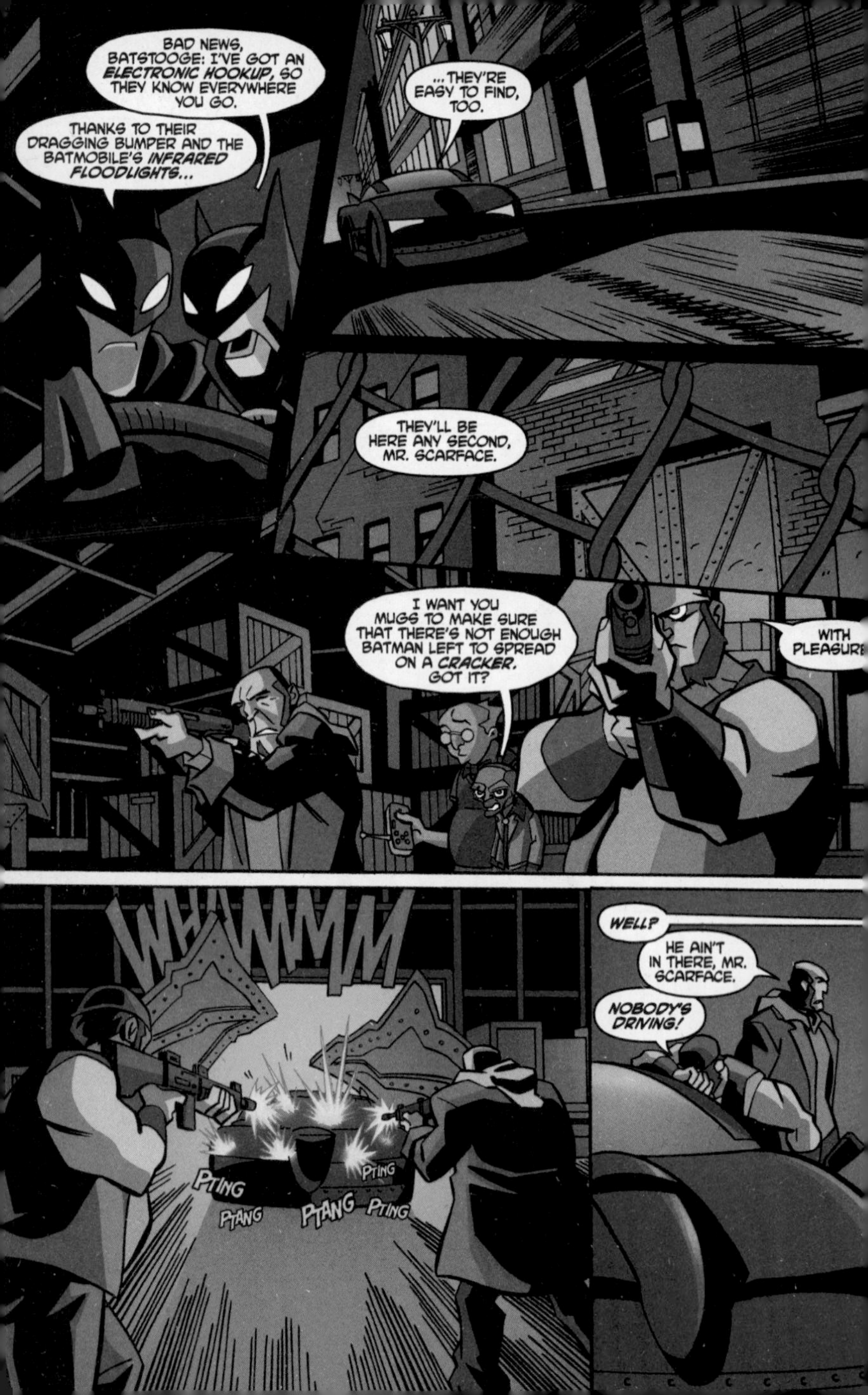
BAD NEWS, BATSTOOGE: I'VE GOT AN *ELECTRONIC HOOKUP*, SO THEY KNOW EVERYWHERE YOU GO.
THANKS TO THEIR DRAGGING BUMPER AND THE BATMOBILE'S *INFRARED FLOODLIGHTS...*
...THEY'RE EASY TO FIND, TOO.
THEY'LL BE HERE ANY SECOND, MR. SCARFACE.
I WANT YOU MUGS TO MAKE SURE THAT THERE'S NOT ENOUGH BATMAN LEFT TO SPREAD ON A *CRACKER*. GOT IT?
WITH PLEASURE
WHAMMM
PTING
PTANG
PTANG
PTING
PTING
WELL?
HE AIN'T IN THERE, MR. SCARFACE.
NOBODY'S DRIVING!

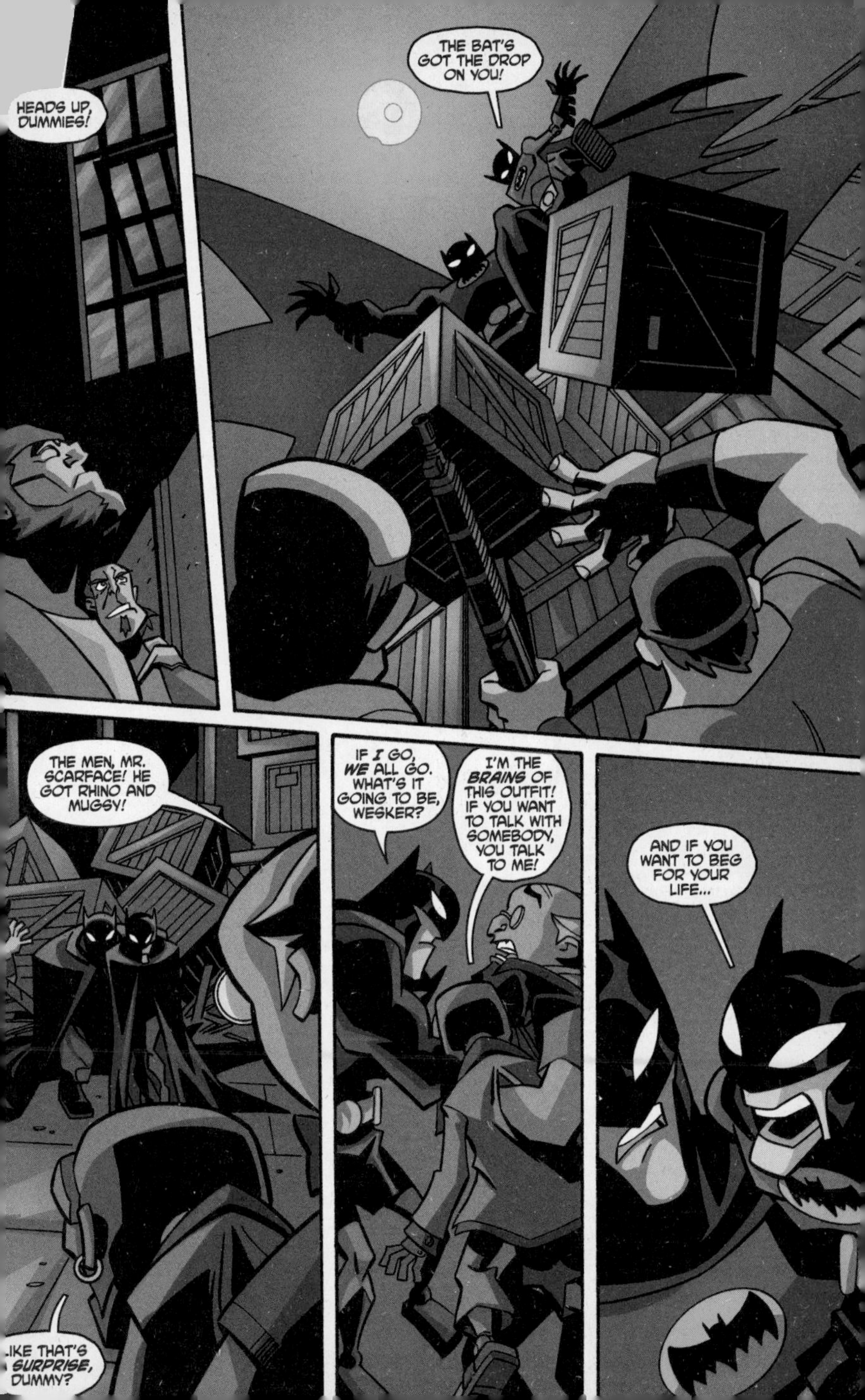
HEADS UP, DUMMIES!
THE BAT'S GOT THE DROP ON YOU!
THE MEN, MR. SCARFACE! HE GOT RHINO AND MUGSY!
IKE THAT'S SURPRISE, DUMMY?
IF I GO, WE ALL GO. WHAT'S IT GOING TO BE, WESKER?
I'M THE BRAINS OF THIS OUTFIT! IF YOU WANT TO TALK WITH SOMEBODY, YOU TALK TO ME!
AND IF YOU WANT TO BEG FOR YOUR LIFE...

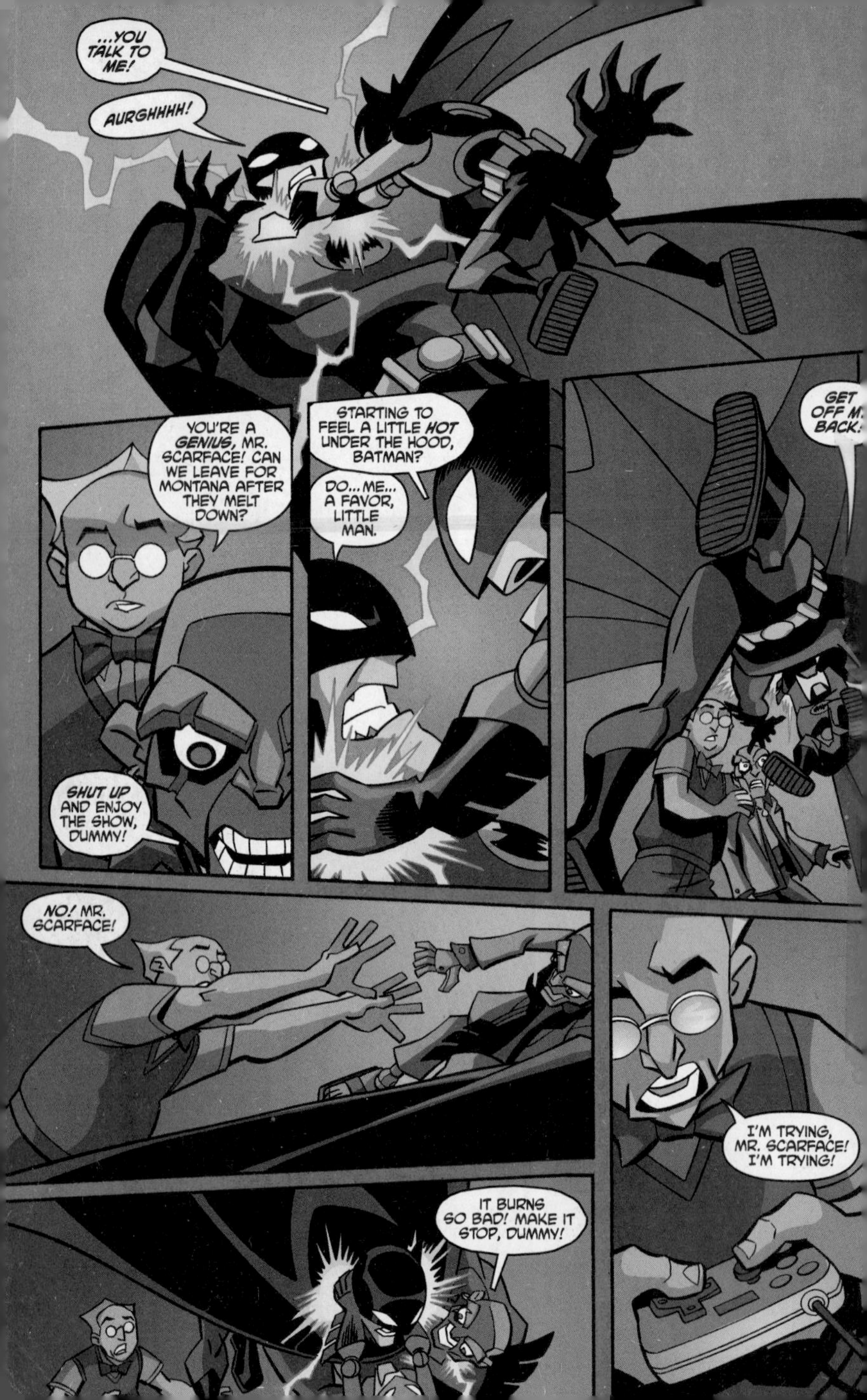
...YOU TALK TO ME!
AURGHHHH!
YOU'RE A GENIUS, MR. SCARFACE! CAN WE LEAVE FOR MONTANA AFTER THEY MELT DOWN?
SHUT UP AND ENJOY THE SHOW, DUMMY!
STARTING TO FEEL A LITTLE HOT UNDER THE HOOD, BATMAN?
DO...ME... A FAVOR, LITTLE MAN.
GET OFF M BACK
NO! MR. SCARFACE!
I'M TRYING, MR. SCARFACE! I'M TRYING!
IT BURNS SO BAD! MAKE IT STOP, DUMMY!

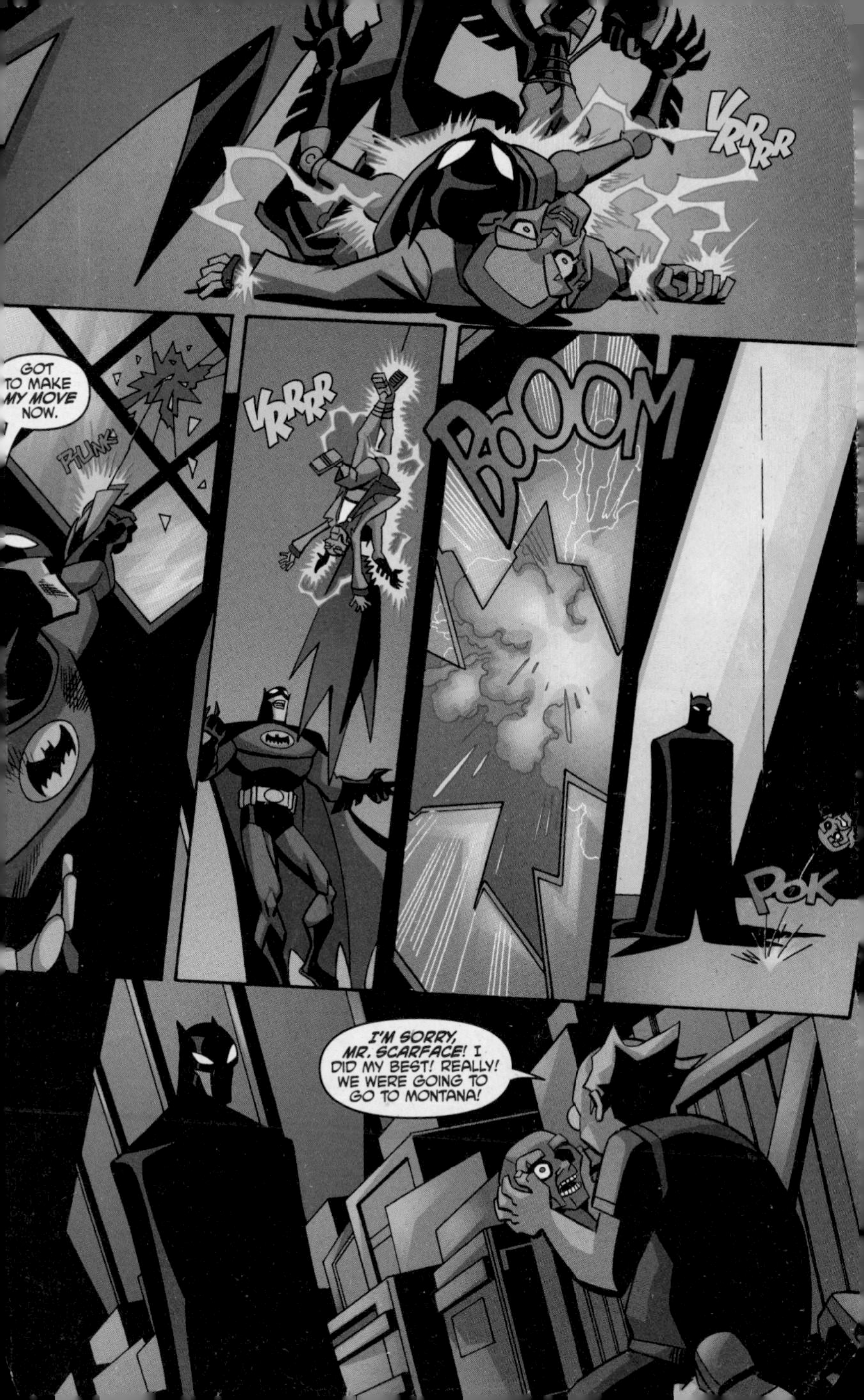
VRRRR
GOT TO MAKE MY MOVE NOW.
PLUNK
VRRRR
BOOOM
POK
I'M SORRY, MR. SCARFACE! I DID MY BEST! REALLY! WE WERE GOING TO GO TO MONTANA!

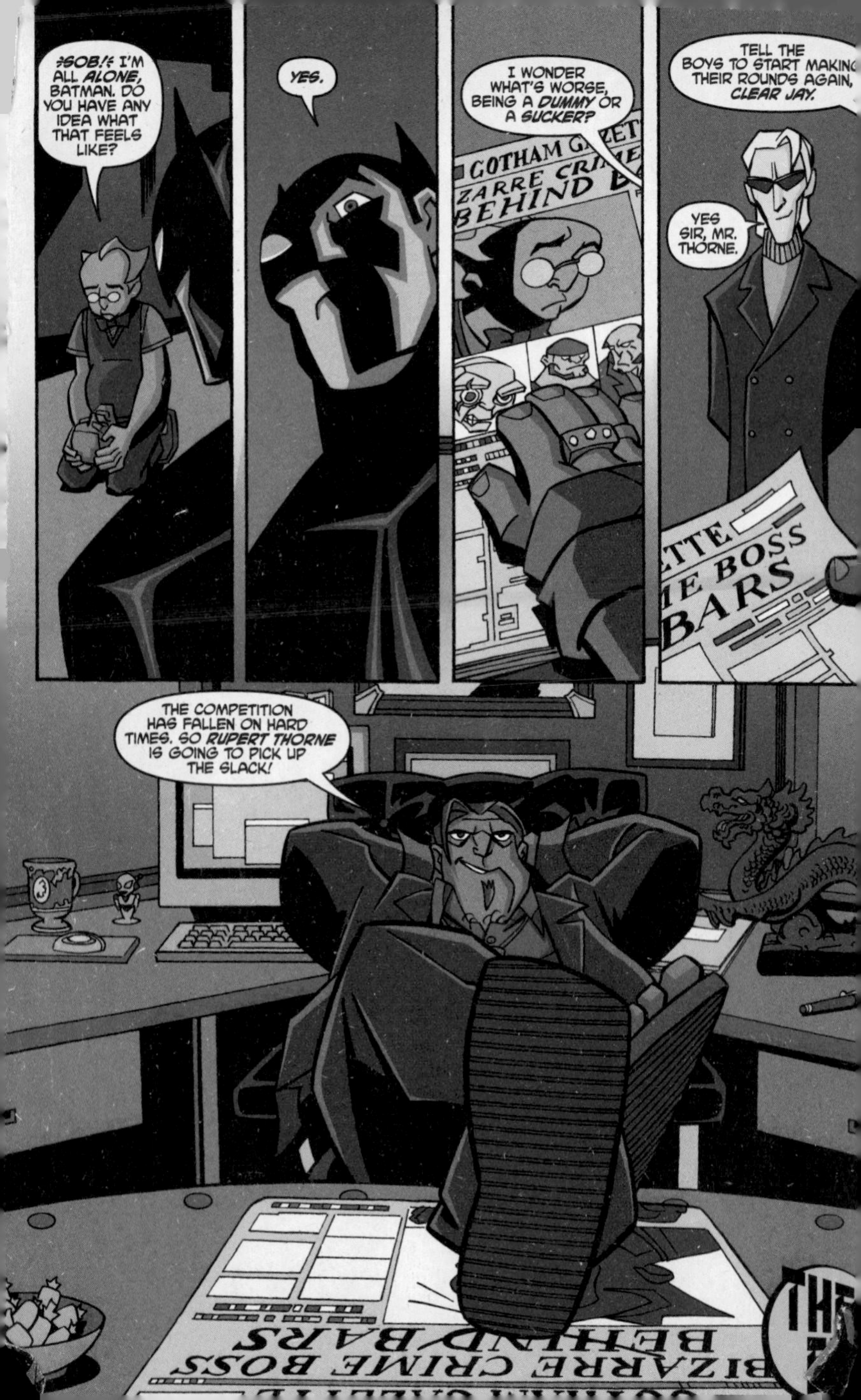

SOB! I'M ALL *ALONE*, BATMAN. DO YOU HAVE ANY IDEA WHAT THAT FEELS LIKE?
YES.
I WONDER WHAT'S WORSE, BEING A *DUMMY* OR A *SUCKER?*
TELL THE BOYS TO START MAKING THEIR ROUNDS AGAIN, *CLEAR JAY.*
YES SIR, MR. THORNE.
THE COMPETITION HAS FALLEN ON HARD TIMES. SO *RUPERT THORNE* IS GOING TO PICK UP THE SLACK!
BIZARRE CRIME BOSS BEHIND BARS

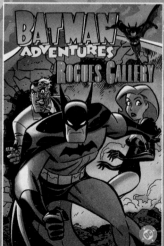

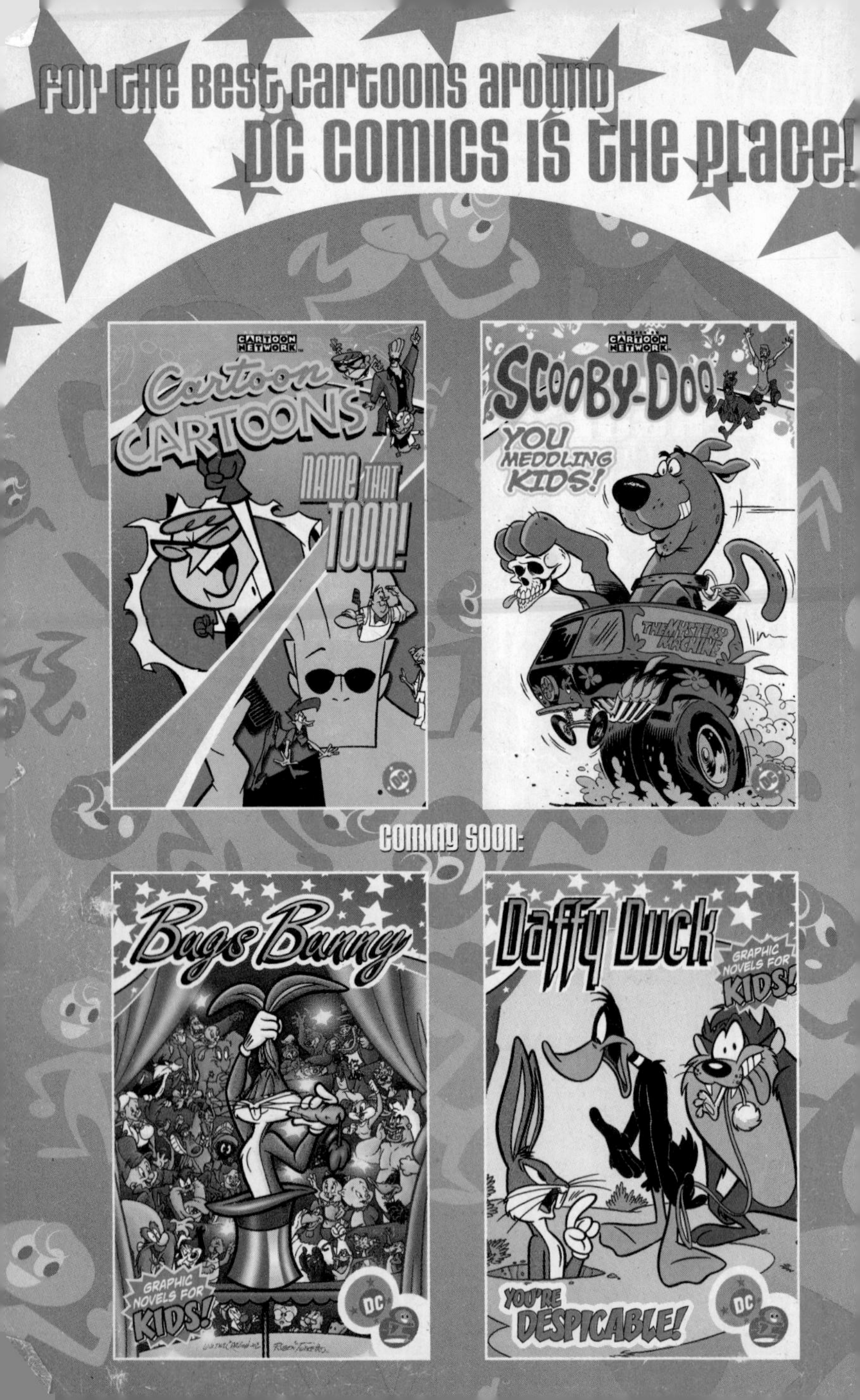

FOR THE BEST CARTOONS AROUND
DC COMICS IS THE PLACE!
CARTOON NETWORK
Cartoon CARTOONS
NAME THAT TOON!
CARTOON NETWORK
SCOOBY-DOO
YOU MEDDLING KIDS!
THE MYSTERY MACHINE
COMING SOON:
Bugs Bunny
GRAPHIC NOVELS FOR KIDS!
Daffy Duck
GRAPHIC NOVELS FOR KIDS!
YOU'RE DESPICABLE!
DC